THE RACE

Bob Judd
THE RACE

William Morrow and Company, Inc.
New York

Library of Congress Cataloging-in-Publication Data

Judd, Bob.
    The race / Bob Judd.
       p.   cm.
    ISBN 0-688-10463-0
    I. Title.
PS3560.U336I54   1991
813'.54—dc20   90-23564
                                                                        CIP

Printed in the United States of America

First U.S. Edition

1 2 3 4 5 6 7 8 9 10

For Cavelli
(who is the absolute best)

Debts

Last year, Al Unser Jr. was leading the oldest motor race in the world, the one half a million people come to watch, the Indianapolis Five Hundred. His father, Big Al, had won four times and this was going to be Little Al's first. Two laps from the checkered flag, Emerson Fittipaldi lost control in Turn Three and knocked Little Al into the wall at 220 miles an hour. Fittipaldi hung on and, genius that he is, got his car pointed in the right direction again. When Fittipaldi came around for his next and winning lap, Al Unser Jr. was standing clear of the pile of oozing junk that had been the Team Valvoline–Lola Stroh Light-Chevrolet. Little Al was giving Fittipaldi a thumbs-up sign to let Fittipaldi know that (1) he was OK; (2) no hard feelings; and (3) congratulations on winning the race. When I told Al Jr. that I thought that was the finest gesture of sportsmanship I had ever seen, he said, 'Yeah. Broke my heart.'

Generosity and honesty like that is a rare combination. Except at Indy, where there is plenty. Mechanics, drivers, team managers and owners gave their time and knowledge generously to 'A what? A novelist?' I owe a special thanks to Al Unser Jr. and Bobby Rahal, two men who don't have 'free time' but took some anyway to teach me what they had learned the hard way. Part of what they told me was first printed in an article I wrote for *Autosport*, '200 mph Driving Tips'.

And I owe a heavy debt to one of America's finest automotive journalists, Gordon Kirby, who gave me the keys to his kingdom and let me act as if it were mine.

I

POP of decompression as I came out of the tunnel into the sun, followed by a rainbow in the mist coming off her rear wheels, followed by a dot coming out of the rainbow. The dot grew until I could see her wings, translucent in the sun, frozen for a thousandth of a second before she hit. She was probably the umpteenth millionth daughter of a runaway father from Damascus, flying with the desert wind at night, picked up by a storm over Beirut, and deposited in the middle of the afternoon in Monte Carlo. Fat with the last hopes of some poor starving farmer she went splat, a thick blob of yellow insect goo and locust wings spreading across my visor.

There should be a name for what happens to mice and men. Just when you think you are in control, when the hard nights without sleep and the long days of working flat out are a breath away from paying off . . . just when you reach for the prize, some clown in the cosmos slips a banana under your foot and whoof, you find yourself falling through darkness, picking up speed. Like they say in Indianapolis, you think you hold the wheel and the wheel holds you.

The world went yellow for an instant and the video replay showed my car making a little wobble left and right when I caught the bug on my visor. And I remember that being hit in the face, even though it was only my visor, made me furious. I was irritated before, but now I was in a rage. Fade from yellow goo to red mist.

Abbey wasn't just holding me up, she was flinging fat greasy locusts at me. She was over her head on the wet track with the big boys. With 700 horsepower underneath her little right foot and a car so sensitive it would twitch at the arch of an eyebrow, she was too busy to check her mirrors.

The number two driver on your team doesn't hold you up, the number two driver holds other drivers up. The number two driver pulls over for the number one driver and waves him past. With a smile. God damn her.

She knew better. I had taught her better. I spent hours with her out on the tracks, showing her the line. Where to lift off, where to stand on it. Showing her another hundredth of a second here and two thousandths of a second there. And I'd told her fifty times to keep her eyes on her mirrors.

Every race I've ever entered I've always expected to win. Even when I knew I didn't have a chance. Nobody expected me to win this race. Nobody except me.

Some teams thought they'd won the race before it started. They'd won it with their backup teams on their private test tracks, with their computers linked by satellite to the aerospace mainframes in California, and in their wind tunnels. Usually they were right. Usually the big money won. But this time I had a chance. Syfret had slid his Williams into the Armco at Mirabeau. Aral had driven his McLaren into the pits half-way through the race and never came out again. Both Ferraris were out with electrical problems. Cartablanca's engine swallowed a valve and the lead was mine. And if none of the thousand ifs happened I was going to win.

If.

If none of the five thousand bits of delicate machinery stressed to the breaking point didn't break. If the tiny delay in the steering when I turned into the corners didn't mean that the left front wheel was starting to work loose. And if the little screech in the automatic gearbox that I'd never heard before wasn't the first note of box full of neutrals. Or a bearing on a gearshaft was about to turn into shrapnel. And if it was just my imagination that the left front tyre was going soft. And if the ragged sound I heard when I accelerated out of a corner didn't mean that the engine was about to blow up. And if I didn't make a mistake. And if nothing fell off. And if Priaino and Faenza didn't catch me . . .

If none of that happened and if none of the other thousand worries that chew on you like piranha fish when you're leading a race . . . If none of that happened and the goddamn woman moved over, I was going to win the Monaco Grand Prix.

I had lapped her twice before. I moved left and right before the chicane, filling her mirrors with Formula One car. She still didn't see me even though I was inches behind her. But unless she moved over, I couldn't pass until the main straight half a lap away. Monaco is too narrow to pass except down the main straight past and going into Ste Devote.

God damn Monaco. If it wasn't Monaco, they'd never race here.

It's too narrow and too dangerous for the 700 horsepower racing cars that weigh less than a little Honda Civic. Like Piquet says, it's like trying to race a bicycle in your living room.

Abbey braked fifteen feet too early for the chicane and then slowed down too much. She was only a few thousands of a second early but at 170 miles an hour you cruise for nearly twenty-five feet in the dark while you blink an eye.

There was no way I could get around her. At this rate, Faenza and Priaino were gaining five seconds a lap. They were nine seconds behind. Five laps to go.

Abbey turned into the chicane. I followed behind, single file, swearing revenge.

We accelerated, towards Tabac. Even though our cars were identical, I could get around corners a little quicker and get on the power earlier, which gave me a little more speed down the straights. But I had to wait for her, and once we both got on the power, I didn't have anything extra to get alongside her. So I trundled along behind, losing time. She braked too early for Tabac, got on the power too late coming out. Damn, damn, damn.

The track was drying out and she was treating it with too much respect. 135 miles an hour felt like crawling. Why didn't she see the blue flags the marshals were waving at her? Maybe they'd been waving them at her for the whole race. Maybe she was just tired. I nudged closer to her urging her on.

Abbey wasn't a bad driver. She had finished third in the European Formula Three championship the year before. Which meant she'd finished at the front of a gang of ferocious kids who happily risk their lives and yours for a half-inch in a 150 mile an hour corner. So finishing third in the European Championship is nothing to be ashamed of.

But it isn't normally enough to earn you consideration for a drive in Formula One, where the cars have another five hundred and fifty more horsepower. And where the drivers are the world's best and the least forgiving. But Team Arundel was not a normal team. And if there ever was a normal time, this was not it.

Coming out of the first kink around the swimming pool, Abbey ran a little wide, off line where the cars hadn't dried the track. As she got on the power her car slewed sideways for an instant showing me the pink Women Unlimited logo on the side before she caught it and I was left staring into the back end of her suspension, tyres spitting grit and a fog of exhaust.

Now Girls was an international employment agency specializing in office temps. But when they started to move women into the boardrooms of the big multinationals, they decided it was time to move their name and their image upmarket. So Now Girls changed their corporate colour from green to pink, and changed the name to Women Unlimited. And allocated $12 million to sponsor a Formula One team.

Rumour has it that McLaren spends £95 million on their two cars. And they get their engines free from Honda. Our engines cost us around £65,000 apiece. And that doesn't include a guarantee. If one just happens to lunch its insides for no reason, too bad. Throw another one in the car and kiss £65,000 goodbye. With two cars we can usually count on using four engines a race. McLaren brings eight. So $12 million doesn't buy a lot in Formula One. But it did buy us Team Arundel. Provided we painted our cars Women Unlimited PINK. And provided one (or more) of our drivers was a woman.

A few journalists raised their eyebrows about a woman driving a Formula One car, saying that women didn't have the concentration or the physical stamina. Rubbish. Desiree Wilson won a Formula One race at Brands Hatch in 1980.

Then there is Shirley Muldowny, America's World Champion Drag Racer. You know drag racing; two supercharged 5,000–horsepower monsters looking like a cross between a baby buggy and a bedframe line up at the start line, the light goes green, you put your foot down and after 4.9 seconds of carefully guiding an exploding bomb, you're crossing the finish line at 289 miles an hour. They use nitro for fuel and a parachute for brakes.

It is the American Proletarian Orgasm and the macho men with the sunburned necks flat out love it. Little Shirley painted her car pink, her son was her crew chief, and she beat Big Daddy Don Garlits, Danny Ongais, she beat all the hard men.

There is no reason why women can't drive as well as men. Although trying to keep their helmet off their shoulder while cornering a Formula One car tends to give them a thick neck.

Women Unlimited said they wanted somebody 'vibrant', 'current', 'glamorous', 'sophisticated'. They wanted 'today's woman'. Somebody like Desiree Wilson. Or Divina Galica.

You could argue, if you felt like arguing, that Abbey was 'today's woman'. And maybe one day she would be glamorous and sophisticated. But the twenty-year-old who showed up for the first day of testing was a short, tough kid from the Midlands with big eyes and a mop of black hair who called men 'dorks'. When the other little girls were off to riding school and dreaming of show jumpers, Abbey had been pounding around the go-kart circuits. Spectators, thinking they were seeing the next Juan Manuel Fangio were astonished at the flood of dark curls that tumbled out of her helmet after she'd won a race. The next Juanita Manuela.

Going into the hairpin at La Rascasse, I slowed down, letting her draw ahead a little. By the time we went through Noghes and into the main straight I had my foot to the floor and I flew past her so fast she almost drove off the track. I checked her once in my rear view mirrors to make sure the kid was OK and forgot her.

Four laps to go.

I blasted up the hill, driving hard, taking charge of the race. The big yellow blob in front of my right eye was irritating, and made my depth perception a little shaky. Too bad. I wasn't going to let up. Ayrton Senna let up for an instant when he was leading the '88 Monaco Grand Prix ten laps from the finish line and took off a front wheel. It cost him the race and it almost cost him the World Championship.

I knew I was losing air in the left front tyre and that the wheel was working loose. And I knew the engine was about to blow any second, that the transmission was chewing its insides to bits. I could tell, I could feel it in my bones, I knew something nasty was about to happen.

But I won the race anyway.

Monaco is the best place in the world to win a race. The beautiful people lining the course cheer for you. Backed up by the vibration of three hundred million people around the world watching the race on television cheering for you. Of course they would cheer for a gorilla if a gorilla won the race. But they're not cheering for a gorilla, they're cheering for you.

The sun shines on the white yachts in the harbour, it is spring and warm and Princess Caroline kisses you when she hands you your trophy. Her eyes shine with admiration. Her pictures do not do her justice. Prince Rainier solemnly shakes your hand and multimillionaires surge forward to press multimillion-dollar contracts in your hand. Warm and sexy girls smelling of the new perfumes strain to get close to you, and the heavy glooms of winter rise up and disappear into the endless Mediterranean blue sky.

Abbey smiled and said how glad she was and I forgot I had been angry at her or at anybody. The photographs show me spraying the crowd with a jeroboam of Moët et Chandon and holding the trophy in front of a big goofy Evers grin. One of Hollywood's biggest agents said he was lining up a feature film that I was 'a natural hundred percent right for. Two mill net, guaranteed.' And Ken Arundel, the six foot seven-inch owner and team manager of Team Arundel, my boss and my friend, told me that Women Unlimited had sent me a telegram. And that it wasn't just congratulations. They wanted me to fly Concorde to New York so they could fire me.

2

Concorde saves you time, but that's not why people fly the world's only supersonic passenger aeroplane. The real reason they fly Concorde is because everybody else can't. It's not a particularly exclusive club. Anybody can join as long as they can pay the dues. Some men had paid with their days and weeks, their weekends and their wives to rise to the level where they could sign their own expenses. 'An extra thousand pounds to save three hours? Certainly. Goddamn right. Worth every penny. It's my time.'

Their briefcases carried the freight of corporate tedium; sales targets, market shares, production forecasts, restructured retirement plans, prospectuses for golf village condominiums on islands off the East Coast where they were going to retire one day if they got there before their careers went smash in a takeover. They carried recommendations from their brokers saying don't worry, the market's going to be just fine again soon. Sell some, buy some more.

They were the men who spoke soft in public and loud in private, who testified before Senate subcommittees and made meaningful contributions to the candidates of their choice. Their dues went on.

For others there are no dues at all. A ride on Concorde, just another one of the perks of privilege that they have long since grown numb to. I suppose I was a member of this last group. I have too much money and too little time to spend it. The world is getting divided between those who spend money to save time and those who spend time to save money. I'll cheerfully spend thousands to add to my beggar's stash of time.

Concorde is a narrow and noisy little plane. Low ceiling and two seats a side. But the grey leather is as soft as a glove and vintage champagne fizzes in the crystal glasses and the air hums with the confidence of men and women of power. And there is the sexy rub of speed when the Machmeter at the front of the cabin reads Mach .56, Mach 1, Mach 1.2, Mach 1.7, Mach 2. Speed, my mistress, my lover. The nervous, sweet-faced girl who will kiss me goodbye one sunny afternoon and smash me head first into a wall.

Departure: Paris, 11 a.m. Arrival: New York, 8.30 a.m.

Concorde gives you a head start. And lunch at 1,400 mph. At 40,000 feet, the air is so thin the blackness of space shows through like a dark halo following overhead.

I had none of the champagne. None of the canapés. And helped myself to none of the lunch. I wasn't hungry. And I could wait. Ken had said that there was nothing he could do. The Women Unlimited contract locked him in for a year. And although he hadn't realized it when he signed the contract, they could fire me if they wanted. He could resign their sponsorship. Now that we had won a race, he could probably find the money. But not immediately and he couldn't promise anything. No, they hadn't consulted him. And no, he didn't know what they wanted.

While the other planes circled slowly, stacked six deep over the Eastern Seaboard, Concorde jumped the queue and went straight in, landing easily, right on time, a needle gliding into the haystack of Manhattan.

Life down on the ground in New York City was crawling along at bug speed. Did you know that one year they raised the average speed of traffic in Manhattan by 20% just by installing a few million dollars of computers to synchronize the lights? Crosstown speeds soared from 3.8 to 4.6 miles an hour. But of course, that was years ago. Morning rush hour these days from JFK isn't that quick. Stop, crawl. Stop, stop crawl on the Van Wyck Expressway. From Mach 2 to 2 mph. with the slam of a taxi door.

You used to be able to take a helicopter from JFK to the roof of the Pan Am Building where Women Unlimited have their corporate headquarters. But one day a chopper flung a rotor blade through a neighbour's window seventy storeys up, frightening everybody to death. And that was it for helicopters on the roof in midtown Manhattan.

Lurch, crawl, stop, stop, stop. Maybe it would cheer me up to fling a few rotors through a few windows. This was a pointless trip. If they wanted to fire me, let our lawyers squabble over the details. I pulled their Telex out of my pocket and read it again.

Congratulations on an absolutely fabulous win for us in
Monte Carlo. Unfortunately circumstances unrelated to
marketing and promotion compel me to terminate as soon as

possible our agreement with you. Have reserved seat for you on next a.m. Concorde, Paris-New York. Can you come straight to my office, 09.30 EST? See you tomorrow. Let's talk.
E. Channing

Talk about what? The lawyers could sort out the terms of separation if that's what they wanted. I could probably get another ride. Or Ken could get another sponsor now that we had won. But why were they throwing away their good fortune? They'd already spent millions and it was working. Three hundred million TV viewers around the world saw us win. If they had to cut down the team, why me instead of Abbey? Abbey had finished ninth. I had finished first. I won.

My sagging taxi pulled alongside the Pan Am Building on Vanderbilt, leaking precious bodily fluids. A crowd of commuters surged forward to grab it before it died, elbowing each other on their way to morning in Corporate America.

I was twenty minutes late, but it didn't matter. She kept me waiting out by the reception desk for another twenty-five. Plenty of time to stare at the enormous sculpture on the wall, my craggy face reflected along with the chrome tubes that rose and fell like waves on the mirrored surface. A small plaque said that this timeless artwork had been created for the 1964 World's Fair to represent the unending achievement of women. Maybe it looked better from a distance. I certainly did.

I was inspecting my crags close up, wondering if Concorde accelerated jet lag when I heard my name behind me. 'Forrest Evers? Forrest . . . good morning, Mr Evers. I'm sorry we had to keep you waiting. Would you follow me please.' She was busy-busy with things to organize and I was one of them. Neatly tailored brown suit, narrow ankles, high heels and a professional secretarial air led me on, past sleek young men and women at their desks. A few of their gazes lingered on me as I walked past, taking note of my soft leather shirt, my baggy cotton trousers, my paper-thin and buttersoft Italian loafers; perfect for Monte Carlo. Cornball for New York City. I rated a three out of ten on the lifted eyebrow scale.

Most of them were more interested in the computer screens on their desks than the thirty-two-year-old racing driver with the seamed face and the brown curly hair who'd just won the

Monte Carlo Grand Prix. Fifty-five storeys in the air, they could go all day without seeing a window, let alone the sky. Under the hidden fluorescent lights their pale green faces had the uneasy and sleepless look of life in the aquarium. Little fish hoping to be the one in a million who grew up to be a big fish.

We turned a corner into the executive wing. Softer light, thicker carpets and more suits. Evidently most of the senior executives at Women Unlimited were women. And judging by their secretaries they were having an in-house competition for whose secretary was the cutest fella. The woman leading me was definitely female. She stopped and turned suddenly.

'Gee, I'm sorry, Mr Evers. It's a real zoo this morning and I forgot to introduce myself,' she said holding out her hand. 'I'm Bonnie.' A quickie shake of the hand, a big wide friendly smile, freckles and green eyes and she was turning to lead me down the soft carpet highway to the chairwoman's office before I could even begin to smile back. And I thought I was quick.

I'd met Ellie Channing in London. The Chairwoman and Chief Executive Officer of the world's largest employment agency had been in London for a European board meeting. Her European management put Team Arundel on her calendar to make sure the press showed up for the launch of the new Women Unlimited Formula One car. They showed up and they were more interested in E. Channing than the car. But then she always did command attention. I remember I felt her presence before I saw her. I had been talking to Nigel Roebuck from *Autosport*, and I turned around. At the time I thought there was something between us, an extra half-second looking into each other's eyes. We shook hands and she was gone, a head of state surrounded by her cabinet, security guards and press. A week later, I read that she had fired her senior European management team. 'They will not be replaced,' she'd said in a magazine interview. 'Personnel management is a contradiction in terms. Given the right direction, people will manage themselves. There is no need for all these layers of managers between the chief executive officer of this company and the people who work for her,' Chairman Ellie said.

'Forrest Evers,' she said, coming from behind her desk to meet me. 'I'm sorry we had to drag you across the Atlantic at such short notice.'

Her office was as efficient as a kitchen. Polished blonde wood floor, the walls a dusky red, like terra cotta but with a glaze. Large white canvases with big streaks of primary colours, red, yellow, orange and blue. A curving desk of blonde wood, brushed aluminium, and black leather with a chair to match. Two banks of computer screens, a wicker bench in place of a couch and not much else except open space. No resting place for the lazy. Behind the desk, a wall of glass framed the East River and in the distance, jets gliding in and out of La Guardia like slow bees taking turns on a succulent flower.

'What's a nice girl like you,' I said . . .

'. . . doing in a place like this,' she said. Letting me know she'd heard the joke before and smiling as if she still enjoyed it. She sent Bonnie to 'round up' some coffee, sat on the wicker bench and motioned me next to her. Two strangers on a love-seat. Her perfume was light and distracting.

'Sometimes I wonder myself what I'm doing here.' Her voice was straightforward, just talking, making me feel comfortable. 'Being an executive isn't something you set out to do. At least not if you have any brains. It just happens to you.'

Bonnie brought us coffee. Her legs were long and tan and strong and smooth and she left. 'How did it happen to you?' I asked Ellie.

She looked at me for a moment, then smiled again. Maybe it wasn't corporate protocol for me to be asking the questions. She was thirty-eight, *Fortune* said, the youngest chief executive officer of a major corporation in America. She was fair with tousled light brown hair piled loosely on top of her head, a high wide forehead and clear blue-grey eyes. She wore almost no make-up and no jewellery. And an off-white linen sports jacket several sizes too large and a plain grey linen suit vest and loose pleated cotton trousers. No blouse, no scarf, just bare unadorned woman underneath. It made her look all working woman, as if she really didn't care how she looked, and at the same time, as if she had just stepped out of a fashion page in *Vogue*. As if she had nothing to do with the sexy glow around her. As if that was my problem, not hers. She had clear, flawless skin. Smiles came and went easily leaving traces in the lines around her mouth. She had a full soft mouth and . . . maybe it would help if I thought of her as the chairwoman. The tough old battle-axe who was about to fire me.

'Yeah, well,' she said after a moment's pause, 'how did I get here? Where did I go wrong? I graduated from Smith, and thought I wanted to teach music to little boys and girls. After a year of that the State of Massachusetts cut the education budget and fired all the teachers who had less than five years' experience. The only job I could get was as a secretary. I didn't like being a secretary so I worked hard, paid attention and moved up a step. And so on. Now there's no place to move up to, so I'm stuck. Unless they throw me out.'

She looked away from me, towards the banks of computer screens winking green numbers mindlessly. 'You know, they don't give the money away. Some of my work is extremely unpleasant. This for example.'

'This?'

'I'm sorry.' She looked back at me as if she were anxious that I understand. 'We're in a credit scissors. You know the credit scissors? We've got rising interest rates to pay on the money we owe, and we've got falling income because unemployment is going up. We're an employment company and we rise and fall with rate of employment. Rising interest payments, falling income and snick, we get it in the neck. So we have to cut back on all of our expenditures. I'll tell you how tough it is, Mr Evers. Some of the toilet paper rollers in our loos are empty and they're going to have to stay that way. You hear what I'm telling you, Mr Evers? We, I, can't afford to run two racing cars.

'You flew me to New York to tell me that?'

'I wanted you to hear it from me. We've lined up a promotional tour for you . . .'

'You're contracted to pay me one million six for the season.'

'One hundred thousand a race,' she said. 'Pounds.'

'Pounds,' I said. 'Some drivers are paid more than six million a year. I beat them. I won the race.'

She stood up and shut the door, leaning against it. No more Ms Nice Girl. 'I'm sorry, I don't have the money to support two cars and two drivers. It doesn't matter if you won. If Women Unlimited are going to sponsor just one driver, that driver is going to be a woman. I'm sure you see the point of that.'

'No, I don't see the point of that. I always thought the point of racing was to win.'

'The point of our racing is to promote Women Unlimited

and whether or not you see the point you are fired. If you want to do promotional work for us, I'm sure we can work something out. For commensurate compensation.'

I was about to tell her that if I didn't drive, there wouldn't be anything to promote when there was a knock on the door.

She stepped aside and opened it, and a tanned face with hair gel giving him that just-stepped-out-of-the shower look stepped in cautiously. 'We're waiting for you, Mrs Channing.'

She looked at him with no expression. 'Tell them I'll be there.' He gave her a little mime of pain. 'And shut the door,' she said.

The face withdrew, shutting the door. Ellie walked over to her desk, picked up a crystal ashtray that looked antique. She weighed it in her hand, and then flung it at the door. She had a good arm. Some of the glass stuck like small daggers in the door but most of it broke into bits on the floor.

She looked at me for moment. Then she said, 'I'm sorry. Will you get out?'

'Is it that bad?'

'Worse. Now if you'll excuse me.'

'Maybe I could help.'

'Look,' she said, her voice rising, getting red in the face, 'my board is waiting. They cost me around $450 a minute and we are through here.'

'If it's that bad your board can wait another couple of minutes. Why don't you tell me what you need? You never know.'

'Look, Evers, if you had what I need you wouldn't be fooling around with racing cars. Or maybe I'm wrong. Maybe you've got twelve million dollars in your piggy bank. Fine, write me a cheque. Otherwise will you please just get out?' She ended it like a question.

Maybe I should have left her then, her fists clenched, her face angry. Except. Except she was over her head and she was crying for help. She didn't know she was but I heard her. When you are on a beach, and there is the clamour of kids playing and screaming in the water, and you are lying in the sun in a half doze, thinking of the sexy girl across the sand, the one in the blue suit and the dark hair, lying on her stomach smiling at you with her top pulled down, and there is a real cry for help, you hear it and you are moving before you think how or where.

Forrest Evers, lifeguard, flexing his muscles, diving into the sand.

So I said it without thinking. 'I can raise twelve million dollars,' I said.

She shook her head. 'Please, it's not funny.'

'I'm not trying to be funny. I'm trying to help.'

'You're a racing driver.'

'Well, it looks like I'm free from now till Christmas.'

She gave a little snort that could have been a laugh. 'You think you can really raise twelve million dollars?'

'Will it put me back in the car?'

'To tell you the truth Mr Evers, I don't think you could raise twelve dollars. But if you could raise twelve million, sure, that'll put you back in the car.' She looked at me for a minute as if I was a door to door insurance salesman. Then gave another little snort. 'Bonnnieeeeee.' Bonnie opened the door. 'Tell the board I'll be there in five minutes.'

Ellie sat back down on her wicker bench and motioned me to sit down beside her again. 'Well Mr Evers,' she said, 'just how do you plan to raise twelve million dollars?'

So here I was, brave, courageous Evers, the lifesaver. Honest and true Forrest, the liar. I had jumped in and now Ellie was looking at me with those beautiful grey-blue eyes, full of hope and suspicion as I took her hand. Later I would think that I really did it for myself, as a way to keep talking to the bright and beautiful woman who was leaning towards me and whose long slender fingers were giving my palm the slightest touch, urging me on. Save her, rescue my battered, wounded pride.

'Well, first, what I need to know,' I said, 'is why you need twelve million.'

3

'She's a smart lady. But she ain't that smart. Where you staying?'

'The Tuscany down on 38th. It's exclusive; they don' 'llow no Lumber Barons.'

'You a rude fucker, Evers,' he said with some seriousness. Then he smiled. Two men in America, sparring. 'Now how come she don't just go to a bank? All banks want to do these days is give you money, the interest they getting.'

Orrin Fenstermacher leaned back in the big leather chair at The Bull and Bear at the Waldorf, pushing an imaginary ten-gallon hat back into thinking position. He was of a size and a presence to make himself heard over the lunchtime din of a hearty businessman's bar with no apparent effort. 'Last I read, her balance sheet look pretty good.'

'What she says is that William Fraser . . .'

'Billy Fraser?'

'Billy Fraser.' The Rupert Murdoch of America. The man who had turned a group of Southern Fundamentalist Christian Newspapers into the largest media corporation in the world. William H. Fraser. Billy to Presidents and friends. 'He talked her into a management buyout, saying he'd fund her. So he holds the junk bonds. And with interest rates going up, and a shrinking job market, she doesn't have the money to pay off her debt. Her board's pushing her to start selling off franchises to raise the cash, but that's going to shrink her income even more.'

Ellie had explained all this slowly and patiently, using simple words until she realized I spoke the language. With contracts that pay up to ten million dollars a year, most Formula One drivers are multimillionaires. We have 'business interests', and when we get together we talk more about cash flow than lap times. My letterbox in London overflows with 'investment opportunities', and my telephone rings with advice from stockbrokers and accountants. The only benefit, if you could call it that, was that I'd learned to speak the cumbersome language of money. I could throw around 'debt ratios' 'debentures' and 'demand curves' fast enough to fool a banker. Which is to say, medium speed. Peel away the heavy phrases, and the simple truth was that Ellie was borrowed to the hilt. The bailiffs were pounding on her door. Because good ol' Billy had stolen $12 million from her.

He'd set up what he called a 'blind asset trust'. A secret, offshore cookie jar that either he or Ellie could raid, with the agreement of the other, if the buyout ran short of cash. Both he and Ellie contributed $12 million. The week after the buyout went through, Fraser had withdrawn all of it, his and hers. I'd said I didn't think she was so easily fooled. She said she wasn't normally. But his lawyers had buried a clause that, under an obscure chapter of Bahamian law, gave him, as the male in a male-female agreement, special drawing rights. A clause so encrusted with the jargon of international law, her lawyers hadn't understood what it meant. So now she was $12 million short of cash she couldn't say she'd lost.

I'd asked her if she'd fired her lawyers and she said she couldn't. Who else, she said, could she trust to cover up the $12 million hole? Which is what lawyers do, I thought. First they put you in a hole. Then they tell you, don't worry, they know how to pull you out. For a fee.

What I said to Orrin was, 'Women Unlimited owes Fraser twelve million in interest on his junk bonds. And he won't answer her phone calls.' Stalwart Evers, protecting the lady's honour.

'She's one pretty lady,' Orrin said with a pickerel grin. 'She call me, I'd do more than answer her phone calls.'

'You lend her twelve million?'

He stopped grinning. 'Just because I got money to throw away on racing cars, Forrest, don't mean I got money to throw away.' Orrin took a sip of his Wild Turkey and put the heavy glass back down on the table. 'Billy did that to her, huh? She can't pay the interest, he owns the bonds, he owns the company.'

That of course was the double whammy. Fraser not only took her twelve million. But unless she could come up with another twelve million to pay the interest on the junk bonds, she would lose the whole multibillion dollar company to him too. First he knocked her down. Then he kicked her in the teeth.

Orrin said, 'I thought he was all communications, newspapers, magazines, TV, satellites, that media shit. What's he want a damn employment agency for?' Orrin's massive fore-head furrowed like a ploughed field. 'It ain't like they got capital assets like plant, real estate or, God help me, lumber,' he said, working out a theory. 'All they got is their good name. They lose that, all those franchises go poof in the night.'

I toyed with my Perrier. Disgusting drink. 'Ellie says Women Unlimited are Billy's biggest newspaper advertiser. All those Personnel Ads add up to a few million a week.'

'US?'

'US, UK, Europe, South America, Japan, South East Asia, Australia, Canada.'

'Ooooh,' he said, drawing the word out across the table. 'I see what he's after. Integration. Big word now in Communications, "integration". He own the employment agency, he discounts the space to himself, maybe drive the others out of business. Or at least he give himself an unfair advantage. Kinda game you can play if you big enough. You gonna drive for me?'

'How can I get hold of him?'

'Fraser? Shit, don't ask me. I'm just a dumb lumberman. Man like that prob'ly got six layers of lawyers around him. Moves around a lot too.'

'You ever meet him?'

'Yeah, I did once. He gimme a long song and dance about how if we link up my lumber with some paper mill he was gonna buy then the whole newspaper process be fully inte-grated: "From the tree to the breakfast table," he said. I noticed that he's got a habit of rubbin' his chin when he's bein' tricky. The ol' philosopher pose. He like you to think he's just one of the folks.'

'And?'

'Well he can be a charmin' man when he so desires. But he's also one mean sonofabitch when he wants to be too. Besides, what I want to sell my business for? What am I gonna do, be a playboy? I already got more women than I can handle.' He grinned a big wide grin that spread across his big wide pockmarked fifty-year-old face, motioning for another round.

Orrin had watched the Monaco Grand Prix on cable, and phoned Prince Rainier when I'd won the race. ('I was gonna ask him, "Prince, where can I get ahold of that Evers?"') Naturally he didn't get through, but he did get as far as a clerk at the Royal Palace who told him I was staying at the Mirabeau.

Orrin rang me, and a day later, here I was. And here he was, fresh from Indianapolis, drinking bourbon. Big as life.

'You didn't answer my question,' he said, turning serious again. 'Goddamn it, I flew all the way out here to New York City to get an answer and you keep pussyfootin' around.'

'I've got other obligations.'

Fenstermacher acted as if he hadn't heard me. 'The doctors tell me no way Hewitt is going to drive again this year let alone come Memorial Day. I gotta have another driver and I'll tell you I'm accustomed to havin' the best. From what I saw of you, you'll do just fine.' He spread his big, speckled hands on the table and leaned forward. 'It ain't the deal, is it? We could work on the deal if that's what's holding you up.'

'Orrin, what do I know about driving at Indianapolis?'

'Shit, you don't need to know nothin'. All you got to do is put your foot down and turn left.' Technically, Orrin was right. Compared to Formula One, where you drove on a road course with up and down hills and lefts and rights around corners, accelerating, braking and turning . . . all you had to do in the World's Oldest Motor-race was put your foot down and turn left. The two-and-a-half-mile oval has just four identical turns, it is as smooth as silk, and all you have to do is drive five hundred miles on the razor edge.

'I'll get back to you,' I said.

'Sure, you get back to me. Just don't be too leisurely about it. There's plenty hotshoes's give their ass for that ride. Call me 'fore the end of the week, if you would, please. I don't nominate a replacement for Hewitt by Saturday, I don't race.'

'Orrin, I appreciate your offer. But I need to tie up one or two things first.'

'You do that.'

4

I left Orrin Fenstermacher with my stomach weeping and gnashing its teeth. He'd had a sirloin steak, two inches thick, sizzling on a platter. I'd had a cold fish salad. Which reflected my mood, but my stomach howled for the steak. One day I'll understand why a grown man my size wants to be a racing driver. At six foot one I'm too tall, too broad across the shoulders to fit into most Formula One cars. I give up the power of several horses to the drivers whose cars don't have to haul around the extra Evers muscle and bone. One day, when I stop racing, I'll take my stomach to an American stomach heaven, maybe Heavy Henry's Steak House outside New Orleans or Janice's in Pittsburg and wolf down the dozen oysters, juicy sirloin, home fries, Caesar salad and key lime pie made with real key limes, accompanied by Château Grillet, Chambertin and Château Latour Blanche. Or maybe just a pitcher of cold frosty Rolling Rock. Until then, I was going to have to live with its complaints. And I was going to be edgy and rude to gentlemen who offered me heavy money to drive their racing cars. Another bottle of Perrier, waiter, if you would be so kind.

On my way back to the Tuscany, I gathered up a pile of the current business magazines; *Forbes, Fortune, Businessweek,* and *Barrons,* along with a copy of *The Wall Street Journal.* Britain has The Government as its national religion. America has Business. Capital B. Nowhere are the comings and goings of business reported with such pious devotion as in America.

I spent a couple of hours in my suite going through the predictions, pronouncements, lifestyles and fears of America's businessmen. Sifting price-earnings ratios, debt structures, poison pills for corporate raiders, profit differential analysis and marginal cost curves. IBM was being restructured. GE's new president was a hell of a guy. By three-thirty I'd found Sunwest, and rang Fraser Communications Corporate Headquarters in Danbury, Connecticut.

'Fraser Communications.'

'William Fraser, please.'

'Ringing for you.'

'William Fraser's office.'

'I'd like to speak to Mr Fraser.'

'Whom shall I say is calling?'

'Alistair Hampton, *Fortune Magazine*.'

'I'm afraid Mr Fraser is unavailable now. Would you care to leave a message, Mr Hampton?'

'I'd like to set up an interview with Mr Fraser.'

'I'm sorry, Mr Fraser doesn't give interviews to competitive media. We have our own reporters.'

'Would you tell Mr Fraser we plan to do a *Fortune* cover story on him as The Businessman of the Year?'

'Hold on.'

I held on.

'Mr Fraser is out of the country at the moment. But he will be giving a press conference in Miami on the, uh, ninth. That's tomorrow. Perhaps you could reach him there.'

'Perhaps I could. If you have the address, maybe you could set up an appointment.'

'Well, I can give you the address. And I can set up an appointment but I'm afraid it wouldn't do you much good. Mr Fraser doesn't very often keep to a schedule. What I could do is clear you with his assistant, Mr Hillburn. Then you could go to the press conference and if Mr Fraser wants to see you he will.'

'What's the press conference for?'

'Fraser Communications is purchasing the Miami Star Media Group, and that consists of – ' there was a fifteen-second pause, ' – The *Miami Sun-Tribune*, that's a newspaper. The *Miami Star*, of course. The *Hialeah Times*, the *Boca Raton Daily Investor* and the *West Palm Beach Sandpiper*. Those are all newspapers.'

'He must be pleased.'

'I'm not finished. WPRA, Delray Beach; WRHJ, Delray Beach, WBLA–FM, Miami, and WMCA, Carol City. Those are all radio stations.

'And MIM–TV, Miami, that's a TV station. Together– ' there was another pause while she consulted her computer screen, ' –together they form an important and strategic new link in the Fraser Global-Village Network.'

'No doubt. And he will be at . . . ?'

'Mr Fraser's press conference will take place on the a.m. or p.m. on Thursday the ninth at IND–TV. Would you like the address?'

She gave me the address. 'a.m. or p.m.,' I said. 'Doesn't that make it hard on your reporters?'

'Oh no,' she said. 'Not at all. What I do suggest is that you call the station first thing in the morning and they may be able to give you an update on the timing.'

'And you'll tell Mr Hillburn?'

'Mr Hillburn will be expecting you.'

I rang Fenstermacher at the Waldorf.

'Hey, Evers, whatcha doin? I was just gettin' out of the shower. Perks me up after a good lunch.'

'If you haven't changed your mind, I'll take the ride.'

'Jesus. You got your business taken care of, huh? You drive fast as you take care of business we gonna be holdin' some lap records. The money's OK with you? I know it ain't what you get paid in Formula One, but nobody gets paid that kind of money at Indy.'

'The money is fine, Orrin. But I still have one or two things to do. And I need to borrow your jet for a couple of days.'

'Hold on. Just a minute. What days? Where you takin' it? These things aren't that easy to arrange. I got stockholders to report to. We keep that plane pretty damn busy. It gets booked up months in advance sometimes. I can't just let folks take it joyriding. You have any idea how much that sucker costs to fly? $3,000 an hour in the air. Sumbitch costs $1,000 an hour parked. Twenty-four hours a day.'

'Orrin, I appreciate it won't be easy. And I'll have to get back to you on the flight plan. But this is important. If you can fix it, I'll drive for you.'

'I just don't know, Forrest. I don't think I can square it with my board.'

'Then lease it to me. Tell your board you're making a little money for them for a change. I just read you own 53% of Fenstermacher Industries. Your board has to love you, you own them.'

'Yeah, well, it won't be easy. You mind telling me how come you got to have my company jet?'

'I think I'm going to need a couple of days' vacation.'

'Horseshit, vacation. How soon you be out there?'

'Tomorrow's Tuesday, I'll be in Miami. I should be in Indianapolis Wednesday afternoon, if I can get a flight.'

'Leave it to me. I'll get your tickets delivered to your hotel.

Along with a room at the Speedway. You know the Speedway Motel? You can have Hewitt's room. I never got around to cancelling it. You could hit the track with a rock from your hotel window. Oh yeah, you'll need wheels. I get you hooked up with a rental. If you heard it's a tradition for Indy drivers to bust up rental cars let me make it clear here and now it's not a tradition I hold with. I'll have the crew leave a message when you can get together. Sooner we get started the better. First qualifyin' is this Saturday.' (He pronounced it Saddiday.) 'We'll need to get you past the rookie tests before then.'

'Rookie tests? I thought you said there was nothin' to it,' I said, egging him on.

'Nothin' but eight hundred right-angle corners at 220 miles an hour. Y'all gonna enjoy it, hear?'

'I'll let you know when I need the jet.'

'Don't count on no jet. All I can give you now is a definite maybe. I gotta know more about this deal.'

'The deal is, Orrin, I need it for two days. If I can have it for two days, I'll drive for you.'

Then I rang Ellie.

She was in a meeting but ten minutes later she rang back.

'What's up?' she said.

'You don't sound like a Chief Executive Officer.'

'You think I should be more pompous?'

'Well, you do sound kinda girly to be chairman.'

'You want I should talk with a lower voice?' she said in her imitation of a man's voice.

'Now you sound goofy,' laughing for the first time since Monaco. 'Something good happen?'

'Nothing good happened. What else am I supposed to do, cry?'

'You free for dinner?' I asked.

'You mean you've reconsidered the promotional tour.'

'I mean I'm asking you to dinner. Doesn't anybody ever ask you to dinner?'

'You mean like a date?'

'Like a date.'

'I guess I'm free from now till Christmas,' she said.

5

New York is the tropical rain forest of cities. The buildings tower overhead, rising and falling with tropical speed. Look one day and a building has fallen in the night. Look again and another one has taken its place. When Manhattan gets its way and declares itself a foreign country outside American borders, its National Anthem will be sung to the rhythm of wrecking balls and pile drivers. Even the Empire State Building, 102 storeys high, has a built-in device to make it easy to take apart. Nothing is permanent except the high-speed cycle of hope and no-hope zooming up and down so fast it feels like a vibrator. Yessir, I thought as I turned the corner on 39th and headed up Park Avenue, New York gets you running.

It was just before eight in the evening, that time at twilight when the sky is the darkest blue before black, when the neon signs flicker on and you feel that restless impatience before the curtain goes up. I walked through Grand Central, rode up the escalator into the Pan Am Building, crossed 45th, through the Helmsley Building, (golden light, like the promise of money, leaked from behind the bronze elevator doors) and out again on Park Avenue at 46th. The last limousines were still moored outside the Park Avenue skyscrapers, waiting to take the last of the executives back to Westchester. While the central islands between the uptown and downtown traffic bloomed with flowers and rats.

The Four Seasons is where you take the Chairman and Chief Executive Officer of a major corporation to dinner. Or Chairwoman as the case may be. It is in the matt black and bronze Seagrams Building, designed by Mies Van der Rohe and the classiest building for miles. A façade big enough and elegant enough to hide the foundation of the Seagram's fortune. Corporate respectability for the bootleggers.

Inside, in the restaurant, the ceiling is high and the room absurdly large for the few tables scattered around the central fountain and pool. This mostly empty space on the most expensive real estate in the world is decorated in different shades of money. Copper for the tall mesh-link curtains that shimmer like an endless flow of coins. Banker's marble for the floor. Gold and platinum for the credit cards.

Ellie arrived wearing a soft and silky blue dress with a short swishy skirt that showed the chairwoman had knees, and long legs, and probably played a lot of tennis. Heads turned as the maître d' led her around the pool to my table. She held out her hand before sitting down, the way professional women do to avoid the awkwardness of the kiss on the cheek. She wore a thin gold chain around her neck, no rings, no ear-rings. She sat down and looked at me with those clear blue-grey eyes ready to face the world and those lines of intelligence at the corners. And again, that artless, casual look as if she had no idea how beautiful she was. Or if she knew, she didn't care.

We began with Ellie waiting patiently, me smiling nervously. A racing driver dates an executive. Why is that so surprising?

'I didn't know,' I said, 'that Chief Executive Officers had free time.'

'From now till Christmas you mean?' She looked around the room seeing who she knew. Then she looked back at me. 'I don't, really. I don't think I can remember when I had free time. On the other hand I don't get asked out on dates all that often either. Men scare so easy. Or maybe they just prefer adoring little softies. Anyway, most of my evenings are spent with regional managers, financial analysts, and women looking for a place on my board. The only men who ask me out are the financial whizz kids who see me as a short cut. Or married men who think I'll be grateful and they won't have to get involved.

'So thanks to you our Southwestern Sales Manager is dining alone this evening.' She gave me a nice tidy little smile and picked up the menu, started to look at it, then looked at me. 'This is a date, isn't it, Forrest? Because if this is an attempt to get me to reconsider, forget it. We're dumping franchises, we can't afford to carry an extra racing driver.' She said this smiling easily, looking from item to item on the menu.

'What makes you think I'd take you back?' I said.

She raised an eyebrow. And let the smile come back, only this time to herself, looking at the menu.

'You see,' I said. 'You're not so tough.'

'No, I'm not so tough.'

'You remember I said I might find you that twelve million.'

'Remember? It was the best thing I heard all day.'

'I lied.'

'Forrest.' She stopped smiling and put down her menu. 'I never thought you could. Get the money, I mean. But I thought it was sweet of you to say you'd try.'

'Yeah, and I'm cute too.'

'I don't mean to patronize you.'

'Then don't. I was bluffing then. But I'm not now. I think I can get your money.'

'How, steal it?'

'Not really. But I need your help. Let me order you a drink.'

'Whatever you're having.'

'I'm having Perrier. For my sins.'

'God, they must have been stinkers, your sins.' She made a little face at the thought of bottled water. 'A little white wine?' I ordered a bottle of the Dry Creek Flintwood Vineyard Chardonnay.

The waiter brought the wine, I waved him away from my glass and he poured Ellie a taste. She tasted and nodded approval. The waiter rewarded her with a half glass, and she took a big sip and held it in her mouth, savouring.

'Is it a problem, this not drinking?' she asked.

'No, it's not a problem. It's a necessity. When I was a kid it was a macho thing to brag about how much you could drink and drive. No more. Now the cars are so much faster the slightest delay in your reactions, say a few thousandths of a second, and you fall off.'

'Fall off?'

'Crash. Besides, there's too many calories in there,' I added gloomily, nodding towards her glass of clear pale gold, imagining the delicious pond of wine on her pink tongue.

'You don't look as if you have an ounce of fat on you.'

'You want to hear my plan?'

'Let's order first. I'm a working girl and I'm starving.' She still wasn't taking me seriously.

Later, lifting a bite of lightly smoked lake trout, glistening with a sheen of champagne sauce, to her mouth, she paused. 'Who's waiting for you in London? You're divorced, aren't you?' Then she took her bite, thoughtful and considering.

'I was. It's the way I used to think of myself, divorced. Now I'm just single. But I'm not a good person to be married to. There are sixteen Formula One races a year in fifteen countries on five continents and God knows how many test days. It doesn't make for a cosy hearth at home. But you are.'

'I am . . . ?'

'Married. Don't people call you Mrs Channing?'

'Oh that,' she said. 'That's like being called Mrs Bridges. You know, an honorary title you get if you sit on the shelf long enough. It seems so long since I was married I almost forget I was. But there was a Mr Channing once upon a time. He said he got bored with sitting next to an empty chair at the dinner table.'

'Little Ellie, struggling up the corporate ladder, while her man waits at home.'

She blew a puff of air accompanied by a backhand wave. 'Wait he didn't. And I don't really blame him. But when I started to find pantyhose under the bed I said to hell with it. With him. With playing house. With pretending being married. Anyway, what's this plan?'

'You remember the movie "The Sting"?'

'Robert Redford and Paul Newman?'

'That one. They set up a phony betting shop with fifty crooks pretending to be punters. And the mark thought that they could get the race results before he had to post his bet.'

'You want me to help you set up a betting shop?'

'It gets better. "The Sting" was based on a real sting. The movie was based on a fraud in Canada in the 1920s set up by a Czech con man who called himself Count Lustig.'

Ellie took a long sip, held it in her mouth and arched her eyebrows like a TV viewer thinking about switching the channel.

'He had a better scam. He set himself up in a fanciest hotel suite in Paris, served lobster and champagne and posed as a bent civil servant. And he sold the Eiffel Tower to socially ambitious French scrap dealers. Twice. He even got them to pay him a bribe for letting him in on the deal.'

This time she laughed out loud. 'Forrest, you're not serious.'

'I'm not planning on selling the Eiffel Tower, but I am serious.'

'No way. I wouldn't touch it with a stick.'

'You haven't even heard my plan.'

'I don't have to hear it. It's fraud and it would expose me and my company to legal action. Right?'

'Not necessarily. Listen, was Fraser upfront with you? Wouldn't you say he was fraudulent? You think what he did was any different from sticking his hand in your pocketbook and taking twelve million?'

She nodded a half nod and then dismissed it with a wave of her hand as if it didn't matter. 'Forrest, I have 14,342 employees to think about. People have to trust us.'

'Wouldn't you like to pull Fraser's tail?'

'There's no way I'm going to be involved in any theft or fraud. Clear?'

'There's no theft. It's just taking the money out of one of his pockets and putting it in the other. Your company's going down the tubes and you haven't ordered dessert yet. You might as well listen.'

Ellie didn't order dessert, but she listened. As I outlined it for her I could see her turning it over in her mind, playing with it. 'You can't do it in this country,' she said. 'They'd prosecute you for racketeering in about twenty seconds.'

'Maybe it doesn't have to be in this country.'

'And Fraser isn't stupid, I promise you.'

'He's not stupid, but he is greedy. It's one of the rules of nature. The greedy ones are always longing for more.'

'Well, I don't want to be involved in any way, shape or form.'

'But you will help.'

She laughed and put down her glass, leaning forward, her blue-grey eyes looking straight into me. 'No, Forrest. No. Hasn't a woman ever told you no before?'

'It's all they ever say.'

'Sure. I'd believe in your $12 million before I'd believe that.' She took a sip of coffee and looked across at another table where last year's Hollywood actress was having dinner with the man who owned MGM. The Princess and the Toad. 'There is one thing I don't understand,' Ellie said slowly. 'Why? Why are you doing this for me?'

'I'm not doing it for you. I'm doing it for me.'

'But from what you told me, you won't get any money out of it. As you said, it's like taking the money out of one of Fraser's pockets and putting it in another. I don't see what you get out of it.'

'I get to drive my car again. The deal is I give you twelve

35

million, Women Unlimited renews their contract with Team Arundel.'

'But you just won a Grand Prix. Surely there are other offers. Other cars.'

'There are no "other" cars for me. This is my car and my team and we won. That's the reason you go racing. To win. This car was built for me. For my dimensions. Most of the other Formula One cars literally don't fit me. My feet won't even fit down the footwell. Besides, any other team capable of winning a race has drivers under contract. There aren't any other rides open with a team that can win. And goddamn it, we won.'

'So you keep saying. Surely there is an easier way.'

'Sure there is, Ellie. And if I think of it I'll let you know.'

'Forrest, look, I'm sorry about your car. I didn't then and I still don't have any choice.'

'But you'll help.'

'How can I say that? I don't even know what you want in the way of help.'

'I talked to Fraser's office this afternoon. He's going to be in Miami tomorrow and I'm going to see him there.'

'You ever do anything remotely like this before?'

I shook my head.

'Well what makes you think you can pull it off?'

'There's a saying in racing,' I said, 'that there's only one thing you have to do to win.'

'Which is?'

'Whatever it takes.'

Outside, her chauffeur was waiting with her limo. Before she got in she held out her hand, then changed her mind and put her arms around my neck and gave me a quick kiss. 'Thanks for dinner,' she said.

6

He was walking alongside me on the way into the terminal at Miami International. Looking back at me from the mirror. West Coast Casual. West Coast Smart. Oversize Armani linen sport jacket, lotta pleats on the trousers. Tassels on the soft loafers. $500 attaché case. A corporate man. One of the players on the Pacific Rim. Right at the top of his corporate ladder and looking for a higher ladder to climb. I gave myself a nice big grin. Today the role of Los Angeles hotshot TV executive will be played by Forrest Evers.

I had to admit, I looked like a Los Angeles TV executive. A man who talked ratings and recall. Knew his Nielsen's, liked the sitcoms for the demographics, but was prepared to go gameshow for the payback coming in on day one. An athletic man. A smart man. A confident man. A sincere man with a suntan and Zeiss sunglasses. Alistair Hampton, Senior VP from Sunwest. Alan Mowbray's right-hand man. The kind of man Fraser would eat for breakfast. For the first time I had the feeling I just might pull it off.

I told myself he had stolen the money from Ellie and he wanted to steal the whole company from Ellie. So why not make him pay back what he owed? Ellie would pay it back to him. I was going to take twelve million from his company to give to his other company so his other company could give it back to him, if you see what I mean. I wasn't really stealing his money, I was just stirring it up.

There is a story about Charles Lindbergh after he had been famous for years. It was March, and Lindbergh was standing by the North Atlantic sea in Sweden, looking at the waves rolling in from the Arctic, with some Swedish sportsman standing next to him, saying that it was because Lindbergh was Swedish originally, that he was so brave. Lindbergh looks at him and says he'll bet the Swede that he can stay in the water longer than the Swede can. They make the bet and the Swede goes first. He takes his clothes off, and he gets his courage up and he walks into the water, forcing himself. He stays in for around thirty seconds and he comes running out. Lindbergh takes his clothes off and dives in. He swims around and after a minute and a half he climbs out. 'If you're going to do anything,' he told the Swede as he took his money, 'do it head first.'

Head first then. Whatever it takes. It was just after eleven and I rang the PR lady at MIM–TV.

'Oh yes, Mr Hampton. We've been expecting your call. Mr Fraser is recording now at our Tamiami Studios.'

She had a breathy voice and I pictured her growing up barefoot in a shack in the Everglades, the big ol' 'gators cruising on by, giving her those crooked wraparound grins. 'What you do,' she said, taking her time, 'is loop right coming out of the airport and head south on Le Jueune around two miles.' Her voice made it sound like a question. 'Then turn left on the Tamiami. Two and three-tenths of a mile on down and you can't miss it on the right. Big office building. Number sixteen Tamiami Trail. We're on the twenty-third floor. Take good care and have a happy.'

Even with the sunglasses and the tinted glass in the Lincoln Marshmallow Mark Whatever the sun made me squint. But she was right, I couldn't miss it. It didn't look like the home of America's Dream and The Major News Stories of Our Time. It looked like a big office building with two banks and a Woolworth five and dime on the ground floor.

When I got out of my car in the parking lot in the basement and walked to the exit, another car door opened and a rentacop stood in front of me with a gun in his holster. He was fresh and cool from the air-conditioning in his car, the creases on his trousers and his shirt, sharp. A muscular cop, bored with his job, working part-time. Behind him, in his car, I could see the heads of two other men. Fraser was one of the richest and most powerful men in the world. So there was bound to be some security around, covering the entrances and exits.

'Can I help you, sir?'

'No thanks.'

'Name?'

'Alistair Hampton.'

'Anybody in particular you want to see, Mr Hampton?'

'Billy Fraser is expecting me.'

'You want to wait a minute, Mr Hampton?'

He went back to his car to look at a clipboard. I could feel the heat soaking in through my cool and casual California pastel clothes. He stayed in his car, telephoning. Then his window went down and he looked back at me. 'It's OK, Mr Hampton, they're expecting you.' His window went back up.

A trim black man with a thick neck was holding open the door to the building for me. 'Hi, Mr Hampton. If you'll follow me, I'll take you to the studio. We've just started taping, shouldn't take more than a few minutes. Mr Fraser's very quick.' He led me down a basement passageway to a lift and we rode in air-conditioned silence for twenty seconds to the 23rd floor. We went past a cute receptionist sitting behind what looked like a newscaster's desk with the letters 'MIM–TV in Miami' blue on the wall behind her, and through a door on the left and down a hallway carpeted in the same Miami blue. My escort opened and closed two heavy soundproof doors, mounted back to back, and I was in a small TV studio. Through one more soundproof door and we were in the control room facing, through the triple, soundproof glass, a small, tired-looking man in a business suit sitting on a simple wooden chair. He had the look of a man waiting for a bus. Billy Fraser's head was too big for the rest of his body with a bulldog face, heavy lines running across his forehead and deep furrows running down his cheeks. Blotches of white make-up hid the purple bags under his eyes from the camera but not from us. The weight of the world weighed heavily, it seemed, on his narrow shoulders. He'd loosened his tie and taken off his jacket. Just another hard-working newsman.

Inside the control room, the recording engineer leaned forward over his console and said into a little microphone, 'That was good, Mr Fraser, but we're hearing a couple of pops on the track so we're gonna dump that and go straight into another take. Any time you're ready.'

There were two cameras with floor mounts in the studio with Fraser. Standing close together, with their backs to the camera, four men and two women. The light on Fraser was intense and was making him squint. In the control booth a woman, sitting alongside the recording engineer at the console, said into the microphone: 'Billy, now that you've got control of the Miami Star Group, are we going to see some changes in the news?'

On the studio monitor, it looked as if Billy was surrounded by reporters, towering over him. He gave his head a shake and a boyish grin. As if to say 'aw shucks, that's a tough question.' Looking up at the camera, he said, 'I'm awful proud to be the new owner of MIM and the *Miami Star* and the Star Group. But I'm afraid I won't get much of a say on how they're run. With over a thousand TV stations in the Global-Village Network, I just haven't got the time to get involved. Even if they'd let me. But you're right, I think you're going to see some changes in the news. MIM and the Miami Star group of newspapers are now part of the Global-Village Network. Which means MIM and the Miami Star Group can call on the resources of Global-Village Newspapers and TV stations all over the world. So I think you're going to see a real improvement in the quality of your news. Just as soon as I get off your screen, heh, heh.'

We watched it play back, the camera going in tight so it looked like Billy was under heavy scrutiny. The director thought there was too much shadow on Billy's face. Billy thought he could do a better chuckle at the end. So they shot it again. Billy thought the camera move in had been too smooth and slow. 'Make it jerk a little and make the zoom faster. Like something is happening.' The makeup girl was dabbing away at the sweat beads on Billy's forehead when he peered sharply into the control booth. 'Somebody's in there I don't recognize. Who the hell are you?'

The man with the thick neck who had led me in leaned forward and pressed the intercom button. 'That's Mr Hampton from *Fortune Magazine*, Mr Fraser.'

Billy waved the makeup girl away and leaned back in his chair. 'Oh yeah. I been expecting you. My friends tell me *Time-Life* doesn't have any Alistair Hamptons on their payroll. And that tells me you're a lying sonofabitch. What the hell are you doing here, Mr Hampton?'

I leaned forward to speak on the intercom and the man with the thick neck leaned with me. Not threatening, just staying close. Another large man was leaning back against the door.

I pressed the intercom button. 'I apologize for the deception, Mr Fraser, but it was the only way I could get to you quick without sending up a lot of signals.'

'And . . . ?'

'And I'm here from Alan Mowbray.'

'Mowbray's damn near dead.'

'Mr Mowbray is terminally ill with cancer.'

'So what's so damn important you have to lie to tell me about it?'

'Mr Mowbray would like to sell you his train set.'

'What's that supposed to mean?'

'It means forty-nine per cent ownership of Sunwest prior to Mr Mowbray's death converting to fifty-one per cent after his decease for fifty per cent of book value.'

He looked around at the room. 'Let's get this wrapped up fast and set up a meeting room for Mr Hampton and myself. Hillburn, you got that?'

A dry voice behind me said, 'Yes, Mr Fraser, I got that.'

When they assembled the tape it was a 45-second insert for the local evening news with recommended pickups via satellite for the other hundreds of TV stations around the world on Fraser's Village Network. On camera, a blonde female newscaster with a fibre-glass hairdo said, 'This afternoon, Mr Billy Fraser, owner of the Global-Village Network, faced some tough questions from reporters over today's purchase of the Miami Star Group.'

This was followed by the 'question' about control, followed by Billy's answer. No wonder the lady at Billy's corporate headquarters said that Billy's unpredictable schedule wouldn't be a problem for reporters. There weren't any reporters.

'Hampton,' Fraser said, looking into the control booth. 'I'll be with you in five minutes. I got a couple of phonecalls I gotta make.'

The producer and recording engineer were rewinding their edit, gathering up their notes, and my escort seemed to have lost interest in me, so I walked past the man with the big shoulders at the door of the control room and went back out to the lobby. Maybe read a magazine, see what the receptionist had to say. The receptionist looked up, saw me, and went back to her novel. The trim man with the thick neck came out of the control room and sat down on the leather sofa, picking up a *Post Production News* from the stack of magazines on a chrome and copper coffee table.

'Hampton,' a bony hand on my shoulder and the same dry, flat Southwestern twang with a whiff of dead fish. 'If you could spare a moment.'

I turned around. 'Phillip Hillburn, Hampton. My pleasure.' Hillburn's hair looked like badger bristle; straight back and sides, short-sleeved business shirt from J. C. Penney, and three pens in his shirt pocket. He was a tall spare man who was either smiling at me or having a gas pain. From the dead fish on his breath I guessed he was having trouble with his digestion. Either way, it wasn't a natural expression. Or one that did much for him. An advanced case of gingivitis made me wonder if any of Hillburn's teeth were loose. 'Mr Fraser has suggested that I show you around while he makes his phone calls.'

'We have a great deal to be proud of in, ah,' he checked the call letters behind the receptionist, 'MIM–TV and the Miami Star group. Course I expect none of this will be new to you, but it's new to us and we're proud of, uh, MIM. I haven't had a chance to uh, personally preview the operation here, but we do our homework pretty thoroughly and I think I know the floorplan well enough to keep from getting lost. Shall we have a look?' He scooped out a handful of jelly beans from a bowl on the receptionist's desk and transferred them to his trouser pocket. 'It's the most modern broadcast facility in the South.'

'You must have made a killing,' I said. Judging by the fast fade on his grin, it was the wrong thing to say. Global was going to control the media for nearly twelve million people and pocket an annual profit of nearly twice that. But one did not call it a 'killing'. Especially since 225 people were slated to lose their jobs. One called it 'a rationalization of resources', 'an aggressive acquisition', or even 'maximizing profit potential'. But in the intricate laws of business etiquette, 'killing' cut too close to the bone.

A dimmer version of his gas pains returned and he said, 'We expect a positive contribution to our score card.'

I made a pleasant noise and followed his back into the bowels of the modern TV station. Apparently his mother hadn't made him wash behind his ears. Like the offices of Women Unlimited, the studios and control rooms of MIM–TV had an unreal, underwater feeling. Where the sun never shines. In one long, unlit and unfinished room with no windows, cluttered with cables and air-conditioning ducts, banks of computerized tape machines whirred back and forth to the commands of distant control booths. Monitors showed silent pictures of what was being broadcast, edited, copied, or altered by computer.

'I understand they do considerable post-production work here,' Hillburn said, nodding towards the rows of humming electronic slaves. 'TV commercials, features, and of course, a certain amount of drama production, although, after tonight, that'll change. We can source a drama from the corporate pool.' It was like being in the engine room of a ship controlled by some other, distant, and unknown power.

But what struck me most was the FM station. We were in the control room of an audio production studio, and Hillburn was toying with the rows of levers and switches set into an oak console for mixing twenty-four tracks, telling me from memory how much it all cost when he said, almost as an afterthought, 'and that's the FM station over there.'

'I don't see it.'

'Sure you do,' he said, getting up from the swivel chair in front of the console, taking two steps and patting a cassette deck, 'this is the whole shebang, right here. You could just about fit it into your briefcase. We're supplying all our major market FM stations with this equipment. We manufacture it ourselves, in Korea, so it's a very cost-efficient unit.

'With this stack loader,' he said, with a trace of excitement in his sandy voice, 'and computerized programming, we can simply load in the cassettes, plug it in and switch it on. It will be timed to patch in the news updates and weather from their AM station, bookended with our signature tune.' He gave the stack of cassettes another affectionate tap. Maybe he just didn't have the time to clean his fingernails. 'We can load in a whole week's programming and you'd swear it was all live. No reason you couldn't run a TV station the same way. The way we're moving you could cover half the earth with one machine like this, a computer to encode time delays, and a satellite. Take two satellites and except for a few Eskimos and penguins, you could cover the earth. 'Course I expect you have something similar in your setup out at Sunwest,' he said, putting his face in front of mine and treating me to another exhalation of dead fish.

I nodded uneasily. Sure I knew all that. Youbetcha.

Five minutes later we were led into a small bare meeting room. The sort of room where they have script conferences and the stale smoke circulates in the air conditioning for ever. Grey carpet, beige walls, and a long cheap Scandinavian-looking table with cigarette burns and ballpoint-pen doodles engraved on the surface. Fraser sat at the head of the table and Hillburn sat down on his right. I sat opposite Phillip Hillburn, thinking he was either ex-FBI or a Mormon without God. Maybe both. Somebody who resisted regular dental checkups. But was a very good imitation of a human being. Somewhere in there, there was probably a man struggling to get out. I didn't want to be around when he made his escape.

There was a faint, musty scent of perfume. I didn't really look up, I was concentrating on Fraser. But she had large brown eyes, and a wide mouth too big for a small oval face she emphasized with long straight hair. A plain yellow frock that was too short, like a little girl would wear. But the movement underneath was fully grown woman, of, I guessed, twenty or twenty-one. She wasn't tall. Her mouth was too wide and her eyes set just a little too close together to be called pretty. And she was a little overweight, like an over-indulged child. But something about her was powerfully sexual and disturbing. I couldn't tell if she was a child dressed as a woman or vice versa. As if she hadn't grown up but she wasn't a child any more. She sat by herself at the far end of the table, and her expression said she was bored out of her skull. At the time I thought she might be one of those children you sometimes see of powerful parents, emotionally dwarfed by the shadow. She stared intently at her father. She said, 'Daddy?'

'Not now, Caroline,' Fraser said, impatient. He turned his attention to me. He looked lazy and indifferent. Small dark eyes under heavy dark eyebrows, his bulldog look, looking at me as if he expected me to say something nasty. 'Now,' he said, 'I can give you ten minutes. Can you tell me the whole story in ten minutes?'

'No problem.' It was what the low level hot-shots like to say, and what the biggies like to hear. 'No problems, Mr Big-time, what we're serving here today are solutions. Solutions to your problem. One less thing you have to think about.'

I said, 'Let me outline Sunwest's position. Fifteen stations in fifteen prime West Coast Markets, thirty-eight million house-holds with an average Nielsen of 4.75.' Fraser was nodding impatiently. He knew all this. 'The company is wholly and privately held by Alan Mowbray and his wife Lisa Ann Mow-bray. Mrs Mowbray has been in an institution for several years and Mr Mowbray holds power of attorney over her holdings. Mr Mowbray has had a disagreement with his heirs and is determined to sell the company he built from a home transmitter in Pasadena into one of the nation's most profitable television broadcast companies . . .'

Fraser held up a hand. 'I don't want the commercial. I want the meat and potatoes. Why don't you begin with why he wants to sell it to me.'

'Mr Mowbray admires your operation. He feels his business would be in good hands.'

'Bullshit. Look, talk straight with me or forget it. Believe it or not, I have one or two other things to look after this afternoon. Why me?'

'Mr Mowbray gave me a list of names and you are first on the list. He said you were the most likely to have the cash.'

'Cash? Cash is for little old ladies to pay their mortgages with. I never pay cash. What's he want cash for?'

'Only as a goodwill gesture. The deal is contingent upon three things. Speed, secrecy and $12 million cash up front as a goodwill gesture.'

'I'm not sure I got that much goodwill.'

'Mr Mowbray knows he doesn't have long to live. He knows that. That's why if we do this at all, and my instructions are to seek out other potential buyers if you are uninterested or unable . . .'

Fraser made a dismissive wave with his hand.

'That's why, if we do this, we have to do it quickly.'

'You still haven't told me why he wants to sell.'

'Because, before he dies, he wants to put up a Sunwest satellite. He needs the twelve million cash up front to borrow the rest of the $220 million.'

Caroline pushed her chair back, stood up and began to walk around the room slowly, swinging her hips. Nobody paid her any attention. Hillburn said, 'Mr Fraser . . .'

Billy Fraser said, 'Shut up.' Then he turned to me and said, 'Twelve million up front deductible from fifty per cent of the book value of forty-nine per cent repayable from future receipts and/or shares in Village Network. Interest to be negotiated.'

I said, 'Roughly, yes. I don't think Mr Mowbray is particularly concerned about how the majority is paid since it will be after his death. His primary concern is the twelve million cash up front for the satellite. That is not negotiable. He needs the twelve million now as seed money for a $220 million satellite launch.'

'What kind of satellite? $220 million is cheap.'

'The launch vehicle will probably be a Ford Aerospace Probe VI. I can show you a model of the satellite in a week.'

His face had the same flat, uninterested look he'd had in the studio before the camera turned on. 'We've had a lot of experience putting up satellites. Maybe we could help you there. Who determines book?'

'The auditors of your choice ... But unless you want the FCC in on the deal, you should ask them to be discreet. Mr Mowbray is very anxious to maintain absolute security. He doesn't want his staff upset. And even after purchase, he doesn't want your holding announced until after his death.'

'I already got the FCC sitting in my lap, never mind looking over my shoulder. But I take your point. What's book?'

'Current estimates are $235 million.'

'Why doesn't he just go to a bank? A bank would give him twelve million for his shoelaces.'

'Well, officially, Mr Mowbray feels banks are too slow and they can't keep their mouths shut. Off the record, the banks don't want to put up money for a dying man.'

'He doesn't know the right banks. How fast does he want to move?'

'He would like to sign a letter of intent, including and accompanied by twelve million cash, by next Thursday in the Grand Caymans.'

'Maybe he does know the right banks. Look, we got a lotta homework to do. 50% of 49% of $235 million is, what, $57 million for potential, I mean what if he doesn't die, $57 million for potential control of a $235 million network plus a $220 million satellite. Spend 57, get 51% of 455. I like the leverage. And I have to tell you our satellite footprint is a little weak on the Pacific rim, so it's a natural fit. I guess you know that or you wouldn't be here. We have to take a good look at this, but I have to tell you my first reaction, off the cuff, is positive. It would help us in-house, give us a little more muscle to do the kind of vertical integration I keep talking about, wouldn't it Phillip.'

Phillip nodded automatically and Fraser threw his head back, staring at the ceiling. 'Most of the security analysts think broad-

46

cast media is a mature business. Most security analysts are looking up their own ass. Television isn't out of the cradle yet,' he said. 'You think it's big now, wait till you've seen the future. People in America watch TV an average of six hours a day. They don't have to, they could do something else. But they do. They watch six hours a day. If Goebbels had TV in Germany in the thirties we'd probably all be wearing swastikas.' He looked back at me with a low-watt smile. 'Where can I reach Mowbray?'

'A week from today in the Grand Caymans. I'll let you know the address. As I said, if you try to reach him before then, he'll deny the whole thing. He doesn't like being disturbed. And he's a very suspicious man.'

'I can understand that. I'm a suspicious man myself.'

Caroline had stopped behind my chair and rested her hand on my shoulder. She had long slender fingers and she chewed her nails. I couldn't tell if the musty scent was her or her perfume, but it had a high erotic note.

Fraser glared at her and her hand shrunk away. 'Sucker,' she said, quietly under her breath.

7

371 Park Avenue between 71st and 72nd is old money, layers of granite mansions fourteen storeys high. When it was built in 1897 there were fifteen spacious rooms and one family per floor, with extra, smaller rooms for the servants. Nearly a century later, there were fifteen spacious rooms and one family per floor, with extra, smaller rooms for the staff. Old money changes slowly.

A doorman in a green, Bosnovian Army Major-General suit opened the bronze and glass door for me, nodding deference and obedience as I passed. Inside, J. Edgar Hoover, Jr., a gent in a black suit and black tie and a greenish face lit from below from a bank of video screens. He had that look of suspicion and resentment that men in Security carry like a wart on their foreheads. I could be a kidnapper. Or an axe murderer. Dope fiend. Or a sexual pervert. (Sexual perverts were the worst. They were out there, doing it to each other all the time. Most people were sexual perverts. Rotten fuckers having fun all the time.) 'Somebody expecting you?' said the J. Edgar Hoover Jr. lookalike. There was a gameshow on one of his monitors.

'Mrs Channing,' I said, looking at my watch. It was just after 1 a.m. and I was feeling a surge of jetlag, my stomach asking my pulse and my nerves what time it was and getting conflicting answers. I'd called Ellie from Miami to tell her about Fraser and she'd said she was too busy to talk on the phone. But would I mind stopping by her apartment? I said I'd be late. She said, 'Wake me up.'

Hoover asked, 'What's your name?'

I told him and he went down his list of sexual offenders until he found me. 'Forrest Evers,' he repeated. He pressed a button. There was a pause and then a squawk from his console. 'Mr Forrest Evers to see you, Mrs Channing.'

A few more squawks from his console and he said, 'Top floor,' pushing buttons.

The inner security doors slid open and I walked across a wide marble and mahogany lobby, lined on each side with Louis XIV love seats that no one had ever loved.

The lift rose slowly, one light, one family per floor.

At fourteen it stopped and the doors slid open on a small,

oval, marble room. There were niches in the walls with vases full of fresh flowers and green tufted leather benches on each side of Ellie's door. The marble walls made it look like a railroad waiting room from the sepia days when the American railroads wanted passengers.

I rang the bell and after a while she answered, eyes looking up at me through the crack of the door still on the latch. She was shorter without high heels. She unlatched the door to reveal a smile and pink pajamas. 'Hi, Forrest. Thanks for stopping by.'

The princess in her tower, acting casual about the gent who'd scaled the walls in the wee hours. She turned and led me down the long hall. Polished blonde wood floor, pink silk bottom. I must try to concentrate on my work, I thought.

'Poor little working girl, working her way up,' I said, following.

'Well it's where I grew up,' she said, leading me through an open door. 'My mother's and my father's. I know, it's too big, but I don't seem to be able to bring myself to sell it. So I keep changing it. You know, redecorate it. Maybe when I can't recognize any of it any more, I'll move.' She stopped at a sideboard and offered me a brandy.

A brandy would be perfect after a long day in a false skin. And it was a Very, Very, Special, Old, Pale, Reserve, Baron du Justafewdropsleftintheworld. Thank you, no.

When she was settled on one of the couches she said, 'You think he trusts you?'

Down below, even though it was early in the morning, the cars on Park Avenue made a silent parade of light. Streaks of headlights coming towards me, red tail lights going away. Ellie's loose, pink, silk pajamas weren't rumpled and she didn't look like she'd been sleeping. She was on a pistachio leather sofa drinking the brandy she'd offered me. She looked soft and pale and sexy but her manner was strictly business.

'About as much as anybody who offers him a deal,' I said. 'So no, he doesn't trust me but he thinks there's a deal.'

'Some deal. Dying TV station owner wants twelve million in the Grand Caymans next Tuesday. Cash. Hey, great, Forrest, let me write you a cheque.'

'He wants to believe it. So the way he sees it, there's a big juicy network and a satellite going for half price. And he knows if he doesn't jump quick, he's not going to get it before Mowbray dies or somebody else hears about it. If you were as greedy as he is you'd think it was a hell of a deal.'

'I can be very greedy,' she said, dismissing her room with a little backhand wave. Under the pink silk there was a helpless little wobble of breast that treated me to an instant sexual stab. If Pavlov had studied me instead of a dog he would have got quicker answers. Her eyes, as usual, said nothing and I looked away.

High ceilings, tall windows . . . the room we were in was immense and felt half empty, that same spare look her office had. No doubt it was to emphasize the big splashy abstract paintings and the sculptured wood and leather furniture the Museum of Modern Art would consider 'major acquisitions'. It was an interior decorator's dream, not mine.

'You're not greedy,' I said, 'you're just rich. What's he like?'

'Fraser? You met him.'

'I met him, but he's a poker player. He doesn't give away anything he doesn't have to.'

'He doesn't give anything away. But I have to admit, when I first met him he was charming. It was one of those conferences the Pentagon runs, you know,' her voice shifted down to a mock baritone, 'The Leaders of American Business meet The Leaders of America. To discuss the Future Defense of America.

'It's mostly angling for contracts and jobs when they retire, but the golf is good. Fraser told me he was impressed with my management but that we were undervalued on the market and a natural target for a takeover. Naturally, I agreed. I'd been trying to get the market to notice our performance for months. And I like praise. It's something you don't get much of when you're the chief executive officer of a big company. The next thing I knew he was in my corporate pants, talking numbers, spinning out alternate strategies for a leveraged buyout, saying he'd finance the deal, make it easy. "Free up all those shackled millions," he said.'

'The great cash liberator.'

'It wasn't that simple. But he made sense. I mean his numbers made sense. What I didn't know was that he had a couple of my board members in his pocket. And I think he was behind another bid that came through Salomon Brothers, but I can't prove it. He was like an octopus, shaking hands with you with one hand, raiding your cash till with another, stabbing you in the back with another, touching you up with another, drumming up hostile bidders with another; he was all over the place.'

Ellie got up off the sofa and walked across the open space to stand next to me. She was wearing fur-lined slippers that looked as if she'd had them since she lived with Mommie and Daddy. She smelt of the creams women rub on before they dream. 'Love your shoes,' I said.

She looked down and then seemed to notice that she wasn't dressed for the office. 'Oh, shit. Look, I'm sorry. I was just getting into bed. I wasn't really thinking . . .'

'Of anything besides business,' I said.

'Of anything besides business,' she said with a little sideways grin.

'It's all right. You look adorable.'

'Why is it that when you say something that normally I would think is offensive, it doesn't sound offensive at all?'

I gave my boyish 'aw shucks, just me tryin' to do my best, m'lady', shrug, thinking of Ellie pulling the covers back, her breasts swinging beneath the pink silk. 'Maybe you think too much about business,' I said.

'Maybe you don't think enough about it,' she said, giving me a friendly little punch in the arm and going back to pick up her brandy glass off the glass coffee table. She gave me a mock toast, took a sip and sat down comfortably on her pistachio-green leather couch. 'Don't you think,' she said, 'that the first thing Fraser's going to do is find out there isn't an Alistair Hampton at Sunwest just like there isn't an Alistair Hampton at Fortune?'

'There is an Alistair Hampton at Sunwest.' Ellie made a face at me, doubting. 'Vice President in charge of special projects,' I said. 'I rang up Sunwest until I found somebody who was on holiday. "I'm sorry, Mr Hampton is out of the office until the first of June. Would you care to leave a message?" Look him up. He's on the Sunwest board.'

Ellie gave me a little smile and curled her legs up under her as if she was going to be a spectator, not a player. 'I can't condone this.'

'You don't have to condone it. Just give me a couple of your lawyers and accountants for a couple of weeks.'

'I can't do that. I play by the book.'

'God damn it Ellie, didn't anybody ever tell you? There isn't any book.'

'Sure there is. It's what they throw at you when you get caught.' She took a sip from her brandy snifter and leaned back against the leather cushions. My move.

'I'm not easy to catch. It's going to be at least six weeks before they find out they don't have a deal with Sunwest. The Caymans are outside US jurisdiction. They'd have to sort through several million banking transactions in six countries to trace the money. If they knew which countries and which banks to look for. The faster we make it happen, the less they are going to see. He's not expecting a fraud. He's going to devote all his time and money to sorting out Sunwest's assets, figuring out what he can sell off, what he can get for it, and what he wants to keep. He's going to be doing projections on how much he'll want to leverage the purchase, and how he'll integrate Sunwest into his network. Besides, the money is going right back to him anyway because you're going to give it to him.'

'The old Evers "out of one pocket and into the other" trick.'

'Well it's not as if we're going to keep it. Besides, he's going to be too embarrassed to come after me.'

'Forrest,' Ellie said, leaning forward and putting her glass down carefully on the glass coffee table and standing up and walking over to me again. 'You asked me what he's like.' Ellie stood in front of me and folded her arms, choosing her words. 'Maybe an octopus isn't the right image. You're talking about taking meat out of a shark's mouth and you seriously believe he won't come after you?'

I picked her up by her elbows, lifting her straight up over my head so her long hair hung forward and her calm grey-blue eyes were looking straight down at me. 'That's a chance I'll have to take.'

I let Ellie down and she put her arms around my neck. Soft squish of woman under the silk. 'You are a stubborn, pig-headed bastard and I think you're dangerous,' she said. 'I think you could get us both into serious trouble.'

'So you'll do it.' I kissed her, a nice soft friendly kiss.

'Look,' Ellie said, stepping back, all business. 'It's late, and I'm tired. If you'd like to stay in the guest room we could talk about it in the morning.'

'Ellie, I'd like to spend the night. I'd like to spend the night with you. But I don't want to screw up a $12 million deal because of a lover's tiff.'

'Tiff? One kiss, and the little fella's worried about a "tiff"? Look, Forrest, I am not some soft little girl, I am a business-woman.'

'You're both,' I said. 'It's what makes you so sexy.'

When I was at the door, I said, 'I'm flying to Indianapolis first thing tomorrow. I'll call you.' Then we had ourselves another kiss. A good one. Just to be sure.

8

'You'd never recognize it, would you,' Eugene said.

'No fuckin' way. Engine tore out of the tub. Tore the wheels right off that sucker. Musta slid six, seven hundred yards before it come back, smack the wall again. One hell of a sorry fuckin' mess,' Jack said.

'Dumb fucker,' he added, still mad. Jack was short and wide and almost cuddly looking except he had a twitch at the corner of his mouth that made you think a tooth was worrying him. His disposition gave you the same impression. 'Asshole,' he added, sweat rolling down his small, butterball face.

Outside the Fenstermacher garage in Gasoline Alley, heat waves made the people on the tarmac shimmer as if they were underwater.

The two mechanics were showing me Polaroids of my car before it was my car. After the previous driver had finished smashing into the wall.

'Fuckin' a-mazing a man could live through that,' Eugene said. Eugene was tall and lank, about twenty-six, with the sorrow and hollow cheeks of a rock singer who hadn't made it to the recording studio. He had a deep, old man's voice. 'All Tommy got was a broken arm and shoulder bone,' he said.

And a concussed spine and no feeling in his right foot, I added silently. In contrast to the wreck in the photographs the car in front of me was immaculate, brand new. New engine and box, new suspension, only the tub was the same. 'I admire your work,' I said.

'You're gonna find it a lot different from what you're used to,' Jack said, giving me a look. 'It's gonna feel real weird at first. We dialled in the same set-up as Tommy had when he lost it. You'll feel it want to turn left 'cause of the stagger.' Jack was older, tougher and shorter. Short arms and legs on a barrel of a body.

'What do you mean, stagger?'

'Well you probably noticed all the turns go left,' Eugene said.

'I'm glad you told me,' I said smiling. Eugene was trying on a little light humour.

'So what we do, we make the rear left wheel just a bit smaller than the rear right and the left front gets toed out a bit extra. What you call "turn too far".'

'The other thing, is these new radials jump around a bit. Takes a while to get used to,' Jack said, still giving me a look. Maybe he suspected I was going to smash the car too, and give him another week of twenty-four-hour days, putting Humpty Dumpty's fractured chariot back together again.

The car looked like a Formula One car on steroids. But then you'd expect it to look like a Formula One car. Americans rarely mention it, but Indy cars are British from their Dymag wheels to their carbon-fibre, aluminium honeycomb core.

Indy car chassis come in three flavours, Lola, March and Penske, all of them British. And all of the Indy engines, with the exception of a Porsche, an Alfa and a Buick stockblock, are designed and built in Britain. Even their electronic digital displays which can show the driver and the crew everything from a graph of the g-forces through each corner, to revs, lap times, fuel mileage and on and on . . . these too are British.

Indy cars race not only on superspeedways where the top qualifying speed can reach 233 miles an hour, but also on short ovals, road courses and street circuits, which partly accounts for the 350 lbs of extra heft they have over their Formula One brothers. To go over 200 miles an hour around a corduroy track like Phoenix, the car and the driver will either be strong or broken.

Despite being from the same family as F-1, Indy cars are a different kettle of specs. Their tubs are made with a combination of carbon-fibre and aluminium honeycomb rather than all carbon-fibre. (American engineers still believe aluminium honeycomb is safer than an all carbon-fibre tub because aluminium deforms progressively in a crash, like a shock absorber.) Indy cars are turbo-charged and burn methanol rather than gasoline. Methanol has a higher flash point than petrol and if it catches fire, you can douse it with water. So theoretically it's safe, although its flame is invisible in daylight. If a driver says he's on fire, believe him.

Fuel tanks are limited to 40 gallons and the cars burn a gallon every 1.8 miles, so pit stops play a major role in every race. And the Indy car tyres are narrower and taller than Formula One tyres, giving Indy cars a kind of hunched up, antique look from behind.

Like the Formula One cars of a few years ago, the bottom of an Indy car is an aerodynamic ventura that sucks the car down onto the track. Hit a bump and grip goes from good to zero in no time at all.

It was the year the Penske chassis (designed and built in Poole, Dorset) dominated the series, powered by a British Chevrolet.

British Chevrolet?

Team owner, co-founder of CART and the owner of a $2 billion automobile, truck and transportation empire, Roger Penske and General Motors financed a new engine from former Cosworth designers Paul Morgan and Mario Illien. The result, from Ilmore Engineering in Northampton, is called a 'Chevrolet'.

At the pinnacle of American racing, though it bears a name as apple-pie as Chevrolet, there lurks a Brit. Here a Brit, there a Brit, everywhere a Brit-Brit. And an Evers. Part Brit. Part American. Welcome home, stranger.

It looked like there was room in the cockpit for my 6' 1" frame for a change. I put my hands on the sides of the cockpit and was about to climb in when I felt a hand on my shoulder.

'Wait'll we get it out to the pits. Then you get in.' I turned around and faced George Gavoni the chief mechanic. His face looked like it was made out of barbed wire and cement. A crew cut that must have been just right in Indiana High School in 1957 was grey now and his eyebrows were steel wool over his grey eyes. If he had a sense of humour, I hadn't found it. He had built five Indianapolis winners and his cars usually finished the race. Like everything and everybody I'd met at the brickyard he was a 'legend'.

So Eugene climbed behind the wheel and the other mechanics looped a strap from the roll bar to a little garden tractor and towed the car out into the sun . . . a glittering candy-apple red and chrome, 800 horsepower ground missile on the black tarmac of Gasoline Alley rolling towards the launch pad.

'You're gonna find it's a lot different here from Europe.' Gavoni was watching the car as it was towed past the other garages, speaking out of the side of his mouth as if he was giving me an inside tip. It was the sixth time in two hours somebody told me it was going to be different.

We started walking to the pits. 'How'd it happen?' I asked.

'How'd what happen?'

'How'd the car hit the wall?'

'Fuckin' Hewitt,' he said. 'He goes into Turn One, and he feels it start to get a little loose and he tries to dirt track it. Thinks he can slide it around like it was a fuckin' sprint car. He turns into the skid and bang – ' George smacked his fist for emphasis ' – he's headed into the wall.' He turned his head to face me. 'You see, the car starts to slide, you lose your downforce.' He made a motion with his hand sliding sideways.

'You turn into the slide maybe you get your grip back, except now you got your wheels pointed at the wall.' He slapped his fist into his palm again. 'You fuckin' rookies.'

'I'm not a rookie.'

'Yeah? What the fuck are you then? That's what Hewitt said. He's not a rookie. He's National Sprint Car Champion. And that's where he belongs, on the fuckin' dirt. You feel the back get loose, you feel the back end start to go, don't even think about tryin' to save it. You're gone. You turn down to the inside of the track, stand on the brakes, and maybe you get lucky and don't hit nothin'.'

'What George is telling you is you take it real easy at first.' Orrin Fenstermacher had come up behind us. 'You be cautious, real cautious. All USAC wants to see, and all I want to see is you go around here on the line nice and smooth at 160.

'Normally, as a rookie you'd have to do over a hundred forty laps, you know, build up to 160. But since you're a Formula One driver, and you won in Monaco last Sunday, they waived most all that stuff. You do four laps at 160 nice and smooth, then we can talk about some serious driving.' Orrin drove a big calloused hand up over his forehead, ploughing the shiny scalp under the thin strands of hair. He was looking past the concrete garage blocks down the track towards Turn One. 'Ya'll go easy out there and for God's sake don't try and drive it like a road course. You get off the racing line a few inches and you are in deep shit. You try and slide that sucker and you can kiss your ass goodbye.'

'So I've heard.'

'You take your time. Ease into it. Nobody's expecting you to go fast yet. You ever ride a bicycle on a skating rink?'

George said, 'Keep your head down, your mouth shut and your ass off the wall and you'll get along fine.'

'George,' I said, 'I don't care about getting along fine. If I wanted to get along fine, I'd find some other line of work.'

As we walked past the immaculate concrete garages with polished linoleum floors shining like Mrs America's kitchen, and teams in freshly laundered designer uniforms, there was a ripple of nods and waves for Orrin and George. And blank stares for me. A rookie at Indianapolis barely exists. A driver who hasn't passed his rookie test doesn't exist at all.

Across the tarmac, walking the other way, with a driver's arm around her waist, there was a girl with long dark hair and a pink mini-skirt. I thought that it wasn't the swing to her walk that made her look familiar, but something looked . . .

Orrin interrupted. 'Like you to meet T. D. Jackson. T. D., Forest Evers. T. D. is our number one driver.'

A short compact man with a chiselled face and a permanent squint gave me a nod. I'd heard of him, three-times Indianapolis winner. A tough man from the dirt tracks of Oklahoma.

'Number one driver,' I said. A detail Orrin hadn't mentioned.

'Until you pass your rookie test, you ain't no driver at all on this track,' T. D. said. 'But don't let it bother you. It ain't hard.'

'It's just different,' I said.

'Yeah,' he said grinning, 'different.'

'T.D. will show you around the track,' said Orrin. 'Give you an example of how to drive one of these cars.'

'I don't drive that sucker,' said T. D. 'I just pull the trigger.'

We'd walked out of the chute that led from the garages in Gasoline Alley through the Tower Terrace Grandstand and into the pits for my first real look at the track.

It was like looking down the wrong end of a telescope, everything too far away. The main grandstand rose up in layers, ten storeys high and extended into the distance, curving around Turn One. To the right there was an even longer sweep of grandstands all the way to the horizon, curving around Turn Four before vanishing in the distance. A deserted beach on the Pacific, stretching as far as the eye can see can give you that same, just a grain-of-sand feeling. The Indianapolis Motor Speedway is a global Coliseum scaled for global television; too big for a man, too small for his machines.

I loved it. I loved the huge arena, the shock of the action about to begin, the feeling of the wild beasts about to be let loose. Said the Christian as he walked into the ring.

Even though it was a Wednesday, and even though the second (and last) qualifying session wouldn't be until the weekend, the immense grandstands were peppered with racing fans come to watch their favourite drivers drive and the others crash. For five dollars, you could sit in any seat. In Formula One, you couldn't look through a knothole for five dollars. But then, that's another difference. In America they care about the fans. There was a screaming in the distance. The old soul-tugging wail of machinery stretched to the limit; a sound that automatically makes a racing driver press his right foot down.

'Markovitch,' Gavoni said. 'His grandfather won three times in the fifties. His father won twice. Sounds like he's gonna make the cut.'

Seconds later, a purple and gold car appeared at the exit of Turn Four, suspended for a moment as it headed towards us and then, in the next instant, blurred by the pits, the screaming rising and dropping in pitch as he passed.

'Entropy,' Orrin said. 'Entropy's why people love racing cars. You know what entropy is, Evers?'

'Third law of thermodynamics,' I said, vaguely remembering my schoolboy physics, 'energy dissipating into confusion.'

'Dissipation exactly,' Orrin said, staring down the empty track where the car had been. 'Every place you look, things are breaking up, and dissipating. These days folks have fifty-six kinds of beer, two-hundred fifty kinds of magazines and three hundred TV programmes to choose from. Entropy is why there ain't no more movie stars worth a damn like there used to be, just a pile of celebrity names that change six times a year. There ain't no Marilyn Monroe, or Cooper, or John Wayne. What we get is a buncha ten-minute wonders and ten minutes later you wonder where they went. Who gives a shit what Meryl Streep does on Sundays? I tell you the half-million people who fill these grandstands on race day and the hundred million who watch at home on television – ' we could hear Markovich's car attacking the back straight ' – you can't imagine how complicated their lives are. And they keep hearin' they ought to upgrade their lifestyles. Shit, lifestyle's just another word for entropy. Too many voices, too many choices.

'But a racing car on a racetrack there you got the opposite of entropy. You get way up in the stands, you see what I mean. People love to watch fast cars go round and round because a racing car, long as it stays on the track, is simple force headed in the right direction. No dissipation and no complication. Just power in control. People think they want to see a car crash. But then when they see it, they don't like it a bit. Cause all a crash is, is more damn entropy. Energy dissipating into confusion.'

Markovitch went past again, sounding like a jet fighter with a motorcycle gang on supersonic hogs for an escort.

'Two-fifteen,' Gavoni said. 'That'll be a new record for a rookie.' George could tell the speed of a car by the sound, 215 miles an hour average speed for one lap around the 2½ mile track. Meaning 225 miles an hour down the straights. He stopped listening to the race car out on the track and turned to me. 'You're going to have to do a lot better than that.'

'George,' I said. '*We* are going to have to do a lot better than that.'

'Take it easy Forrest,' Orrin Fenstermacher said over his shoulder, looking at the pretty girls in the grandstands behind the pits. One of them seemed to be waving her phone number at him. He turned towards us, a sad look on his face. 'You try and go that fast your first time out,' he said, 'and they'll be scraping my nice pretty race car off the wall with a putty knife. I went to a lot of goddamn trouble to get you exempted from the Rookie Orientation Programme, and you better damn well do what USAC tells us to do. Goddamn it, they made Fangio take a rookie test when he came here in '58, and he was World Champion five times. Just cause you win a Formula One race don't mean you're automatically gonna be quick at the brickyard. Four laps at 140 and four at 160 if you feel comfortable. You go over that and you can just pack up and go home. They won't give you another shot for a year. Let alone qualify on Saturday.'

I shrugged. I was in no hurry to prove how fast I was. Teo Fabi came over from Formula One to Indianapolis in 1983 and qualified on the pole as a 'rookie'. And Formula One World Champion Graham Hill came over to Indy as a 'rookie' in 1966 and won the race. So it wasn't impossible. It could be done.

'What we're gonna do now,' said T. D., 'is I'm gonna lead you around, show you where the lines are. Don't worry about it feeling cockeyed. It'll make sense once you get over 180. Over 200, those chutes, those little short straights between One and Two and Three and Four just disappear. And what you get is two corners, one on each end instead of four. Just like any other kind of racing, the smoother you go, the quicker you go.

'Couple of things to look out for. Don't chop nobody like you do in Formula One. Somebody's got the line, you let 'em have the line. Oval racing, everybody's going a hundred and one per cent a hundred per cent of the time. So there ain't no room for adjustment. Just be real smooth and cautious, you know? Feel your way into it nice and easy and we'll keep you off the walls.' He grinned and shook my hand. I grinned back.

When he got into his car, there must have been twenty fans just behind the pit fence, taking pictures of him, smiling and waving. He got in slowly, lowering himself into the driver's seat of his car, twitches of pain reminding him of the nerves and bones he'd smashed at tracks like Langhorne, Daytona, DuQuoin, Trenton, Phoenix, Mechanicsville, Nazereth, Pocono, Sacramento and Milwaukee. He'd broken more bones than most people have bones. But when the belts were done up, strapping him into his Indy car, he grinned again, a man who loves his work.

I knew the feeling. A single-seater racing car is a wild, and magic high, a million miles away from the phonecalls, the messages, the agents, the sponsors, the girlfriends and the wives ... an 800-horsepower vibro-massage for the ego. Non-stop exhilaration punctuated by jolts of terror. A single-seater racing car is the closest you can get to pure power and all you have to do is put your foot down. Don't let anybody fool you, it is addictive.

I'd had my Formula One seat shipped over. Moulded around the imprint of my body, it fitted like a second skin. So it should. It's hard to go around a corner at 220 miles an hour if you're having trouble sitting down. So I felt right at home and my grin matched T. D.'s, yard for yard.

I let out the clutch and accelerated out of pit lane, hungry to get moving.

The car felt like a truck. It pulled to the left and there was less than an inch of travel in the suspension. Until you load the suspension with downforce from the wings at over 180 miles an hour and the nearly 3g's the car pulls turning into the corners the suspension might as well be set in concrete. Bumpity bump bump bump. I trundled along behind T. D., warming up the engine at a crawling 40–60 miles an hour, keeping inside the white line that runs inside the track. Everything felt bigger, stronger and heavier than it had to be. Colin Chapman's rule in Formula One used to be, 'If it breaks, it isn't heavy enough. And if it doesn't break, it's too heavy.'

Nothing felt like it was going to break. And there was more room. The differences were slight, a quarter-inch there and a half-inch here, but they were enough to give me the feeling that I had elbow room.

I was going to need it. The officials had waved off the other cars while the rookie had his first run. So it was just T.D. and Ol' Forrest out on the open track. No traffic. No 220 mph candyflake cannon balls rolling by on wheels. Just the wide open track with the concrete wall all around the rim. As we went around the track we crossed the scorched tyre marks of the cars that had 'lost it' and gone smash into the concrete. By the next morning the gouges, tyre burns and squashed car marks on the wall would be blanked over with whitewash. But the skid marks on the track were still there. T. D. picked up speed and we moved out onto the track.

From the stands the track looks immense, with steep banking in the corners. From ground level, moving along at 120, it looks much smaller, narrow and flat. Going down the straight with your ass bouncing along an inch off the ground, the first turn looks like a right angle left turn. It opens up when you get into it, but going down the straight for the first time you think it's too sharp. It also looks flat, as if the banking is only an illusion for the spectators.

We did a few low speed laps, 120, 130, 140, and the car was a mess, bounding around like a three-legged rabbit, vibrating, the wheel constantly pulling left. There was just one little bump on the whole track, coming off Three into the back chute.

160 miles an hour wasn't fast enough. There wasn't enough downforce to hold the nose down, so the car felt vague. It felt like the nose wanted to slide wide on the entrance to the turns, what they call 'push' at Indy. And coming out, the tail felt ready to step out, 'loose' they call it. But in a weird way, the car seemed to know its way around the track.

You can't turn in at this marker or that one. There aren't any markers. There was a break in the wall for a little hip-high door at the end of the main straight going into Turn One. And just after that point I started to ease the car into the turn. You don't turn into a corner at Indy, you lean into it.

The car felt sloppy and wilful. And the engine was rough and sluggish. At 160 it wasn't a problem but it didn't feel like it wanted to go much faster. 200 would be out of the question without serious changes.

When I came into the pits, Orrin bent over the car and I flipped up my visor. 'How was it?' he said grinning from ear to ear. Evidently I hadn't blotted my copy book.

'It's a pig, Orrin. An evil pig. But I'll drive it. As long as I can borrow your plane for two days.'

'I don't know. We'll have to see about that. What two days?'

'Thursday and Friday.'

'Next week?'

'Tomorrow.'

'Jesus H. Christ, Evers. We gotta qualify on Saturday and Sunday. That only gives us Thursday and Friday to set up.'

'Don't be such a baby Orrin. We have all afternoon.'

In Formula One you get one morning's untimed practice before timed qualifying starts on Friday afternoon. At Indy, they took the whole month of May, practising and qualifying. The first qualifying weekend had been the week before while I was at Monaco. The second session would be next Saturday and Sunday. Orrin and I argued about it for a while and we agreed that if I could get up to serious qualifying speed that afternoon I could have his plane, 'at cost'.

Serious, we agreed, would be over 218. Over 220 and I could have his jet for free.

The afternoon dragged as I crept up to qualifying speed. George set the car on a 'soft boost'; 42 inches of pressure from the turbo. This is an old Indy trick that makes the car a little easier for a rookie to drive. As I got the feel of the car and the track, George turned up the wick to the maximum 45 inches of boost that the rules allow, adding another 50 horsepower. But the adjustments took time. For the USAC officials, in their wisdom, don't allow you to work on the car in the pits. Every time we wanted to make an adjustment to the car we had to tow the car back to Gasoline Alley.

'The thing is,' T. D. was saying when we were back in the Garage, waiting for George and Jack and Eugene to make their thousands of minute adjustments, 'thing is, trundlin' around like you were in the morning, the car feels rough and sloppy. They all do. You get up to 180 and you'll feel it settle down. Then it's real easy to drive as long as you pay attention to it. Up to over 210, then it starts to get nervous again, starts talkin' to itself, trying to decide what wheel's gonna break loose first. That's when you got to listen real good.'

Eugene looked up from bending over the front suspension. 'T. D. comes in and he can tell us what each wheel was doing on every corner. That's 'cause he was born with his asshole inside out.'

T. D. smiled. 'That's right. And you,' he pointed a finger at Eugene, 'was born without one and that's how come you're so full of shit.' T. D. turned back to me. He'd been a tremendous help. You could say that since he had qualified on the front row last weekend, he could afford to be. But he didn't have to be here. He could be back at his 2,000-acre ranch in Tulsa. Or lying by some glamourpussy's pool in Beverly Hills. He had his own jet and $50 million in the bank. He could be any damn place he pleased. So I was grateful he was spending the afternoon coaching me.

'You pay attention to what your backside tells you,' he said, walking over to the car. 'Your head tells you to watch out for that bump coming off Three. But your backside says don't worry about it. Your backside says worry about coming into Turn One. That One'll fool you if you don't look out.'

My last lap, I'd turned 211. About as fast, I thought, as a human being ought to be allowed to go on the ground. I'd been 211 in a Formula One car. But I hadn't been turning left at the time.

At that speed the track turned liquid, a grey rushing blur, almost without features. At the same time, my head was pounded around in the wind so it was difficult to get a good look at the track and the car started to get jumpy again, darting off to one side and another down the front and back straights. The short straights disappeared and the trick was to keep the suspension fully loaded turning left all the way around One-Two and Three-Four. On a road course, there are plenty of places to go if you make a mistake, if you're, say, a hundredth of a second too late or too early. But hesitate at the Indianapolis

Motor Speedway, and the wall swings out at you at 200 miles an hour.

But I didn't have a real problem with 211. It was hard. It was terrifying. It was as fast as I could go. And it made me ask myself why I did this for a living. But I felt I could handle it. The only problem was that 211 didn't count. As George Gavoni pointed out, 211 would not get us into the race.

'What you got to realize, Evers,' Orrin said, 'is that even if you just get on the outside of the back row, even if you qualify dead last and blow up on the first lap in the race, we take home $60,000 in prize money and none of the sponsors want their money back. You don't qualify, we don't get a damn thing except a lot of bills to pay ... Shit, it costs me $35,000 just to enter that car. And I didn't bring you to Indy just to help me pack up an' go home.'

T. D. was kneeling behind Eugene. 'How's it feel going into One, Forrest?' he asked.

'Still a little soft,' I said.

'Why don't you give him a touch more right wing, and trim the left about the same. And don't fuck with the ride height.'

'T. D., why aren't you playing golf?' Gavoni said, rising up from where he'd been lying alongside the car. 'Play around with those little white balls before my big angry ones get in an uproar.'

T. D. and George had set up a thousand cars for a thousand oval races. An Indy car has an infinite number of adjustments. And every time you make one adjustment, however fine, it affects all of the other spring, shock, height, wing, tyre, weight and roll adjustments. So you have to remake all of those again too. The process of making these trillion adjustments is called dialling in. And the difference between a car that is dialled in right enough to win the race and one that won't qualify is finer than a frog's hair.

But they weren't really that concerned with the set-up. They knew the car was close to perfect. It was the driver that needed adjusting. They were giving me a break, a chance to catch my breath and think about what it would take to get around the course a few hundredths of a second faster.

T. D. read my thoughts. 'You know what it takes to qualify out there?' he asked me. I waited for his line. 'Balls the size of basketballs,' he said.

'I thought you said it takes keeping your ear plugged into your asshole.'

'Well,' he said, 'it's both. It's what makes us race drivers so funny lookin'.'

Outside, in the shimmering heat, the long legs again, the swishing pink mini-skirt.

'Trouble with you is,' said T. D. 'you're still a little wall-shy.' Everybody had lots of advice. T. D., I listened to.

He said, 'Coming off Two and Four, you want to whitewall it. Coming off the exits you want to be right up against the wall, so close it melts the white letters on the tyres. You exit too low, you scrub off too much speed.'

'You just flatfoot it,' said George, 'and this car'll turn 220 easy. Keep your foot down and don't fuck around with no goddamn wall.'

222 miles an hour down the back straight. In the old days it was the rev counter that sat on top of the dash. Now that electronics won't let you over-rev and the gear ratios can change five times a day, a little digital readout is your lap report card. How fast are you going? Not fast enough.

I was going 222, 223, 228, 230 and easing into a left-hand turn. The day had cooled and clouds covered the sun.

Speed, like its cousin, time, is relative. An hour before, under the sun, I had been struggling at 211. Now the track was cooler, giving me more grip. And the adjustments they'd made, made the car feel more relaxed and predictable. But the biggest change was the driver. I had driven this fast down the Mulsanne Straight at Le Mans and, until the corner at the end of the straight came rushing up, felt relaxed. Now I was used to the car and the track. Specific points stood out in crisp detail (the windsock behind the stands in Turn Three, a skid mark on the inside white line going in low on the same turn) . . . and I kept my foot welded to the floor, flat footing it all the way round. Which meant thinking ahead, knowing exactly where you want to place the car before you get there. Travelling across the surface of the earth at hundreds of feet per second, your mind has to race ahead, because by the time you imagine the car in the perfect position for turning into the corner, it's no longer there. And all with a delicate balance. As Orrin said, it's like riding a bicycle on ice, except that you are trying to change the direction of 30 tons of force while skimming across the surface of the earth at nearly four miles a minute.

Easing into Turn Three, I came off the wall and dove down to the inside line, just keeping my outside wheels outside the line, following the line around and coming off it, feeling the back end starting to step out, keeping my foot down, trusting the banking to keep the back end in line, feeling the outside rear tyre get back the grip it had almost lost, easing up into the wall on the exit of Four feeling the buffeting of the air trapped between the car and the wall, letting the car ride through the rough air until I was six inches from the wall, coming out of the turn so smoothly I couldn't tell where the exit was. It was the old feeling from Formula One, when I was driving well, that there was plenty of time, time to relax and feel the blip of the one-yard strip of bricks pass underneath at the start finish line and see the checkered flag wave before lining up for Turn One and turning in, letting my foot come off the pedal easy, slowly, keeping the car balanced and in control, slowing down to come into the pits.

'220.013. See, I knew that car could do it.' George was in charge again. George, The Legend. George, Indy's leading mechanic, taking his record-breaking car back to the stables. The record, which was unofficial, was for the fastest lap by a rookie. If I could do it again on Saturday or Sunday, they'd give me a $25,000 prize.

'George, don't you touch a thing. Just leave it set up exactly the way it is.'

George stopped what he was doing, which was acting as parade marshal for the little procession of car, mechanics, tyres, tools and fans that was headed back to the garage. 'You see, that's another thing you damn rookies don't understand. Every day is different. Hell, every damn minute is different. A cloud comes over the sun, the track changes. The temperature goes up or down a couple of degrees, the track changes. The humidity goes up or down, or you get a little more rubber on the track and the track changes. And every time the track changes, you got to change the car.'

'George,' I said, running my hand over the heap of rusty nails he had for a crew-cut, 'don't change a hair for me.'

People don't believe me when I say this, and maybe it was

gas pains, but George Gavoni bared his teeth at me in what I took as a grin.

What he said was, 'Keep your fuckin' hands off me.'

T. D. shook my hand and said that wasn't bad for a rookie. Before I left I asked Eugene if he could get ahold of some decals, and the best car painter in Indianapolis and meet me at the airport at seven. He said sure.

9

I was stalled, as still as the furniture inside the motel at four o'clock in the afternoon. Dry cool air-conditioned air, served with a hum. Pea-green cotton bedspreads on twin king-size beds. A blank colour TV, a brown ice bucket, dark green carpet, beige floor-to-ceiling drapes pulled shut to keep out the Indiana sun. Two blue, grey and green pastel landscapes of Muzak centered over the beds. And a blonde wood built-in dresser full of empty drawers, topped with a mirror reflecting a barefoot racing driver in blue jeans and a plain white t-shirt fresh from the shower. Time to start moving.

I picked up the phone and dialled.

'I'm sorry, Mr Fraser is unavailable right now.' Her light, clear voice filled with regret at having to give me such disappointing news. In the evenings, she probably went to acting class. In the evenings, I should probably go to acting class. I tried feeling tough, hungry, aggressive, determined and all those other hard words they use to praise linebackers and businessmen.

'Do you mind checking and seeing if he's available for Alistair Hampton?'

'I don't mind checking at all, Mr Hampton, but I'm afraid Mr Fraser really is unavailable. Just a second, yes, you are on Mr Fraser's priority list. Would you care to speak to Mr Hillburn? Mr Hillburn may be able to assist you.'

'I'd be happy to talk to Mr Hillburn.' There was a thirty-five-second interval of the musical drivel that corporations like to think the 'public' likes.

Hillburn came on, his voice bristling with the same artificial goodwill as the music. Walt Disney has a lot to answer for.

'Yes, Mr Hampton,' said Mr Hillburn, 'how can I be of assistance to you?'

'Can you take a message?'

'Yes, Mr Hampton, I believe I can take a message.'

'Mr Mowbray has instructed me to request a meeting with Mr Fraser on Friday to confirm your interest in purchasing Sunwest.'

'Well, we're very interested in purchasing Sunwest. I don't think we need a meeting to confirm that.'

'Let me put it another way, Phillip. Mr Mowbray wants the $12 million "goodwill" payment on Friday.'

'Mr Hampton, I appreciate the circumstances forcing Mr Mowbray to accelerate the timetable . . .'

'He's dying,' I said.

'I appreciate that. But no company in the world is going to be forced into making an acquisition of this size without time for sufficient appraisal and preparation.'

'We're not asking for you to buy it now. Mr Mowbray's asking for a deposit to give you exclusive negotiating rights. Deductible from the purchase with interest. A goodwill gesture, as I said, to ensure good faith on your side.'

'How much interest?'

'We'll discuss that on Friday.'

'I'm sorry. We're not going to be rushed into this.'

'Fine. Then my instructions are to accept another buyer in New York.'

'New York? What buyer in New York?'

'Tell Mr Fraser goodbye for Mr Mowbray.'

'Wait a goddamn minute. You said this was an exclusive deal.'

'It was.'

'Hold on.'

There was another long pause although, this time, no Muzak. Then Fraser came on, teased out of his hole, bristling with irritation. 'What's all this crap about forcing payment on Friday?' he said.

'Nobody's forcing you, Billy.'

Next, I rang Bash on the West Coast.

'Forrest, you old fucker. What're you up to? Hey, congratulations on Monte Carlo. You sound like you're next door. You passing through LA before Mexico?'

'I'm not driving in the Mexican GP. I'm driving at Indy.'

'What do you know about driving Indy cars?' Bash is a big man with a big genial face and the instincts of a barracuda. He makes his living these days building road-going props for movies. P–51 Mustangs with four wheels and no wings and bridges that collapse in slow motion when the quarter-scale model car drives over them.

But once upon a time, Bash had driven Indy cars before a crash fractured his spine. He knew all about Indianapolis.

'I'm learning,' I said. 'Bash, you know how I'm always saying if you want it built fast and right, you are the man?'

'No, I never heard you say that. What do you need?'

'I need an accurate scale model of a communications satellite in the Cayman Islands the day after tomorrow.'

'Sure, no problem. You want that sucker to fly by or just hover overhead?

'A nice plastic case would be good.'

'Forrest, what are you jerking me around for? A good model, you know, camera spec, would take me a month and cost you forty grand. I don't even know what those suckers look like.'

'I'm not asking you to build one. I just want you to bring one. One of the prop companies is bound to have one. Ask around. Or Hughes Aerospace in Long Beach. I don't care what model or what scale, but the smaller the better. I want to put it on a table in a hotel meeting room. It also has to be current. You know, next year's not last year's.'

'And you don't care what it costs.'

'I want to rent it. I don't want to buy it. But hire a plane if that's what it takes to get it there.'

'Where can I reach you?'

'I'm in the Speedway Motel, you know the Speedway Motel in Indianapolis? Got the number?'

'Strictly speaking, Forrest, the Speedway Motel is in Speedway, Indiana, not Indianapolis. Yeah, I got the number.'

'Tomorrow and Friday I'll be at the Caprice on Grand Cayman.'

'When do you want this thing for?'

'Friday. Can you do it by then?'

'Morning or afternoon?'

'There's another thing. Can you bring an actor with you? An old man who looks like he's dying of cancer? Somebody who can improvise. With a thin face and thin grey hair. Find a recent picture of Alan Mowbray, and use that as a guide. And if you can get any recent clips of Mowbray from his TV station, bring those too. Tell the actor we'll pay him triple scale for a day and worldwide rights, plus expenses.'

'Can I tell him what it's for?'

'Tell him we're casting for a feature.'

'Forrest, what the hell are you doing?'

Then I rang Ellie. Naturally she was in a meeting. It's what corporate executives do all day, go to meetings. In the evenings, after the phone dies, they work at their desks until they slump.

'What is it?'

'It's hot in Indianapolis.'

'Forrest, I'm in a meeting with a room full of people who have stopped discussing what we were discussing and are staring at me wondering why I've interrupted them to take a call. Can you make this quick?'

'No.'

'I'll call you back in half an hour. Leave your number with my secretary.'

'I want to tell you that except for a few moments on the track this afternoon, you have been interrupting me all day with your pink pajamas. And that I need your two best corporate lawyers and an accountant in the Caymans tomorrow and Friday.'

'Half an hour,' she said.

'You're missing a button,' I said.

There was a pause while she looked.

'On your pink pajamas,' I said.

I used the half-hour to make reservations for the Sunwest Development Corporation at the Caprice on Grand Cayman. If you've been to the Caymans you know the Caprice is a little thousand-acre whim of International Investors built to resemble the grand Victorian scale of the 1890s. A resort built to bring back that carefree time when people spent whole summers at grand hotels and when we childishly thought the world was going to last for ever. That carefree time before we punched holes in the Polar skies and peeled back the skin of the earth in the Amazon.

The Caprice has a choice of swimming pools, tennis courts, golf courses, saunas, ballrooms and beaches. And yes, they had a suite suitable for a business presentation. And yes, they had in-house video, satellite links and rooms for myself, Bash, and three other gentlemen, names to follow. In May, they always had rooms.

Ellie was punctual: thirty minutes to the dot, the phone rang.

'Forrest,' she said coolly, 'I don't like being interrupted. And I especially don't want to be interrupted by coy little personal remarks.'

'How are you?'

'Not too bad. I have a meeting with the finance committee in ten minutes and I should be going over their quarterly report instead of talking to you. What's this about lawyers?'

'It's the one four down from the drawstring.'

'Forrest, cut it out. I'm busy, damn it. Now why the hell does this have to happen so fast? I don't see how I can get you anybody, let alone two good lawyers and an accountant who don't mind risking their careers on a dodgy financial scam.'

'It has to be fast, before Fraser has a chance to think about it. The less chance he and his troops have to think about it, the better. And it has to be fast because Alan Mowbray really is dying. And if he dies there is no deal. Besides, it is what I do, go fast.'

'Should we be talking on the phone? I have this feeling someone's listening.'

'Who could be listening?'

'Just my secretary.'

'Well look outside and see if she's blushing when I say I wish I'd spent the night with you and fucked your brains out.'

'Forrest. You really know how to romance a girl.'

'Is she blushing?'

'Bonnie's not even at her desk. She's filing.'

'You checked.'

'I checked. Is that really the way you think?'

'Blame the button. Ellie, look, I know you're rushed. But so am I. I've set up a corporate jet, I've got a model of a satellite flying in, I've reserved the hotel and I'm flying out at six in the morning. And Fraser will be there on Friday. But I have to have the lawyers and the accountant and I have to have them here, I mean in the Caprice on Grand Cayman, tomorrow so we can draw up the papers.'

'Do they have to be real lawyers?'

'Real good lawyers. It has to look good and it has to protect us.'

'You're not just bluffing.'

'No, Ellie, I'm not just bluffing. I'm getting your money back.'

'That's not what I'm talking about.'

'Well what are you talking about?'

'If you had any brains, you'd know what I'm talking about.'

Finally I rang Tom Castleman. Sir Thomas Castleman, a man

who buys and sells companies the size of Brazil. We had crossed paths twice, and both times he had come away with a sizeable pile of money.

I had put him onto Texon. I hadn't meant to, but when I'd met him at a dinner in London, I'd mentioned a testing programme Texon were having trouble with. A little over a year later I'd read that Texon had paid him $85 million to go away and stop threatening them with a takeover. He'd also picked up a small British textile company for nothing thanks to me. So I felt he owed me a favour although I doubted that's how he saw it.

'Yes, Forrest,' he said, sounding positive and committing nothing. I pictured his sleek brown seal's head and his mild brown eyes as deep as optical instruments. At fifty-five he still had the long legs of a long-distance runner.

'Who should be my banker in the Cayman Islands?'

'Depends on what you want to do and who you don't want to know about it.'

'What I want to do is set up a company to take $12 million in a lump and distribute it to an American company without anybody knowing where it came from.'

'The IRS will want to know where it came from.'

'I have that covered.'

'What company in the US?' he said. 'If there's a company you want to invest $12 million in, maybe I could help.'

'Tom, I can hear your teeth grinding. But no, this isn't anything you'd want to be involved in. There's no profit.'

'I can usually find a profit.'

'That's what scares me. You were going to give me the name of a tame bank in the Cayman Islands.'

'Well, there are over thirty banks registered in Georgetown and any one of those can handle a twelve million laundry. There's also a couple of hundred guys sitting at their desks calling themselves private banks. But unless you're doing something really stupid I'd stay away from them. Give David Webb at Providential Commercial a call. He'll bend over backwards.'

'Can I use your name?'

'Not unless you tell me what you're doing.'

'I'm doing,' I said, 'whatever it takes.'

'That may not be enough.'

'You ever have any dealings with Billy Fraser?'

'We've met. But we never danced.'

Another idea was edging forward. Ellie's lawyers had led her into trouble in the first place. And what if Fraser recognized them? And what other time-bombs was I planting around my feet? I said as casually as I could, 'Have you got two lawyers and an accountant who can keep their mouths shut?'

'Forrest, I have fifty lawyers and accountants who can keep their mouths shut. It's what I pay them to do.'

'Let me borrow a couple for two days. I'll pay their fees.'

'Forrest, you sound a little desperate. My guys are not stupid. They are not going to do anything that might besmirch their standing.'

'Bullshit.'

'Unless, I was going to say, unless it is very much worth my while. Now come on, fess up. What little prank do you have in mind? I mean you can't seriously believe I would get involved or allow my people to get involved in anything I didn't know everything about.'

No, I didn't think he would get involved in anything he couldn't control. Which was why I didn't want him involved if I could possibly avoid it. He would take control and I would lose it. So I did the only thing I could think of to keep him out. I told him my plan.

'Seems straightforward enough,' he said. 'Straightforward fraud. And you're right, I wouldn't touch it with a barge pole. But I do like the idea. It's about time somebody pulled Fraser's tail. I think I could help you with your personnel problem for a small fee."

'What small fee?'

'I think I know just the gentlemen. Just the gentlemen,' he repeated for effect. 'I know two lawyers and an accountant who could construct a bullet-proof legal shell around you. And you'll like them, Forrest, they enjoy their work.'

'What small fee?'

'Oh, my usual consultancy rate, four per cent. Round it off to five hundred thousand.'

'Tom, I can't pay you that. I can't pay you anything. The twelve million has to be clear or there's no point.'

'Then have my guys write an extra half million into the contract. They're good, they'll find a way.'

'If they're that good, they can find a way to do it for nothing.

You owe me for Texon and for Courtland Mills, Tom. That's about a hundred million in assets you owe to me.'

His voice got softer and slower. The big shark putting his arm around your shoulder and showing you his smile and his teeth. 'Forrest, one of the first rules of this business is that you never owe anybody anything. I busted my balls for a year and a half for Texon. And I haven't made a dime out of Courtland yet. So don't give me that shit about owing you anything. If you want me to owe you something, lend me a dollar.'

'I can't go another half million. Fraser won't stand for it. I've told him twelve. And if I raise it up to twelve and a half he's going to have to go find it. Even if he agrees, he's going to need more time. This has to be fast and clean or it won't happen.'

'All right. So he's not going to buy an extra half million. Suppose I give you two guys for two twenty-five, plus their expenses.'

'I don't know. He might stand still for two twenty-five if we find a good reason for it. But two hundred and twenty-five thousand has to cover your guys' expenses. I don't want to haggle with you about their telephone bills.'

'I'm only doing this as a favour.'

'If you want to do me a favour, give me the second lawyer.'

'What the hell do you need two lawyers for? Give me a reason.'

'Sure, I'll give you a reason. If this thing doesn't look right, and smell right, nobody's going to get anything. Suppose this was your show. Would you walk into a $250 million sale with just one lawyer?'

'OK, you can have a second lawyer. But two days and I got to have them back here in New York.'

'Two days, starting tomorrow. Have your secretary get their tickets. They'll have to fly to Miami, then get a flight to Grand Cayman.'

'Sure, but you buy the tickets.'

'Tom, it hurts me to find that one of the richest men in the world is also one of the cheapest.'

'Believe me, two twenty-five won't cover my costs. How are you going to pay me? I don't need more taxes.'

'If those guys are as good as you say they are, they'll find a way. What's their names?'

'Sharfman, Gutierez, and Orsi.'

When we hung up I dialled Ellie again. Bonnie said, 'Oh hi, Mr Evers. I think your last phonecall upset her, she's really in a state. You're not going to upset Mrs Channing any more, are you?'

'What do you mean, upset?'

'She yelled at me twice and she's been on the phone for the last half hour yelling at our lawyers. I mean usually she's pretty calm.'

When Ellie came on the phone there was a hard edge to her voice. 'Forrest look,' she said. 'I don't know why I ever agreed to any of this but I am backing out now.'

'Wait,' I said when she drew a breath.

'You wait. Our lawyers are scared witless over this thing. They don't even want to talk about it let alone go down to the Cayman Islands. And I don't want to talk about it either. I have a company to run here.'

'Forget the lawyers. And the accountant.'

'I haven't even talked to our accountants. And I'm not going to.'

'Will you shut up and relax just for a minute. I have the lawyers and the accountant. The only thing you are going to have to talk to your accountant about is what you want to do with the twelve million.'

'Forrest, what do you know about finance? I mean, for example, do you know how arbitrage works? How much do you know, really?'

'Not much.'

'Let me put that in a more positive framework for you, Forrest. You know fuck all about finance and buyouts. Fraser will eat you alive.'

'I don't have to know anything. I'm not buying, I'm selling. And I'll let the accountant and the lawyers do the talking.'

'I think I'd better come down there. You need someone to coach you, show you the ropes, keep you from falling flat on your ass. I know Fraser, Forrest and believe me, you need me.'

'All right, I need you, but I don't need you for this. If Fraser or any one of his crew sees you or even think they see you, it would screw up the whole deal.'

'I'll hide in your bed.'

'No.'

'When's Fraser flying in?'

'Friday morning.'

'I'll fly down tomorrow and take the first plane out on Friday.'

'Ellie, no.'

'Yes.'

10

Indianapolis: incorporated, 1832. William H. Hudnutt III, mayor. Rising out of the flat farmland on the west fork of the White River. Home of the Eli Lilly Corp. and RCA. A growing communications centre. Looks just like a real city from a distance. A skyline, smack dab in the middle of Middle America. Up close, though, it feels real neighbourly, just like home town.

Across the black asphalt, another jumbo was trundling towards the terminal, gorged with race fans, race officials, celebrities, journalists, hookers and pit poppies. The Indianapolis Five Hundred is the biggest sporting event in America, and a half a million people come to Indianapolis to see it.

The second biggest sporting event in America, if you can believe the local papers, is qualifying. This was going to be the second weekend in qualifying, and, as the fans will tell you, it ain't nothing compared to the first. The first weekend, they say, is where the big money fills up the front of the grid. On the second weekend, the drivers who didn't make it on the first try to squeeze in at the back of the field. So there's an air of desperation and hope, but most of the big-name drivers and teams are someplace else, playing golf. And still, the fans come to Indianapolis in waves to see the last do or die dash to make the grid.

It was a quarter past seven on Wednesday evening. On the horizon, against the darkening orange sky, the tall outline of Indianapolis was beginning to sprinkle with lights. In the foreground, in the dusk, Orrin Fenstermacher's corporate jet was undergoing a cosmetic facial.

Air rushing along the skin of an $18 million Gulfstream IV at 600 miles an hour sounds like the rush of air over any other corporate jet. But there, the resemblance between ordinary corporate aircraft and a Gulfstream ends.

Orrin hadn't wanted to loan me his plane, and now that I was in it, I could see why. He'd fussed about regulations, insurance, the FAA, fees and stockholders. But the real reason he didn't want me to use it didn't have anything to do with money, rules or stockholders. The reason Orrin hadn't wanted me to use it was because it was his toy.

In the old days, financiers and lumber barons had yachts. Now they have jets. And if they are wealthy enough they have a Gulfstream. It's what the President of Ford flies. David Rockefeller has two. A Gulfstream IV can carry up to twenty-five passengers. Orrin's had seats for six and space for sofas, coffee tables and a bar. The leather sofas doubled as beds if you felt sleepy or sexy. And after that there was a small shower in the back just big enough for two very good friends. The walls, the ceiling and the floor were panelled with Fenstermacher's stock in trade; birch, walnut, birch, cherry, hickory. The effect was light, spacious, opulent and reassuring, like a high-tech men's club in the sky. But of course I didn't care about the interior, the interior didn't matter at all. What mattered was that the largest private jet at the Cayman Airport no longer had the Fenstermacher 'Touch Wood' logo on its tail, it had the Sunwest logo, a big W in front of an orange sun. I wondered what the penalty is for kidnapping a logo over international waters.

There was a crackle from the hidden speakers. 'We're just passing 34,000 feet over Key West, Mr Evers, and we'll be touching down in George Town in thirty-four minutes, ETA 904 local time. We'll light up your seat-belt sign in around twenty minutes. In the meantime, if there is anything else we can do for you, just buzz us on the intercom.' He switched off.

Maybe Ellie was right. Maybe I was rushing into this too quickly. I was getting the same it's-all-coming-apart feeling I had on the last laps at Monaco. Fraser might find a direct connection to Mowbray. Somebody in Fraser's group might know the real Alistair Hampton was short, bald and paunchy. Mowbray might die. Or worse, get better. They might recognize Ellie. Recognize her? Fraser *knew* her. They might recognize Forrest Evers, racing driver. My craggy face has stuck out of a few sportswear ads and a catalogue. And three hundred million people had seen me in close-up on television when I won at Monaco. The chance that someone would recognize me was real enough, up into the double figures of paranoia. What the hell did I know about international finance. Sweet fuck all.

I picked up the phone and started to dial the banker in George Town. Then I realized the number would go on Fenstermacher's bill and hung up. Part of the con-man's creed. Leave no footprints. Or at least take your shoes off.

From the air, Grand Cayman looks like a long arm with a bent wrist, enclosing a shallow sound. It is mostly mangrove swamps except for George Town, the capital, on the elbow. And for a long strand of sugar called Seven Mile Beach running up the forearm from George Town. For centuries the only creatures tough enough to live there were the mosquitoes. Now the Cayman government loads up flying tankers every morning to dose the air with bug spray and the mosquitoes are almost all gone. Except for a few berserk kamikazes who live in the swamp and still think there's a war on. Their welt will outlast your suntan.

We landed at 904 and taxied over to the private section of the airport where the Gulfstream dwarfed the jets of mere millionaires. It took a little extra time, but yes, it was possible to park the plane where the incoming aircraft could see it. Suppose, I thought, one of the incoming holidaymakers was from Sunwest. Or a Formula One racing fan. Cue Nightmare 606; I greet Fraser just as some fan says: 'Can I have your autograph, Forrest?' Only last year, somebody had asked for my autograph. Twice. The first time I didn't believe him. But it was true, the risks were mounting into a pile you could see for miles.

One thing about flying in on your own plane, you don't worry about your luggage taking a side trip to Chichicastenango, and you don't have to wait for it. On the other hand, having your own jet doesn't impress the customs officials. It was hot, and sticky, and the customs officials took their time looking at my passport. Maybe they were slow readers.

'How long will you stay, Mr Evers?' said a tall black woman with a frown engraved on her face.

'Two days.'

'Two days. Holiday?' She said it the way you would say "funeral".

'Holiday.'

'Enjoy your stay, Mr Evers,' she said, committing my face to memory. I wondered if the real VIPs breezed through; if it was just the bogus ones they slowed down to ground speed.

I was wearing blue jeans, Reeboks and a Ken Done T-shirt I'd picked up in Adelaide during last year's Grand Prix. 'Thunda Downunder,' it said, screaming bright colours. I'd assumed the bright colours would blend in with the tourists. Silly boy. The tourists were Norwegians from Minnesota, wearing all the colours of the rainbow between grey and beige and sandals with beige or grey socks. One of them tugged my sleeve and gave the back of my blue jeans a playful feel.

'Hi, conman,' Ellie said cheerfully.

'You really shouldn't be here,' I said. 'Who's minding the store?'

'I talked to my accountants. If this doesn't work, there won't be any store to mind. Aren't you glad to see me?'

'Not really. I mean, I'm glad to see you. I'm just not glad to see you here.'

We were moving out of the airport building in the middle of a wave of tourists, businessmen and returning islanders looking for taxis. The sunlight was a shock as we stepped off the kerb and out of the shade. Ellie wore loose khaki trousers and an olive drab Army t-shirt several sizes too big for her. I suppose it was her idea of going undercover but she looked as inconspicuous as Marilyn Monroe in Korea. Heads turned to watch her, mine among them, entranced by her clear, uncomplicated, grey-blue eyes, and the gentle wobbles underneath her t-shirt. She wasn't just distracting, she was the centre of attention. If there was anybody at the airport who hadn't noticed me before, they did now as she stood on tiptoe to kiss me.

I grabbed her hand and pulled her into the back of a ram-shackle American station wagon that looked like it had been abandoned on the beach twenty years ago and been doing penance as a taxi ever since. Its springs groaned when I got in.

'You don't have to be so rough,' Ellie said, staring out of the window on her side. 'And you forgot the luggage.'

I got out again and helped the driver throw our luggage into the back of the wagon. There wasn't much. A suitcase for me, an overnight bag for Ellie. 'Where you goan?' he asked with the pleasant unhurried voice of a man who is already where he wants to be.

I leaned inside the cab, feeling people were still watching. 'Where are you staying?' I asked Ellie.

'Wherever you are. That would be the simplest, wouldn't it?'

'It would be the dumbest,' I said. It would be bad enough if one of Fraser's people saw Ellie on the island. If she was seen with me . . . with me would be unthinkable.

'We'll find you a nice place,' I said.

'Forrest,' she said calmly, 'if you're going to treat me like a little bit of fluff, I will tie your balls in a bow-tie. I am the chief executive officer of a major multinational corporation. I'm here because it is my money and because you are in over your head. You need me, and it's only because you are so obstinate that you think you don't. And I miss you.' She added a smile to this last little twist.

I asked the driver if he knew of the Cayman Caribbean Providential Bank.

'We have one lotta banks in George Town,' he said.

'On North Church Street. In the West Wind building,' I said, giving him the address Tom Castleman had given me.

'Hang on, mon,' he said.

Ellie was sullen on the way in, staring out of the window at the low ramshackle buildings as the car wallowed along the two-lane blacktop at 20 miles an hour. The driver stopped for pedestrians who he thought might be considering crossing the road, and slowed down to a crawl when he saw someone he wanted to wave to and grin at. He knew lots of people.

George Town is the capital of the Cayman Islands, the centre of all Cayman trade, industry, finance communications and commerce and you can just about hold it in the palm of your hand. It's a sleepy little Caribbean seaside town with a scattering of new financial buildings that look unreal, as if they had been dropped out of the sky. We drove past five or six of them, modern, five- and six-storey buildings with banks, drug stores and glossy duty-free jewellery stores facing the street, turned left down Fort Street, and pulled up after two blocks. The West Wind building was on the corner, overlooking the harbour, the dock and the sea. Two cruise ships had anchored offshore and launches awash with tourists ploughed towards us. At 945 in the morning the air was humid and an electric sign in a shop selling Caribbean T-shirts said the temperature was 84°. It felt like 94°.

Ellie was out of the taxi first, her hair damp and sweat running down her cheeks. 'Who are we seeing?' she said, playing chief executive etc.

'The fence,' I said.

The lobby of the West Wind building was air-conditioned and mercifully cool. We rode up to the top floor in silence, Ellie wiping her face with a Kleenex and peering at herself in the elevator's mirrored button panel. She gave a little snort as if her face would have to do.

It was a quiet week at the Cayman Caribbean Providential. Thick dark green carpet cushioned our feet, dark mahogany panelling lined the walls. Green leather chairs and sofas sat empty. If you didn't know better, you would have thought it was an ordinary bank. A chubby teenager behind a receptionist desk pushed aside the telephonist's microphone that hung in front of her face from a headset. 'Can I help you?' she said without a trace of interest.

I told her my name was Forrest Evers and that I'd like to see David Webb.

'Does Mr Webb know what this is in relation to?' The girl looked doubtfully at Ellie. I looked at Ellie. By a zinging leap of the imagination, someone might think that Ellie in her olive drab outfit was a member of the Dingbat Revolutionary Army, but her manicure gave her away. Maybe the girl thought Ellie might be a replacement receptionist.

'Mr Castleman suggested that Mr Webb would be interested in my problem.'

The girl looked up at us, pushed her microphone back into place and swivelled in her chair so her back was to us. Judging by her back and the tiny movements of her head she was talking to Webb. Or her mother. Evidently the Cayman Caribbean Providential Bank was big on secrecy. Outside a breeze gave the sea a hard glitter skittering across the opal and aquamarine-blue surface. The launches were going back to the cruise ships for another load of tourists. I felt a pang of longing for a simple life.

After a couple of minutes the girl stood up and said follow me. When she had herded us into a small room with no windows she said, 'He'll just be a minute,' as she was already walking out of the door. Maybe she wasn't happy with her work. Maybe she was unhappy because the gauzy blue flower dress she'd chosen to hide the width of her bottom wasn't doing the job. Maybe I'd better start concentrating on mine, I thought as a man said good morning from the darkness of the hall.

David Webb was six foot four and greying at the temples; he held out a big heavily-veined hand towards two suede chairs. He sat in the other chair behind a small Regency desk. He wore a finely-tailored dark grey pinstripe standard investment banker uniform that would have looked at home in the Bank of England or on the Corporate floor of Chase Manhattan, but must have been unbearable without his air-conditioning turned up high. Bankers still wear those suits for the same reason they still put marble on the floors of bank lobbies: to give the impression of institutional stability and propriety. Priests in cathedrals of commerce. Button-down collar, Harvard striped tie. The room was small, and he and I filled it. Ellie stood behind her chair.

'Please,' he said. 'Do sit down.'

'When I'm ready,' Ellie said.

'Your friend Tom Castleman rang to say that you might stop in.'

'That's funny,' I said. 'He told me not to mention his name.'

'But you did anyway. And I don't blame you, I would if I could. How can I help you?'

'I expect that by tomorrow afternoon, I will have $12 million. And I'd like to move it into America without attracting a lot of attention and without letting anybody know where it came from.'

Webb didn't react but sat behind his desk. Waiting. Patient. I waited. Impatient.

'Well, first, let me reassure you,' he finally said into the silence, 'there are no bugs in this office.' He leaned forward, resting on his elbows, the friendly banker. 'I'm paranoiac about security. If I saw you on the street I wouldn't recognize you. You appreciate, some of our depositors are the richest people in the world. And I have to tell you if there was disclosure today, some of them would be shot before tomorrow morning.'

'You mean,' said Ellie, 'that what you are doing is illegal.'

'I mean,' he said, leaning back, 'that when I was an airline pilot for Pan Am, the regulations that covered taking off were in two volumes about this thick.' He held his hands about two feet apart. 'And every time I took off, I knew I had to be breaking some regulations. You can't avoid it.'

'I can avoid it,' Ellie said, sitting down.

That won Ellie a don't-give-me-that-shit smile. 'There are two ways of looking at money,' he said. 'One is that what you have is everybody's business, the government's, the police, your competitors. The other view is that your money is nobody's business except yours.'

'And yours is the second view.'

'If you've got the money, as far as I'm concerned, it's yours. You were talking about $12 million.'

'It will be liquid, cash transfer.'

'Drawn from where?'

'Jersey.'

'We do a lot of business with the Channel Islands,' he said. 'A lot of Brits are finding out their money isn't really very well hidden there.'

There was another pause. Then he said, 'Well, do you want to deposit it, set up a trust fund, invest it? We have some excellent money management schemes, and I suppose you know the Cayman Islands have no personal income or corporate taxes.'

Ellie was surprised. 'No income taxes.'

'It's a charming story,' he said, shifting into his friendly banker mode. 'Back in the eighteenth century, a merchant ship crashed into our barrier reef in a storm. It was leading a flotilla of ships and when she tore a big hole in her bottom she lit her lanterns to warn the other ships. The other ships misunderstood the signal, after all it was a very stormy night, and they thought it meant to close up their formation behind the lead ship. So one by one, all ten ships smashed into the reef.' David shifted easily in his chair, with the professional pause of someone who has told the same story three hundred times.

'The Cayman Islanders managed to save everybody on the ships, among them a cousin to King James II. The King was so grateful he granted the Caymans freedom from taxes for ever. It's what makes our island such a safe harbour for, uh, windfall money. And since our own government can't tax it, they are totally incurious about whose money is doing what. Now, what would you like to do with your twelve million, Mr Evers?'

'What I'd like to do is transfer the money to an American corporation as quickly and as quietly as possible.'

'We invest a great deal of money in American securities every day.'

'What do you mean, a great deal of money every day?' Ellie said.

'Billions,' he said, giving the word an emphasis to let us know we were small players in his game. 'The easiest thing for you would be to set up a corporation. You may know there are 23,000 corporations in the Cayman Islands.'

'And 17,000 inhabitants,' Ellie said. 'And lots of lovely restaurants,' she added quietly to me.

'Right, Mrs Channing, 17,000 inhabitants. I was in Switzerland a couple of weeks ago for a banking conference and I have to tell you I was looking into some of their new disclosure laws, and Christ, are they porous. You know, the Swiss banks absolutely won't disclose. Except if this happens or except if they happen to suspect . . . You might as well keep your money in a glass jar. It's not the country it used to be.

'But what I would suggest for you, Mr Evers, is that you take one of the corporations we've got on the shelf. We'll provide a board of directors and you would be the unnamed director and you'd have total control. And I guarantee that nobody anywhere can find out where the money came from or what you do with it or who you are. On the other hand, since you're in a hurry then maybe you should have one of the corporations that we've aged. To avoid attracting attention.'

'What would it cost?' I asked.

'For one off the shelf, around $5,000. An aged corporation is $8,000.'

'Sounds reasonable,' I said, looking at Ellie.

'Sounds dumb,' said Ellie. 'There are ways, are there not, of tracking down laundered money.'

David Webb spread his veined hands on the table giving us his patient banker's look of confidence. 'There are ways. Major banks use the Swift Satellite for their financial transactions and that memory can be accessed by certain investigators. On the other hand, there are over thirty licensed banks on Grand Cayman. And even assuming you knew the bank, and the day, each bank makes an average of some 20,000 international transactions a day. Beyond that, if I were particularly concerned about protecting your confidentiality, I might go down the street to Barclays and deposit your money, along with some other depositor's accounts. Then I could move it anywhere in the world as CCP's account. And bring it back bit by bit from time to time. The book-keeping is complicated, but it's nothing a computer can't handle. Let's just say that any investigator would have to be highly motivated and highly funded. And even then . . .'

'That's how you launder drug money? Use Barclays?' I asked.

David looked at us with the same confident look. He must have been a fine poker player.

'Wouldn't it be better if we made it legal?' Ellie said, tucking a loose strand of blonde hair into the loose whirl on top of her head.

'I don't recall that we were discussing anything illegal. But yes, of course, that is what I always tell my clients. Just because they wish to keep their financial affairs confidential doesn't mean they have to break any laws. It's always wise to be as legal as possible.' David leaned back, the old capitalist philosopher.

What we worked out was simple. We set up a Cayman Corporation called Sunwest Developments. Sunwest Developments would use Fraser's money to pay Women Unlimited $12 million for Women Unlimited Bolivia SA and for Women Unlimited Venezuela SA. The money would go by satellite to Women Unlimited accounts in those two countries and then be transferred by satellite to Women Unlimited in Canada and then to New York, in varying amounts not exceeding $25,000 so as not to alert Swift's flag system for large international transactions. 'We could go up as high as $500,000 without attracting undue notice,' Webb said. 'But I like the cushion.'

'And the transfer fees,' Ellie added unkindly under her breath.

David had offered to skip the money, via satellite, to half a dozen countries around the world before landing it in Women Unlimited's accounts in Venezuela. But we agreed that it wasn't necessary.

When Fraser found out that Sunwest Developments had

nothing to do with Sunwest TV and that all he had bought with his twelve million were leases on two shabby offices in two shabby office buildings in South America with six months past due on the rent, there really wasn't anything he could do about it, even if he knew where the money went.

David would be happy to set up the transactions.

'How long will it take for the money to clear from here to South America to New York,' Ellie wanted to know.

'From the time we verify the banker's order,' David said, 'about thirty minutes.' He looked at his watch, a busy man.

'Is there anything else I can do for you? We have contacts around the world and if there's any service I can provide . . .' his voice trailed off, as if we were both men of money and power and understood these things.

'There is just one more thing you could do, if you don't mind, David,' I said. 'Would you call Mrs Channing a taxi?'

12

Ellie pushed the stop button on the lift and it stopped. 'What the hell are you doing?' she said quietly.

'There is an eleven-thirty flight back to Miami. You should catch it easily.'

'You arrogant son of a bitch,' she said. I hate to think what you and that clown up there would have cooked up if I hadn't been there.'

'Ellie, it's great you're here. And you'd be a tremendous help if you stayed. But the flip side is that sooner or later, somebody, some assistant, some lawyer or Fraser himself is going to bump into you. And that would be the end of it, your career, your company, your twelve million. You can't take that risk and neither can I. Besides, I have two good lawyers and an accountant.'

'Oh, for God's sake, Forrest, lawyers and accountants don't know anything. They're like computers. They'll just bang their heads against a wall if you don't point them in the right direction. This is my money and my company we're talking about. What makes you think they won't recognize you?'

'They've met you. They haven't met Forrest Evers. Even if somebody thinks I look like some guy who races cars in Europe I can say, "Yeah, a lot of people say that." '

There was a buzzing. Somebody was calling the lift. Ellie kept her finger pressed against the button.

'Anyway it is a risk I'll have to take. You staying here is a bad risk and we don't have to take it. If you stay, fine, I'll drop the whole thing. Fly back to Indianapolis, forget it and find another way to get back into my car. It's what I should do anyway.'

'You really don't understand do you?' she said. She drew a gulp of a breath as if to cry. 'Why I came here. God I hate you big, strong, silent fucking men. You think you're so strong and brave and you're just another weakling. You're too weak to feel anything and if you ever feel anything you're too fucking scared to say anything about it. Another goddamn emotional cripple.' Ellie let go of the button and the lift started to go down again. 'You just do what a man's gotta do, Evers. And fuck yourself.'

As we were crossing the lobby I put my hand on Ellie's shoulder to comfort her, I thought. She stopped and turned to look at me, her eyes clear again. I leaned towards her and she hit me in the mouth. It wasn't a hard punch, but it caught me off balance and split my lip.

'Ow,' she said holding her hand. 'Oh fuck, that hurts.'

I have a theory that the father of the British race was a tortoise. It's the hard shell and keeping your head tucked in that allows the British to walk straight through disaster. My father was British; a proper, stalwart, suffering British gentleman (suffering mostly from an underdose of my American mother who had too much money and spirit to be confined to Norfolk.)

So maybe it was my British father and the father of all Brits that kept me moving, walking to the door, holding it open for Ellie as she walked through into the bright sunlight, and opening the door to the black taxi that had pulled up behind the old station wagon.

'Don't forget my suitcase,' she said.

'Look, Ellie,' I said, 'when this is over . . .'

'Do whatever the hell you want to do, Evers. I don't want to hear about it.'

I watched her car turn the corner onto North Church, heading back to the airport. It was hot and humid, the sun making the buildings, the street and the sea pulse with light. I was sweating and when I walked over to the old station wagon the driver was leaning against the door, looking at my bleeding lip. 'You havin' a busy day,' he said.

We drove along the coast with Seven Mile Beach on our left. Occasionally, in the gaps between the high walls, condominiums and hotels stuttering by, I would see a flicker of pine trees, white sand, and tourmaline sea. I was in paradise, with no time to stop.

Good old Forrest Evers, racing driver hero. The ladies just fell at his feet and he didn't have to do a damn thing but pull back the sheets, did he. Ellie was right, I couldn't find my heart with a searchlight. I really couldn't tell what I felt. Maybe the divorce from Susan and Beverly's death in Mexico had turned me into an emotional zombie. Maybe I always was. But I had pushed a very good woman away on the flimsy excuse that she would be in the way. Sir Forrest, adding insult. Was I afraid of loving her or was I worried she would jiggle the concentration I was going to need to make Fraser believe in this charade? I couldn't tell. Was I really this committed to getting my ride back in Formula One? There had to be easier, less dangerous ways of getting my old car back. I could probably do that with a few phone calls. Maybe the whole point was to do this for Ellie, to get her money back, and be the bright white shining knight on his noisy four-wheeled horse. Pedal to the metal, Evers. Flat out around the track. We of very little brain can only think of one thing at a time.

Or was I more afraid of her loving me?

Three miles out of George Town we turned left, drove through the pink stucco gates of the Caprice, and under an archway of royal palm trees, past the putting greens, tennis courts and parking lots, leaving Grand Cayman behind for the bland and expensive no man's land of an international resort.

When you first see it, the Caprice looks as if it had been built a hundred and twenty years ago, a solid Victorian pile of stucco, arches and balconies. Up close, the workmen were putting the finishing touches on a construction project that began by bulldozing a mangrove swamp eighteen months ago. The concrete, the paint and the plants were all new. And that bright and shining newness made the Caprice feel temporary, as if it were all just painted scenery for a play and in the night a wind would come and blow it all away.

13

'Señor Evers, no?'

I was bouncing on one foot, shaking water out of my ear and rubbing my face with a thick new towel after twenty fast laps in the Caprice pool. When I dropped the towel from my face, the sky and the water were the same shining blue, and the man in front of me was in a dark shiny suit with a cream silk shirt and a black tie. He was just over five feet tall, with a round pock-marked butterscotch face and long black hair combed straight back.

'I am Señor Gutierez at your service and theese, my associate, Señor Sharfman.' Sharfman was two inches taller with broad shoulders and one long, dark bushy eyebrow over a look that said he was sorry. He wore a brown suit with an undertone of iridescent green and he held his hand out to me.

'*Encantado*,' he said.

'I am sorry to interrupt your swimming, but I understand we do not have much time.' Gutierez pronounced the words 'sweeming' and 'onderstond'.

'You can't be.'

'Can' be wha'?'

'The lawyers. You cannot be the lawyers.' They wouldn't have looked out of place in a doorway in Times Square. Except for their manicures.

'What you want, more height? You think maybe because we are Colombian we are not good enough? You want to commit a crime and you think you gonna get to meet a better class of people?'

'What makes you think I am going to commit a crime?'

'If you not gonna commit some kinda crime, you wasting my time.'

'Yeah, well,' I said, furious at Castleman, 'your time is already wasted. Fraser is never going to believe you two work for Sunwest.'

'You want another lawyer, go get another lawyer. I don' give a fuck. But I graduate Harvard Law School, 1981, Señor Sharfman from Colombia Law, 1979.'

'Colombia, South America,' added Señor Sharfman, with a shrug that looked like an apology.

'And you know everything there is to know about laundering money,' I said.

'It is one way we peasants eke out our meagre living,' said Señor Gutierez.

'We draw up a contract, it's bulletproof,' his partner added, rolling his broad shoulders. He would have been easier to believe if he didn't pronounce 'it's' as 'ees'.

'We eat Yankee lawyers for breakfast,' he said. 'Scrambled, fried, sunny side up, how you like them.' Gutierez paused to smile, then let it fade. 'They get offshore, in International Law, they fucking sink. Señor Castleman say you gonna pay him $250,000 for our services, including Señor Orsi. What's your problem?'

'When's Orsi going to be here?'

'Tonight,' Gutierez said. 'He's comin' in tonight. He's having a tough time getting a flight out of São Paulo. Some kinda strike. He'll be here, don't worry.' Señor Gutierez dropped his smile and tilted his head to the side, appraising me. 'Señor Castleman said you talk to David Webb.'

I nodded.

'That's a good start. Now maybe we can sit in the shade and you tell us what it is you want to achieve. Then we see how maybe we can help you.'

We sat drinking iced tea in the shade until the shadows crept across the pool, and the scent of the jasmine vine arching over us began to bloom in the evening. Little brown lizards scurried out from their secret places in the dark plants and stared at us, arching their backs, as still as stones. Then they would think of something, and jerk their heads to one side, trying to remember what it was.

'What I want to do,' I said, 'is take $12 million of Billy Fraser's money, and transfer it to Ellie Channon's company in New York. He owes it to her.'

'And how do you propose to effect this economic miracle?' Gutierez was watching a honeymooner who had just climbed out of the pool hike up her overburdened bikini top.

'I want Fraser to think that he is making a down payment on buying a West Coast media corporation called Sunwest. I've set up a corporation called Sunwest Developments. . . .'

'No relation to Sunwest,' Gutierez said, still watching the girl with the streaming blonde hair.

'No relation to Sunwest. If I can move the money out of Sunwest Developments fast enough, I'll leave Fraser holding an empty bag.'

'An empty, but legal, bag, yes?'

'That's what we're paying you for. To make it legal.'

'The best thing,' he said, pronouncing the word 'bess', is to register branches of Sunwest Developments in Panama and Mexico, backdated, give yourself some history. We have connections that can accomplish this. But first we need to know if Sunwest is registered internationally and the same for any company called Sunwest Developments. We don't want no surprises. Then maybe, I think we route the money through one of our corporations, like Opal, in Venezuela. We got almost 5,000 corporations, you know? Everybody should have a corporation. We got so much money going through that one, nobody gonna notice your little bit.'

Gutierez took a thoughtful sip of his iced tea, set it down on the table and looked at it for a moment. 'It's not a big problem writing a default clause that would give Fraser control of Sunwest Developments. That would make the whole transaction look legal, like a safety net for him in case the deal falls through. But you have to admit, you got a fraud at the heart of this thing and they gonna have tape recorders, witnesses. But as long as you don't come back to the Cayman Islands, we fix it so it take Fraser twenty years to take it through a British court.'

By the time the sun had set we had a draft of a document that seemed to give Fraser Sunwest Corporation but which would, in fact, leave Fraser holding a balloon called Sunwest Development Corporation.

'Are you sure,' I said, 'his lawyers aren't going to find a lot of loopholes?'

'They gonna find two loopholes. We stick 'em in. Makes 'em think they smart when they find them. Makes 'em think they earning their keep,' said Sharfman, swirling the ice in his glass.

'Makes 'em think we're dumb spics,' said Señor Gutierez. The blonde had taken her top off and was sunning herself, facing him.

'And the extra $250,000 for Mr Castleman?'

'That's a little hitch,' said Señor Sharfman, raising a mono eyebrow, dragging the rest of his face up into a smile.

'What hitch?'

'Castleman want to keep the money fifty-two days. He earn around 15% interest, around $256,000, then release the money.'

'That's that Opal Corporation you mentioned. In Venezuela.'

'You not so dumb as you look, Señor Evers.'

'I was thinking we can't wait fifty-two days. The transfer has to be immediate.'

'That's no problem. Castleman lend your lady the money in New York from one of his New York accounts. Only charge 18.5%. Tax deductible. Everybody happy.'

I pictured Ellie's $12 million flying from satellite to satellite 22,000 miles above the earth. 'Above the law' took on a new meaning.

14

Both waitresses were black, wide across the hips, slow moving and graceful, their loose, pink dresses sashaying to the Calypso music. One had pulled her hair back tight and wore a fresh hibiscus in the knot at the back. Her skin was smooth and her head was as sleek as a swimmer's. The other woman was younger, about twenty-five, and smiled easily, her hair flowing over her shoulders. Across the tables of crystal and silver, a bride with blue eyes and hair the colour of sunrise stared adoringly at her new husband as he cruised through the wine list. Near my table, a stockbroker and his wife had left the kids at home in Connecticut and were trying to relight the passion they'd felt years ago, trying to think of something new to say to each other as they looked out at the sea. Her pale skin said they'd just arrived today and the creases across her forehead spoke of housewife worries and two little kids in school where they sell crack like candy. They were trying but it wasn't easy and for a moment she gave up the struggle and looked my way. Her look held me for a moment and she smiled. Then she looked away, having gone as far as she would ever go with a stranger.

It was a warm evening and the soft breeze blowing across the dining terrace seemed to be bringing romance in from the dark blue sea. I felt my swollen lip. I would call her in New York after dinner. Talk to her. I had no idea what I would say.

I had checked the conference room and the video link. They had set up a TV camera in a bedroom and when I flicked on the monitor in the conference room it showed an empty bed where the actor would lie and play a dying man.

Orsi, a shambling bear of a man, well over six feet tall, an oval, olive, pock-marked face, and small black eyes, had checked into the Caprice at six, wearing a new white raincoat and asking shyly for '*Señores Sharfman y Gutierez, por favor.*'

In a racing car, there are predictable forces at play. The rate of deceleration, the aspect ratio of the left front tyre, the coefficient of adhesion of the surface of the track, the weight of the driver. There are hundreds, no, thousands of calculations that could be made to judge the maximum possible speed one might negotiate any given corner in a Formula One racing car.

Or, alternatively, Forrest Evers, lying horizontally an inch off the ground, arms and legs working, head vibrating in tune to the seven hundred horses behind his neck, approaching the same corner at 190 miles an hour, might make the same judgement in a hundredth of a second and alter it a thousandth of a second later as another racing car travelling at the same speed, jerks left three inches. Strap me into a racing car and I will take it to the limit, and keep it balanced on the knife edge of control.

But here in the hotel, sitting comfortably in the mild pleasures of a corporate paradise, having dinner, I was completely out of control. I couldn't tell if I was heading for the cliff or the wall. All I really knew was that I was picking up speed. When I had taken Orsi up to the conference suite where Gutierez and Sharfman were working in a heap of papers, coffee cups, bottles of Perrier and books, Orsi had grunted hello, sat down, and pulled a laptop computer out of his satchel. Apparently he worked in his raincoat, his shoulders rounded under the weight of billions. He stood up to hook up a modem to the phone and sat down again, punching commands into his computer. Gutierez had said that everything would be fine now. I would see, he told me: in the morning everything would be fine.

The waitress with the beautiful brown eyes and the pink hibiscus in her hair looked at me, wrinkling her smooth brow. 'Is it all right, Mon?' she wanted to know.

I looked down at the plate of watery green veg and flakes of mystery fish under a slug of ketchup and mayonnaise. '*Si, bueno,*' I said, handing her the plate.

'*Fucking mullet!*' A shout from the hotel reception desk almost made her drop the plate on the tiles. The reception desk is all the way across a garden courtyard with a fountain in the middle blabbering away. Bash's voice had carrying power.

'Hey, Forrest,' his voice boomed out to the coral reef when he saw me pushing through the reception doors. 'You better talk to this turkey. He says you're not here.'

I put my arm around Bash's broad shoulder and ushered him away from the small crowd of functionaries with gaping mouths behind the check-in desk.

'Alistair. Alistair Hampton.'

Bash looked at me puzzled.

'That is my name here,' I said quietly. 'That's the name I told you I was using. Alistair Hampton.'

'I don't think you told me. But I have to tell you I don't think it's going to make a rat's ass. I can't get that goddamn satellite model out of customs. What happened to your lip, you piss somebody off or what? It looks like it hurts.'

'It hurts. Did you bring it?'

'I brought it, Forrest . . .'

'Alistair,' I reminded him.

'Right. But they are dumber than—'

'Keep your voice down. Where is it?'

'The satellite. It's great, you know. A jewel, a real jewel, of a little miniature, 1/43 scale. But the Cayman customs people won't let go of it. Dexter's OK. The satellite though it pretty much looks like you're definitely going to have to skip.'

'Dexter?'

'Lionel Dexter,' said a light and polished voice behind me.

I turned around and a small, grey, elderly man gave me a nod. The sort of nod he might have given on the edge of the stage in Chillicothe in the 1930s after a matinée curtain call. He had sparse grey hair and watery blue eyes and the shy sadness of a pickpocket. 'How do you do, Mr Hampton,' he said.

'Call me Alistair,' I said.

'If you wish. And if you wouldn't mind, I prefer Dexter, if it's all the same to you. Lionel sounds like a train set.' He smiled an automatic smile at his joke. 'I gather you are asking me to act in some kind of fraud.'

'If you have any doubts,' I said.

'There was a time, Mr Hampton, when I chose my roles. Now I'm afraid, my roles choose me, and I cannot afford to turn them down. And yes, indeed, I have,' he said, pausing to pull a cigarette packet out of the side pocket of his grey pinstripe suit, 'doubts. I have plenty of doubts. But they're only about being paid and being caught. What is it you want me to do?'

'I want you to impersonate a dying media tycoon, Alan Mowbray.'

'Oh, I've met him.'

The concierge in reception had a cousin in customs. No doubt it was just a misunderstanding. 'Ram,' he said, 'he good at fixing.'

Ram, when he arrived ten minutes later, wore two gold chains around his neck, a thin gold wristwatch, and a diamond gold ring. He also wore an unbuttoned sport shirt with giant flowers, white cotton trousers, and sandals. The Cayman's hip dude. 'Is bad now,' he said, 'the customs all close. We go look for my cousin, he know the man with the key.' He looked at Bash. 'What you do, man?'

'Yeah, well,' Bash said tossing his head like it didn't matter, 'I build race cars, stunt rigs for movies, shit like that.'

'Yeah? Maybe we do a deal, you fix me up with a Ferrari.'

'What we want to do,' I said, 'is get our satellite model out of customs.'

'What you want a satellite model for?' Ram asked.

Over the next two hours we found that Grand Cayman Island is not very large, that most of the people on the island are related to most of the other people, most houses don't have windows, only blinds that pull down to keep the rain out and that when strangers arrive they break open a few beers and invite the neighbours in. 'Hey, mon, come see who come here.' By midnight, we had the satellite back in the conference room and the only people on Grand Cayman Island that didn't know about us and our satellite model were either passed out in a bar or out on a boat, fishing. Ram could tell them tomorrow. It would be part of the story of how he made $2,500 from the rich Americans in two hours.

The conference room was stale and close, the curtains drawn, the remains of three dinners congealing on trays at the end of the table and adding the fragrance of fish to the smell of three hot men working in the room. Gutierez, Orsi and Sharfman had been arguing. 'You ask him,' said Gutierez when we walked in the door, pointing his finger at Sharfman, then turning to me. 'You give a fuck about percentages on buyback discounts?'

'What are you talking about?' I asked.

Gutierez spread his palms in triumph.

I introduced Bash and Dexter to the two lawyers and the accountant. The five men eyed each other doubtfully.

Bash put the wooden crate he was carrying down on the table, and said, 'Oh fuck, it's a mess.'

It was a mess. Inside the crate the gold foil of the satellite body had been torn, the sails torn off and the bottom of the crate was sequined with miniature solar cells that had fallen off. 'They must have taken it out of the box and dropped it,' Bash said, looking at the way it had been stuffed into the packing foam.

'Can you fix it?' I said.

'Sure, no problem. Should only take a day or two in my shop.'

'By tomorrow morning,' I said.

Bash looked at the crushed satellite model. 'Come on, Forrest, look at the sucker. Four of the solar panels are bent and the array extending booms are all out of shape and the antennae are a mess. What do you want me to do, ring room service for a screwdriver?'

'You didn't bring any tools?'

'There's a took kit in the plane, but I don't think there's anything in there I can use. This is a model and what I need are things like tweezers, wire, lacquer.'

'Do what you can.'

'Your voice sounds funny. Like a lithp.'

'My lip is swollen.'

'Poor baby. Does it hurt when you suck your thumb?'

'I thought women were the gentler sex.'

'Well stop thinking in generalizations then, and think about me.'

'You're not so tough.'

'No, I'm not so tough. How are you? Apart from the fat lip.'

'I was just thinking about that.'

'About yourself.'

'About how, in a racing car, when you're driving quickly, once you enter a corner, you're committed. It depends on the corner but on the fast ones, like Indianapolis, you have to keep your foot down. If you feel the car start to go, you can't touch the brake, you can't even lift on the throttle, and you can't tighten up or go wide. You're committed. Well I can feel this whole thing coming loose. Fraser's going to see the lawyers are clowns, the satellite is a mess, he's going to take one look at me and call the police. The only part of it that looks right is Dexter, the actor.'

'The guy you got to play Mowbray.'

'He's perfect. The only trouble with him is he wants $10,000 up front.'

'That's blackmail.'

'I told him five up front and another five if we're successful.'

'That's what we call participatory management.'

'Call it whatever you like. I'm spending a lot of your money.'

'Forrest, you're not on a damn race track, if it's not working call it off. Tell Fraser to stay home.'

'Ellie, it's two-thirty in the morning and I don't even know what country he's in.'

'How much? How much have you spent?'

'I don't know how much. Bash rented a plane. He says he had to pay Hughes Tool $10,000 for the satellite model. We just paid a local thug $2,500. But that's just the tip of the iceberg.'

'Spend it. If it works, I'll have it. If it doesn't, I'll just add it on to the list of problems for the receivers.'

'Castleman wants a quarter of a million for his lawyers and the accountant.'

'Omigod. Did you tell him what he could do with it?'

'I told him it was fine. He's going to hold the money for fifty-two days, keep the interest as payment.'

'Wait a minute, I need the money now. What kind of guarantees do I have I'll get it?'

'He'll loan you twelve million tomorrow. And charge you 18.5% which you can deduct against income.'

'What income? And what the hell makes him think he can get eighteen five. I better talk to him. Do you miss me?'

'I realize why I didn't want you here.'

'And?'

'You're a terrible distraction.'

'Sometimes, Evers, you have the grace of an ape.'

15

'At over 11,000 miles an hour, 22,500 miles above the earth, the Hughes Intar IV completes a 164,000 mile orbit in approximately twenty-four hours. Goddamnit, Evers, that makes you seem pretty slow, 11,000 miles an hour.'

Bash was reading the PR sheet that came with the model.

'11,000 miles an hour just to stand over the same spot on earth.'

I knew the feeling. We'd been going flat out and now we were stalled. Fraser hadn't shown up at ten-thirty. At eleven I'd called his office in Danbury. Yes, we were on his agenda for today. No she couldn't say what time, precisely. Mr Fraser was a difficult man to pin down to any specific time of arrival. I asked her if she could tell me where he was coming from, thinking I could at least find out what time he left whatever airport he was leaving. 'I'm not at liberty to say,' she said.

The room was done in different shades of green, lime green for the walls, dark green for the drapes and the carpets. The windows were shut for air-conditioning and through them we could see oily bodies strewn on the white sand. Offshore, where the water turned from light to dark blue-green, a speedboat was towing a waterskier across the horizon.

The long conference table had notepads and pencils neatly placed at each seat. On a separate table in the corner Bash had set up the satellite model in a plastic case. With just tweezers, glue and a make-up kit Bash had performed a small miracle. From a distance, you saw a box wrapped in gold foil with one flat, outstretched arm of solar panels. Bash had folded the other arm into the box to hide the tear in its foil and the missing solar cells. At the same end of the room in the other corner we'd placed a TV monitor. From time to time we switched it on to see Dexter, in off-hue blue and pink colours, propped up on pillows in his bed. He looked ghastly.

At noon we called the airport control tower and they said yes, they would let us know when Mr Fraser's plane landed. If we could just give them the call letters.

At one-thirty we ordered lunch. At two o'clock a plate of overcooked cheeseburgers arrived, saturating the room for ever with the smell of hamburger fat and stale French fries. We rang room service at two-thirty to clear away the plates and at four they did. At four-thirty I switched the monitor on. Dexter was sleeping, his grey head sunk forward into his chest, his snoring an irregular soft grinding sound. I switched it off.

We had worked all night, polishing and rehearsing. At 9 a.m. we were ready. Sharp. Alert. The rehearsed phrases on the tip of the tongue. By 5 p.m., after a day of waiting, doing nothing, we were exhausted.

At 5.47 p.m., the door burst open and Fraser was moving into the room, his nose up in the air, sniffing, blazing with energy, charging onto the field. This was his game. The deal.

'Christ, it smells like dog food in here,' he said in a loud voice, looking around the room, taking it in. 'What're you guys, the leftovers? You got nothing better to do than sit around this fucking hotel room?' Fraser was followed by his daughter, Caroline, Phillip Hillburn looking as if he hadn't slept in a week, and a tall man with a golf course tan, a large Adam's apple, big hands and a look of contempt pinching his long, wolf-like face. He looked like he ate takeover bids for breakfast.

But I wasn't watching him, I was watching Fraser's daughter. Caroline was wearing a soft white cotton top that draped over her breasts and stopped a long way short of her soft tanned navel. And loose white cotton shorts. And, as far as I could see, no underwear. It was an outfit that kept promising glimpses every time she moved, the long curved underside of a breast, the hollow at the top of an inner thigh. Her large brown eyes looked around lazily and stopped at me, with a little snort of recognition. If you told me her job at the meeting was to keep me from thinking clearly, I would have said she was very good at it. She was short and overweight, and her eyes, set too close together, made her look more clownish than sexual. But something about her gave off a powerful sexual invitation as clear as the pulse in the hollow of her throat. Against the background of Wolfman and Caroline, Hillburn in his light green polyester suit looked like wallpaper.

Fraser never stopped for breath.

'Well I'll tell you I got a hell of a lot of better things to do lose a whole day flying down to this dipshit little island.' He grabbed the chair at the head of the table and sat down still talking. 'You assholes ever hear of the telephone? You got a telex here? That's what I got in my office, a telex and a telephone. You guys too fucking dumb to do this on the phone with Hillburn? You afraid of $12 million, you don't think you're going to get your money if you don't see me count it for you. Let me tell you, I could save a lot of time if I didn't have to run all over the place meeting assholes. Global-Village is a rich company. And the reason it's rich is that I run it. I run 2,000 newspapers, 3,400 radio stations and a network of as near as 1,000 TV stations as makes no difference. And every single one of them thinks he has to talk to me. Well let me tell you a little secret. They don't have to talk to me, all they have to do is listen. If they listened they'd know they didn't have to talk to me. I'm telling you this because I don't want you to make the same mistake twice. You read all this crap about participatory management. Well the only thing my management participates in is profits.' Billy motioned impatiently to his daughter, Wolfman and Hillburn to sit down. They didn't move.

'I read a piece in *The Wall Street Journal* the other day that said some guys in business think I'm a dinosaur, almost extinct. A man who runs his own company. And that's right. I don't have a committee to tell me when I can wipe my ass.

'Who's taking notes? For Christ sake, I'm talking and I want somebody taking notes. You think I came all the way down here, three hours stuck on a plane, just so I can repeat myself? Start taking notes, or don't you know how to do that either?'

He looked across the table at me. 'Tell me, Hampton, you go to business school? I hope to hell you went to a real good business school. God bless the Harvard MBAs. They couldn't find their ass with both hands. Profit ratios, market shares indexes, brand profiles, they know all that shit. But I never met one yet knew how to read a balance sheet. I love doin' business with 'em. Like leading pigs to the sausage grinder.' He smiled, having fun. 'Only place you can find a dumber bunch of assholes in Washington. Let me tell you something. Never let politics get in the way of a dollar. That's where I agree with Mr Marx. Politics is money. So's power. And so's just about everything else you care to name this side of the size of your dick. Now who is taking notes?'

I looked over to Gutierez. He shrugged, opened the notebook in front of him and took a pen out of his breast pocket and held it poised. He held it in midair for the rest of the meeting.

'Mr Fraser,' I said, 'we are here to discuss—'

'I don't give a fuck why you're here,' he cut in. 'You can go play on the beach for all I care. I'm here to put down a deposit on Sunwest and get the fuck out of here. You said you want a twelve million deposit on 49% of Sunwest at half price. The 49% rising to 51% when Mowbray dies. You want to make a ceremony out of it wait'll I'm gone. Jesus Christ, what the hell are we waiting for?'

Fraser had turned in his seat and was looking up at his daughter, Hillburn and the hawk-faced man behind him. 'Sit down where I can see you, goddamnit.' They moved forward to find seats. Wolf-face and Hillburn to the right side of the table, facing me, Caroline walking behind me trailing a fingernail lightly across the back of my neck, trailing a scent of musk and apples that promised all the variations the goblins of my mind could dream up. She watched me watching her sit down and she gave me a little smile behind a little yawn, then looked away, a fisherman setting the hook.

'Now here's what I want,' Fraser said.

'Mr Fraser, we have a document,' I said.

'Look, Hampton, I didn't get where I am by reading somebody else's paper. I'm not interested in walking through a hundred and fifty-seven sub-clauses looking for snakes.'

'It's a simple document,' I said. 'Even you could read it.'

He looked at me for the first time, sizing me up.

'You're here, you might as well look at it,' I said, trying to ignore the image of Caroline bouncing on white sheets. The goblins were just warming up.

'This is what Mr Mowbray wants,' I said. 'And if you don't want to read it, then fly home. We're not short of buyers.'

Fraser grabbed the document I was holding and passed it over to Hillburn. 'Read it, Phillip,' Fraser said, not looking at him, 'you know what I want.'

'While he's reading,' I said, 'maybe you'd like to talk to Alan Mowbray.'

'What for?'

'You're buying his company.'

'Is this the entertainment part of the show?'

'We've arranged,' I said, 'a satellite link-up to Mr Mowbray in his hospital room in Santa Barbara. If you have any questions, I'd appreciate you keep them as brief as possible. Mr Mowbray is a very sick man.'

I got up and turned on the monitor. Dexter was still snoring, his head forward, a plastic tube stuck up his nostril. 'Mr Mowbray,' I said into a microphone on top of the monitor. 'Mr Mowbray, can you hear me?' His head jerked up and he looked around puzzled. He stared at us out of the monitor, his eyes blinking. There was a touch of green in his make-up and the bags under his eyes hung down like grey turkey wattles.

'Mr Mowbray, this is Alistair Hampton. I have Mr Fraser with me and you are coming to us live via a satellite link to the Cayman Islands.'

'What?'

'I have Mr Fraser with me on Grand Cayman Island.'

'I can't see you.'

'No, but we can see you.'

'I look like shit.'

'Mr Mowbray, Mr Fraser would like a word with you.'

'Well for God's sake let him have it and let me go back to sleep. I'm going to die soon, I need all the sleep I can get.'

Fraser had stood up and was standing behind me, peering into the set.

'You look pretty sick. You know what's going on?'

'Ask me after I'm dead. Maybe then I'll give you a good answer.'

'What the hell you want a satellite for?'

'Same reason you want one. Depression proof. Better than owning the water supply. Best goddamn money machine ever invented. You got any more philosophical questions, or can I go back to sleep now?' He closed his eyes for a moment, then he opened them again, slowly. 'Listen, Fraser,' he said, his voice crusty with age. 'You do what Alistair says, you'll be OK. He's a good boy. You'll be OK.' Then Dexter made a grimace of pain and closed his eyes. Fraser went up to the screen and watched closely for a few seconds.

'He's breathing,' Fraser said, peering at Dexter. Then Fraser switched off the set. 'He's still breathing. Let's get this sonofabitch signed.'

'Would you like to take a look at the model of the satellite?' I asked.

'I saw that piece of junk when I came in the room. Four

years out of date. You guys really couldn't find your ass with both hands, could you? Don't worry, when we put up the satellite, I'll choose it. We're gonna go with these new microsats as soon as they can prove their performance. Launch 'em from a 707 and you can forget about two-thirds of the cost of a launch vehicle. Jesus, where'd you get that thing?' he said, pointing at the model. 'Looks like somebody sat on it.' He made a dry coughing sound which must have been his idea of laughter. Hillburn had hung his polyester suit jacket over the back of his chair. He said, 'Mr Fraser, I think we need to be careful here.'

Fraser cut him off. 'Phillip, I don't give a monkey's dick what you think. I don't even care *if* you think.' Fraser smiled benignly at Phillip. 'You got a hard job, Phillip. Your job is to do what I tell you to do. Now I know, Phil, nobody likes to do another man's bidding. But goddamnit, I pay you to do mine.

'You want to think, Phillip, you get somebody else to pay your salary. That clear enough?' Then he turned to the wolfish one, saying, 'You got anything you want to add, Meyer?' Meyer's expression of contempt hadn't changed since he came into the room, although whether it was aimed at us, or Hillburn or Fraser or what he'd had for breakfast was impossible to tell.

'Not a lot,' he said with just a trace of guttural accent I couldn't place. 'But there's a faint whiff of bullshit in the air. It doesn't look to me like it's the same company.'

'It's not the same company,' I said. 'It's a separate holding company.'

'Without the charter, I think we need one or two things spelled out.'

Gutierez looked up. 'I appreciate your concern,' he said. 'But I think you going to find, if you read the guarantee clause, that if the deal is not concluded to your satisfaction, you have sufficient remedies. If we default in any way, for example, you can claim 100% ownership of the company.'

'It doesn't give me a good feeling.'

Fraser threw his head back, stretching his arms. 'Oh for Christ's sake, Meyer, you never have a good feeling in your life. If there's a guarantee clause, and it looks OK, let's sign the fucking thing, give them the money and get outta here. We should have been in Tampa six hours ago.' He looked over to me. 'Don't get involved in theme parks. The assholes who run theme parks make Rambo look like an intellectual. Christ, what a bunch of dogbrains.'

He got up and walked over to the window, staring out to the sea, leaving the rest of us staring at his back. 'Look, Hampton, we're a long way apart on price. What you guys are offering is another lump of coal. Everybody thinks, Billy you just lucky. You just see the jewels before anybody else sees 'em. Well let me tell you something,' he said, his voice quiet and weary now. 'I see the same shit as everybody else sees. Only difference is, I know how to squeeze it. Squeeze a lump of coal hard enough and you get a diamond. Christ, knows you got a lot to squeeze in that Sunwest outfit. You guys are sinking with dead weight. You got two dozen salesmen you don't need. You don't need 85% of your production studios and staff. We plug you into the Village Network, you won't need a goddamn thing except transmitters. So don't try to tell me that lump of coal you got is a goddamn jewel.'

He turned back towards us, his arms outstretched. 'But I didn't come here to haggle about the price. We can work that out later. You wanted $12 million to guarantee me 49% rising to 51% on the death of Alan Mowbray for half the book value. Let's just sign the thing, give the bastard his money before he dies and we'll be on our way. We'll talk about book value later. OK Meyer?'

Meyer, the Wolfman, threw his hands up in surrender

On the way out, Caroline stopped in front of me, her eyes level with my shoulders. She took my hand lightly. 'I don't know who you are or what you're doing,' she said. 'But when my father was in his prime he wouldn't have even let you in the same room.'

I drove out to the airport with them in the hotel limousine. It was stifling, Billy was in an expansive mood, laughing, telling stories about private dinners at the White House. 'It's God's truth,' he said. 'I've seen him. He sits down to pee.' They walked Caroline to her little jet and stood and watched as her plane took off and curved off into the distance in the blue sky. Then they got on Billy's Lear Jet, the plane turned to taxi down the runway and the last time I saw William H. Fraser, his face

was behind an oval window in his executive jet. Billy was
smiling and waving.

16

'Hello.'

'Hello, Ellie.'

'Who is this?'

'Come on, Ellie, your secretary just told you it's me. Don't be so damn difficult.'

'Oh yes. The twelve-million-dollar man. What can I do for you, Mr Evers?'

'You can stop behaving like a chief executive officer for two minutes and listen to what happened.'

'It's your dime. Are you OK?'

'Not bad. But nothing went right.'

'What do you mean, nothing?'

'I mean nothing. Not one thing. It cost us six grand to get the model out of customs. And when we got it, it was a mess. The two lawyers and the accountant Castleman charged you $250,000 for were three guys who looked like the doormen in a strip joint. Fraser was six hours late. He took one look at the satellite and said it was the wrong one. He wouldn't listen to a word I said— '

'Probably just as well . . .'

'And he never glanced at the contract. And I think his daughter saw through the whole thing.'

'So how much am I out?'

'You're not.'

'Not what? I mean how much did this idiotic charade cost?'

'Ellie, he bought it. He signed the contract. He sent the money. Ask Castleman. Call your bank. Fraser went for it with a low moan. I think he was just acting tough so we wouldn't think he was a pushover. But it doesn't matter. You have the twelve million.'

'You mean Castleman has it. Where are you?'

'I don't know, somewhere over Arkansas.'

'I never noticed, you have a little lisp.'

'My lip is still swollen.'

'Poor baby. Does it hurt?'

'Next time I hit back.'

'You're not so tough. It really worked?'

'That's what I'm calling to tell you.'

'*Whoooooooeeeeeeeeeee*. Really, Forrest?'

'Your twelve million flew first class, via satellite, to Bermuda, Mexico, Sao Paulo, Buenos Aires to Argentina, safe and sound.'

'No bullshit?'

'When did you start saying bullshit?'

'When I found out what it takes to become a chief executive officer. Did I tell you I knocked down Castleman from 18 to 13.75%?'

'You're so sexy.'

'Fuck you.'

'When?'

'Damn you Forrest. Does it occur to you that there is something missing in this relationship?'

'I didn't know anybody said "relationship" any more. You used to be my employer.'

'Well, all right. I felt a few sparks. Like maybe there could be something more. But you were just thinking fuck and run.'

'How the hell do you know what I'm thinking. You want a lifetime guarantee?'

'I don't know what I want. I don't want to fight. You think maybe we could stop fighting?'

'Sure. Say thank you.'

'Thank you for bringing my money back. Now maybe you could say the same.'

'What for?'

'For giving you your ride back, dummy.'

'When?'

'I don't know. What's the next Grand Prix?'

'The American. In Phoenix. The week after Indy.'

'That's good. That's really good. You know what a Phoenix is, don't you, Forrest? It's a bird that rises up from the ashes.'

'After it burned to death.'

17

We were waiting in line. It was hot, humid and hazy and getting hotter. 185,000 fans across from us, behind us and all around the course, had seen our morning practice, had watched the Armed Forces Day parade and jet fighters in the pale blue sky. And the eleven o'clock bell had sounded opening the qualifying session on the last weekend of qualifying. We were all back-markers. The grid had been filled the weekend before and the only way any of the cars in the pits could qualify for the race was to turn four laps faster than the 212.356 miles an hour Beckowitz had run for thirty-third fastest last weekend. They had all been here for three weeks, working day and night to qualify for the race. If they didn't make it today or tomorrow they would have to wait until next year. I had thought it would be easy and I was wrong.

Arnhower's Red Fox Pizza Lola Cosworth ground away out of the pits, its engine stuttering and grinding. At low speed Indy cars sound like cement trucks.

In the hour and fifteen minutes of practice that morning I felt as if I hadn't driven on the track before. The heat made the surface slippery and a 15–25 mile an hour wind was gusting in Turn Four, pushing the nose towards the wall. That was the easy part. My first lesson came when I followed Phil Cameron's car into Turn One. It was my first lap at speed in traffic. And Cameron seemed like a good man to follow for a few laps while I got the feel of the place again. He had won the race twice, in '69 and '81, and this was his twenty-fourth season at Indianapolis. He no longer had the top equipment, but if he didn't know his way around the track nobody did. A few nice easy laps, I thought, just to get the feel.

I had been bounding along down the pit straight, my head buffeted by the wind at 210 miles an hour, the car feeling shifty, bouncing like an aeroplane in dirty weather because of the air that came boiling off Cameron's wing. I pulled up tight to get a little more tow, and into the vacuum behind his car. Up where the air will be a little smoother, I thought. Not so close to be rude, just about three feet away. From behind the wheel, the difference between 210 down the straight and 225 isn't really noticeable, you check the gauges. But when you turn . . .

We passed the door in the outside wall, Cameron turned in and I followed, easing the car into the turn, foot to the floor, letting the sideways friction scrub off speed. Waiting for the tyres to bite into the turn. And waiting. It was as if the track had turned to ice, Cameron was turning and I wasn't, he was moving down towards the inside of the turn and the wall had suddenly picked up tremendous speed heading towards me. One instant I had been on the edge of control, a racing driver cocooned inside the aluminium and carbon fibre tub of a racing car. Then the edge of the cliff fell away, and the world around me lurched into hyperspeed.

My first instinct had been to turn towards the skid, but the trick at that speed is that by the time you realize something is happening, it happened 100 yards ago. I yanked the wheel sharp left and stood on the brakes and the clutch. And what had been a nice and orderly telescopic tunnel of vision, blurred at the edges, sharp in the middle, turned into a merry-go-round whirling at the speed of a blender. Whop whop whop, like riding on the end of a helicopter blade. The car spun in a long wide arc up into the grey area along the top chute, scrubbing off enough speed for me to start to pick out the white blur of the wall on my right approaching and the green blur on my left getting farther away, so I lifted my foot off the brakes and the clutch, got back on the throttle and steered straight ahead.

At the time I thought I was still going around 180 miles an hour when I straightened the car out. When I looked at a replay on a TV monitor I saw it was more like 50. The car had spun for almost a quarter of a mile through the turn and down 200 yards of the chute before the spin slowed down enough for me to tell what was going on. I hadn't been smart, or especially quick, I hadn't saved the car, I was just a passenger. The weird gods of the Speedway had taken a moment out of their day to give me a lesson and the lesson was over.

I checked my mirrors, dived down inside the white line on the apron and drove quietly back to the pits, the tyres thwop thwopping on the big wide spots I'd scrubbed flat. When I got out of the car, my system had drained the half-gallon of adrenaline it had pumped into my bloodstream and I felt as weak and as poorly informed as a new-born boy. And the bottom of my right foot felt like it had been slugged with a sledgehammer from trying to stomp the brakepedal through the floor.

George, his stubble silver and white on the deep furrows of his cheeks, his bushy eyebrows knit together, grabbed my arm as I got out of the car. He stuck his face about two inches from mine and held onto me as I walked back to the garage to wait while the car was towed into tech inspection time. Grabbing my arm and trying to talk to me as I strode back gave him a peculiar hopping sideways gate. He looked like a testicle with legs.

'What'd I tell you?' he said with that rasping voice of his that made him sound like a parody of a gangster.

'I don't know George, what'd you tell me?'

'I told you you are a fuckin' rookie and like every fuckin' rookie you don't believe me. You think you can go fast right away. You have to learn the hard way. You know what happened?'

'It wouldn't turn in, George. I don't know why.'

'You see, you never drove speedway traffic before. Cameron stole your air.' He smiled a little triumphant smile, and his voice lowered. 'Listen Evers, you get behind somebody, they steal your air. They steal your air, you lose your downforce, simple as that. Any time you run in a vacuum from the car in front, your car ain't sucked down on the track no more and you are embarrassed by no grip. You get behind somebody going into a turn, go above him or underneath him or you go into the wall.'

I nudged George gently against the wall of a garage we were passing. Not hard enough to hurt him, just enough to hold him there. To anyone in the constant crowd of crews, fans, reporters and friends of the corporations it would have looked as if we were having a nice friendly conversation. He must have caught the edge in my voice because he went very quiet.

'George, I appreciate your advice. But it is a little late. Do you have any other driving tips you want to give me . . . before I find out for myself?'

George had been pushing against my chest and he let his arms drop down to his sides. 'Oh Jesus,' he said. 'You got everything to learn.'

Fenstermacher was waiting in the garage. 'You all right?' he asked. 'You know you can't go into a turn like that.'

'George was just giving me a driving lesson.'

'Well I hope to hell they run it through tech in a hurry. You need the track time. What the hell were you doing in Cayman Islands? You run into Billy Fraser down there?'

'How'd you know I was in the Caymans?'

It's in the pilot's log, turkey. That's really something about Fraser, wasn't it?'

'Wasn't what?' I said, my mind still spinning from the car going round and round.

'Man like that, got everything in the world.'

'What do you mean?'

'I mean he must be one of the richest, most powerful men in the world and it don't mean dogshit to him now, does it?'

'Goddamn it, Owen, what are you talking about?'

'You mean you didn't see it? Didn't you watch the news this morning?'

I waited.

'No? Well, here, look at this. Help you calm down.' He handed me a copy of the morning's *Indianapolis News*. The top headline said: STROKE FELLS FRASER. The masthead said the *News* was a 'member of Global-Village Corp'. No wonder they thought the story was front-page news. The story said Fraser had suffered a massive stroke on a flight from the Cayman Islands. He was resting in a Miami hospital, acting Chairman, Mr Hillburn said. Indications were that he may have lost the power of speech, Mr Hillburn said. Fraser's Village news media would continue to provide the very highest standard of news and information, said Mr Hillburn.

I felt guilt and fear.

'You saw him, didn't you,' said Fenstermacher. 'That's how-come you were asking me those questions about Billy in New York.'

'Acting Chairman' Hillburn.

I didn't answer him and Fenstermacher looked at me for a minute and then he said, 'Well I don't give a monkey's fart what you did or who you saw down in the goddamn Cayman Islands, but the time has come to get this car on the grid. You do that one thing and that'll be enough for one day.'

If a racing driver loses his concentration he is no longer a racing driver. (I pictured Billy's face smiling in the oval window of his jet, waving.) The essence of the sport is the ability to take in a huge amount of information in a fraction of time. (Hillburn's suspicious face.) When the world rushes towards you at a hundred and ten yards a second, and another car is one foot to the left and the wall is one foot to the right, and the place to start turning into a corner is twenty feet ahead, there really isn't time for stray thoughts. (Fraser gagging, his face turning purple, his eyes bulging. A stroke?) There were just nine minutes left in the practice session when I rolled out of the pits and back onto the track. I erased Fraser's face. And his daughter and Hillburn and Ellie's kiss, and my sore lip. And concentrated on the car, my arms and legs with wheels for sensors. Only the car.

Only the car. And the track. It is what makes racing drivers the callous bastards that we are from time to time; switching off from the world and concentrating. In fact, if you are unable to concentrate on a race track with total ferocity, you will cease to be a racing driver and become a passenger in a surprisingly rapid series of events beyond your control. Only the car. Only the car.

My practice lap in the middle of the week at 220 miles an hour had seemed almost impossible when I'd done it. But it was a piece of cake compared to what it was like out on the track now. The track was littered with traffic, dodging like carnival dodgems, some slowing down, some speeding up. Some staying along the wall along the straight going by me as if I was standing still. With the ventura on the bottom, the Indy race car depends on a clean slice through the air to give you the effect of an inverted wing. But with the wind gusting in Turn Three, and boiling off the wings of all the other traffic, the limits of the car were changing moment to moment. There was no let up, and no safe place. And the heat and the humidity made the track slick. I put in eight laps after one warm-up lap. And my best time was 206 miles an hour. Way short of what it would take to qualify.

'You need more time,' George said when I came into the pits along with all the other cars. 'But don't worry about it.'

I worried about it. I'd drawn ninth. Hodges went out in his Greyhound Lola-Buick. And on his second lap the Buick went blooey and he had to be towed in. Then there was a ten-minute delay while they swept oil dry across the small pond of lubricant Hodges had deposited in Turn Three. The temperature had crept up to 88° and nobody wanted to try to qualify with the double disadvantage of a track turning to Teflon in the heat and oil dry destroying the tyres. So they opened up the track for practice and I went out again, a mad dog of a semi-Englishman in the noonday Indiana sun.

The surface shimmered in the heat and from my vantage point twenty-six inches off the pavement the track looked like a long strip of oil. With the wind gusting in Turn Four, and pushing the nose of the car towards the wall unexpectedly, even cruising speeds of 199, 202, 203, 204, felt dangerous and uncertain. But as I lapped around and around, I began to relax and feel the rhythm. I wasn't trying hard, there was no point in going right up to the limit in these conditions. But I began to get the feel of the traffic, and started to learn to anticipate the openings before they happened. I also tried different lines around the corners, trying to stay in a flat arc all the way around One and Two and Three and Four, tried to get used to getting right up next to the wall coming out of Four and Two. I'd got to the point where I could relax enough to use the few precious seconds on the front and back straights to check the rear bodywork and tyres in my mirrors and look for the wind sock over Three so I could anticipate the wind in Four. In fact I was just starting to feel at home when the yellow went on and I had to come in. The haze had turned to thin corrugated cloud and some fool wanted to try to qualify.

Tom Martens, the flying Dutchman, went out in his wine-red Waldo's Steakhouse Lola-Chevrolet and turned in four laps over 214. So he was in the race and suddenly it looked like qualifying was possible. But it wasn't easy. The next three attempts failed. Then Bill Campbell, who had entered his own car, a three-year-old March with last year's Cosworth, tried too hard. He just touched the wall in Three, tried to hold it together, stayed up high and touched the wall in Four and tore off the right front and rear wheels. The car went flopping crazily down the main straight, rolling, bounding and sliding to rest just beyond the start/finish line. Campbell was fine and said the crew would have to work all night. Brave words because he was the crew. Even if he succeeded in rebuilding the car, there was no way he could qualify on Sunday. The car wasn't fast enough and neither was he. But when did that ever stop anybody from trying at Indy?

There were several like him. Men who didn't have the money or the talent who came back year after year, hoping for a miracle, slinging their lives and their fortunes into the welcoming arms of the wall. 'You wait till tomorrow afternoon,' George said without sympathy. 'Tomorrow afternoon, he's gonna say, "wait'll next year".'

When it was my turn the air had gone still and a black and white armada of thunderheads was moving in across the sky. It was that low pressure calm before a storm when you feel dull and irritable and the humidity clings to you like steam.

George did up the buckles of my racing harness again, and Eugene shoved the starter motor onto the back of the transaxle and the engine roared and died. And it would not start. It took George just three minutes and forty seconds to diagnose the problem, take out the electronic black box that controls the engine, and fit a new one. And in three minutes and fifty-nine seconds I was on the track, on my warm-up lap. Once around to get the car up to working temperature and once more to heat up the tyres and get up to speed and I was flat out, coming down the straight at 12,700 rpm, thinking I only want to do this once, the starter waved the green flag and I was on it, turning into One. The track was cooler and had more traction. I couldn't quite flatfoot it all the way around, lifting just a little going down into One and Three. And once, coming off Three there is just a slight bump and a little bit of a down hill and I thought the back end was starting to come around and I thought about getting off it, turning down and standing on the brakes, but I kept my foot down. The lap board said 217 for my first lap, 217 for my second and 218 for my third. Maybe somebody else could have gone faster. But those four laps were as quick as I could go without losing the car and they were over, it seemed, about an hour and a half after I started. The checkered flag came out, there was the little blip of the strip of bricks at the startline and I lifted, coasting into One and Two. Coming out of Two, relaxing, knowing I'd qualified, the car wobbled. I wasn't worried. 150 miles an hour after you've been going 225 down the straights feels like a slow roll down the Parkway. I checked the tyres and the body in my mirrors, and nothing seemed wrong. But then I started to feel a sinking, the car leaning back a little and to the right.

If you want to appreciate the impact at 150 miles an hour,

try this simple experiment. Walk slowly, taking your time, with your hands behind your back, forehead first into a wall. Note the tiny sound it makes inside and outside your head and the spreading flood of pain. Also note the crunching feeling at the back of your neck as your head bends your neck back, and the dull aftermath of ache in your head and neck. Since the force of an impact multiplies at the square of the speed, multiply the above sensations several thousand times until you reach 150 miles an hour.

The car lurched right and hurled me towards the wall and I just had time to think: oh fuck, not twice in one day, before the wall rose up and struck like a concrete wave.

18

I've always liked upside-down faces. Oriental eyes in western masks. The close-cropped iron spike grizzled crew cut was a dead giveaway. That would have to be George. The big meaty upside-down face with the receding hairline took a moment to puzzle out, until the name Fenstermacher came floating up to the surface. But there was a third, boyish face with intense brown eyes, green motes in the irises, a thin lace-work of red veins on the yellowish whites, staring at me and I closed my eyes for a moment to see if I could remember who it was.

Years later I came back again, and the faces were gone, just the clutter of mirrored spotlights on the ceiling. A hospital, I thought. Something's missing, I thought. A leg, a hand, an arm. But I couldn't move and I thought of the stories of the men in war who'd had their limbs amputated and still had 'feeling' in their hands and their toes.

'He's coming around,' someone said and I turned towards the voice.

'You can sit up if you feel strong enough,' he said.

I didn't ever want to sit up. I wanted to lie there for ever.

'You had a little tap on the head,' he said. 'You've been out for several minutes.' The voice was coming from my feet.

I lifted my head and George and Fenstermacher and a man in a faded green short-sleeved hospital shirt were standing there. Greenshirt had brown eyes and the weariness of a doctor.

'Nothing broken, but I'd like you to check into the hospital overnight for observation,' the doctor said.

'I thought I was in the hospital,' I said, starting to sit up. A wave of pain started with my neck and flowed down to my shoulders and chest and stomach. My stomach was too sore to pull me up so I pushed up with my arms and that was another mistake.

'You're still at the Speedway, at the Speedway hospital,' the doctor continued as I forced myself up, my head beginning to thump. 'You're probably feeling a mite bruised, but I think you're sound. If we had any doubts we'd have put you on our Lifeline Helicopter Service, nonstop to the critical care unit at Methodist Hospital. But as I say, I'd like you to stop in there this afternoon so we can keep an eye on you overnight.'

Sitting up was, after all, possible. I let my legs hang over the side. This brought me almost to the level of the three heads around me. Staring into their chests, I was too tired to look up.

George's voice said: 'The tub is a mess. We're air-freighting it back to Lola in England. We might not get it back for Carburetion Day next Thursday, but we'll have it for the race.'

'You mean I qualified it.'

'217.654. That puts us up to, I don't know, probably 20, 21 on the grid. It depends on what the rest of the field does today and tomorrow.'

I became aware of the far-off scream of an Indy car going around like a distant bee circling a hive. I lifted my head up with an effort and looked at Orrin. He was smiling his reassuring smile. 'What happened?' I asked.

'Well,' he said with his midwestern drawl, 'you got a flat tyre. That's the simple answer.'

'It was pretty well wadded up,' George said, 'but it was in one piece. We took it off to look at it and the whole inside of the thing was turning to soup.'

I looked over to Orrin. 'We got Goodyear looking at it. They say they never seen anything like it.'

Half an hour later I'd had a shower, and I'd just stretched out on the king-size bed in my motel room. Orrin had insisted I stay with him in his big Newell motorhome with the woody panelling on the outside that he used for his corporate and party headquarters. From the outside it looked like a bus. Inside there was a jacuzzi ('Just what you need,' he said), two double beds, a small living room, a kitchen, a bar ('a half-hour in the jacuzzi with Cindy and Mary-Lou and you'll be feelin' real good').

'No,' I said, 'thank you.'

I'd taken a couple of aspirin for my headache and I was just stretching out having admired the criss-cross of bruise stripes over my shoulders and across my chest and between my legs, a perfect black and blue and dirty yellow imprint of my driving harness, and having taken a couple of aspirin for my headache I was just closing my eyes when the phone rang.

I was inclined to let it ring, but it hurt my headache.

'Forrest,' she said in a low and breathy voice. 'Are you all right?'

'Never better. Who is this?'

'Forrest, this is Caroline. I have to talk to you.'

'Caroline, I don't know how you got my number. I'm sure you are lovely as well as intelligent, but I am having my nap now and I really don't want to be interrupted.'

'Caroline Fraser.'

I sat up.

'Why,' I asked carefully, 'are you calling me?'

'Forrest, please, don't play games. I'm not good at games. I'm scared and I really don't know who I can talk to. Maybe I can't talk to anyone. But please, Forrest, please. I need your help.' Her voice was rising.

'Look, I don't know why you are calling me. But I've just had an accident and I'm not in much shape to get out of bed without help, let alone be any use to anybody else.'

She ignored my plea for sympathy. 'Forrest, I don't need you to do anything, I just need to talk to you.'

I lay back down and shut my eyes. 'We're talking,' I said.

'I can't talk on the phone.'

'It's not that difficult. You just put one word after the other.'

'Goddamnit, please,' she said catching herself, 'you'll understand when I tell you.' Her voice had started to quaver.

'Can you come here?'

'No,' she said. There was a long pause. I pictured meeting her in a bar or a restaurant in Indianapolis and the thought made me sink with fatigue. 'I'm in Carefree.'

'Carefree?'

'Arizona,' she said. 'It's one of Daddy's hideaways. At the corner of Hum Road and Tranquil Trail. My jet will be landing in Indianapolis in about a half an hour.'

'You mean you're on the plane.'

'I mean it's coming to pick you up.'

19

There really is a corner in Carefree, Arizona where Hum Road mets Tranquil Trail.

An hour's drive north of Phoenix, Carefree sits in the middle of the last stand of the saguaro cactus. You know saguaros, they're the ones everybody thinks of when they think of Cowboys and Indians. They're the big green ones that throw their arms up in the air as if the desert was being robbed. Fifty years ago, saguaros ranged south into Mexico and west to California. Now they are corralled in a hundred and fifty square miles of National Park north of Phoenix. Hands up, cactuses. Don't you move a goddamn inch.

I was going north, in the back of a plain jane Ford Taurus, air-conditioning on hi, at a quarter to seven in the evening. The sun was low in the west and we were running over saguaro shadows in the road.

I knew how they felt. Caroline had said please. She had said it would only take a couple of hours on the plane and I could fly right back. She said she had no one else to turn to. She was desperate. There wasn't anybody she could trust.

I said I was sick, sore, lame and disabled. And I was sorry, but no. I had to be at the track for practice at eight in the morning.

Caroline lowered her voice and said fine, she would call the FBI. 'I don't know if they have jurisdiction over fraudulently impersonating an American corporation in the Cayman Islands and stealing $12 million, but I'll bet they can tell me who does.'

I said I'd come.

Caroline's jet was a Falcon. A cute little $4.5 million aircraft. Just right for Daddy's little girl. The pilot looked twenty-six, but he was greying at the temples. Maybe waiting in airports and reading thrillers had aged him prematurely. The co-pilot was more relaxed, a fat man chewing gum, reading a pornographic comic book. No doubt he was a whizz at navigation.

My navigation, climbing in and out of a taxi was slow and painful. But the crew and the jet were waiting by Butler Aviation, just like Caroline said they would be. And when I climbed up the ramp and into the plane, the door shut, we taxied, and took off. No check in, no hanging around the limbo of an airport lounge, no 'Sorry flight 309 to Phoenix will be delayed while we nail the wings back on the aeroplane.' There really are magic carpets, if you can afford them.

But even magic carpets take time. Caroline lied; it was a three-hour flight, not two. I slept and dreamt of cartoon racing cars circling around a big black track, bouncing off the walls and catching fire to the bouncy tune of a merry-go-round.

When we landed in Phoenix, a compact man who I took to be an Indian drove up to the plane and held open the door to the back seat of a new and dusty Taurus. He got in and drove me all the way to Carefree without a single word.

Ah, Carefree, a word reminiscent of childhood days before we knew there were Real Estate Developers. Carefree is a model community for people with wealth and leisure to spare. The street signs say Happiness Road and Contentment Avenue and the desert hills rise and fall just enough for most of the houses to hide. Like Carmel in California and Darien in Connecticut, Carefree is so clean the dirt looks swept. No Burger Kings need apply.

Caroline's house was down an unmarked drive at the corner of Hum Road and Tranquil etc. We drove over a small rise, the rest of the world fell away and we were in a world outside of time.

The driver stopped the car and I got out.

The desert is slow to change. A beer can thrown lightly out of a passing car will shine brightly fifty years from now. But there were no beer cans and no signs of human beings as far as the eye could see. The view stretched a hundred miles to the south, east, west and to the mountaintops to the north. Judging by the view, it could have been five thousand years ago. Or it could have been some time in the future. There were no buildings, no little domestic patches of green. No thin plumes of industrial smoke. And no planes crawling across the sky. The stars were just starting to come out and all around there was the comfort of silence.

I almost had to look twice to see it. But what looked like an eight-foot wall of stone fifty yards away of me was not a wall with a wooden door, it was a house. The stone was from the desert and it had the same sand colours. As I walked up to it I could see that it had been there long enough for the mortar to have begun to crumble in thin trails and that the door had the dull, dark and weathered look of centuries. Probably the door had come from the front of an eighteenth-century Spanish mission razed to make way for Tranquil Trail. Before I could knock or find a bell to push, the door opened and Caroline was saying, 'I'm sorry, I look a mess.'

Her eyes were puffy from crying and she took my arm, leading me inside.

'You look fine,' I said.

She put her hand in mine and led me into the house. When I had seen her before she had been in the shadow of her father. She looked different now. But then first impressions are rarely worth much. You make a sketch from the slightest details – the colour of a skirt, the lift of an eyebrow at a phrase – and you fill in all the lines and the colours in between. And then, after you know someone a little, well enough to recognize a thought behind a smile, you realize that first sketch had more to do with you than her.

She was small and pale and rumpled as if she had been kept in a drawer. She hadn't combed her hair, and the long fine black strands fell across her face. When she brushed them away with the back of her hand, her skin was translucent white, there were bluish patches under her eyes and dry flecks at the corner of a mouth that was too wide for her face. Her brown eyes looked at me with what looked like fear and pleading, like she was drowning drop by drop.

We crossed the polished stone floor, past heavy, low, oak and leather furniture and went down a few stone steps to a jade-green swimming pool. The far wall was glass and a hundred miles in the distance the mountains were red and purple, reflecting the sunset. The pool must have been a hundred feet long, half of it outside the house. Inside the house the pool was the centrepiece of an elegant architectural design; outside it was an oasis in the desert sand and rock. A low cantilevered roof for keeping the sun out on hot summer days, and flooding the room with sunshine when the sun was low in the sky in the winter. In the silence, we could hear the sound of pumps and filters keeping the water as clear as a mountain stream. It wasn't a big house. By billionaire standards it wasn't much more than a comfortable cabin. And yet it had power from the desert and the mountains, as if the house didn't end but went on and on to the horizon and beyond. From outside, facing north, the house was a stone wall that kept out the world. Inside, facing south, the world was yours.

'I can't stay,' I said.

'They've killed him, you know,' she said.

'The newspapers said he had a stroke.'

'He's brain dead. It's the same thing. The only difference is they don't want him in the ground yet.' Her mouth made a quick little smile.

'Who's "they"?'

'C'mere,' she said, suddenly animated, ignoring my question. Like a small girl tugging her Daddy's hand, she led me along to the pool and out of the house and onto the terrace. She was wearing tight tennis shorts and a t-shirt, with a small bird for a logo over a free-moving breast. 'There's something I want to show you.'

I stopped. My problem was that I didn't know where to begin. She was grieving and I didn't know how to ask the awkward questions.

She looked at me for a moment and gave me another one of those quickie smiles. 'I know. There's a lot to explain. And I'm sorry I had to, you know, blackmail you to get you here. You're not easy to move are you? But you're here now and you might as well listen. Come on, you get the grand tour.' She led me down a path that curved away and out of sight of the house.

When I first saw it I thought it might be a covered reservoir, or a paranoid's fallout shelter the size of a football field. The walls, the same stone as the house, were only four feet high, but when Caroline unlocked the door, we went down a flight of steps into the darkness. She flicked on a switch and one by one, row after row, appearing out of the darkness, there was a Ferrari, and another and another. Each one different. The sequential light switch clicked like the snap of a magician's fingers and a scarlet 250–GT short wheelbase California Spyder would appear out of the darkness. Snap, a 250–LM, snap a chrome yellow Monza from the fifties, snap, an original GTO, snap, a Vignale 340 America. Snap, snap, snap, a collector's wildest dream coming true. Snap, a $2 million F–40 against the far wall. Snap, snap, a Daytona Coupe alongside a Daytona Spyder.

The lights continued to snap on. 'Daddy started collecting them when I was born. There aren't any Grand Prix cars because Mr Ferrari had most of them broken up after every season. You know how collectors are, Daddy wanted a complete set. So there is one of every road-going model Ferrari ever made. He said whatever happened, whatever he did, these would be mine.

'Or my responsibility is more like it. We have a staff of six to look after them, funded by a permanent foundation. There's a climate control system, but sunk here in the desert in this dry air, there's almost no humidity and the temperature stays pretty constant. Over the hill there's a track where Daddy used to take them out when he had the time.'

It was a stunning display. Stunning in the profusion of the sensual curves and the ferocious aggression of these hollow rolling sculptures. Stunning in the variety and beauty of Enzo Ferrari's imagination. Not to mention Vignale, Touring, Pinin Farina, Zagato, Scagliatti. And stunning because here were over two hundred cars whose average value was probably a half a million dollars each. As a complete set they would have been worth more then the GNP of Venezuela.

We walked down the last few steps and onto the polished stone floor. Like acolytes in a cloistered garden, we walked among scarlet, silver, yellow and blue cars and Caroline told her story.

'My mother died when I was three,' she said, looking at me as if she wasn't sure she was saying the right thing. 'And the week after she died Daddy took me with him to Chicago. And then we went to London and Sydney and Tokyo and we just kept going. Almost from the time I can remember,' she said, slipping her hand into mine, 'he took me with him. There was a whole parade of nurses and nannies and teachers and tutors that had to come with us, just to look after me. But I went with him.

'When I was seven I knew the first name of the managers of, I don't know, probably fifty hotels and they all called me Miss Fraser. When he started buying places for us to stay in, like you know New York, Paris, London, Sydney, San Francisco, Maui, they all had my clothes and stuff and at least one fulltime staff so we didn't have to pack and unpack. I used to wonder what it would be like to be a real little girl. I wondered what it would be like to have a friend. Apart from Daddy.

'Sometimes he'd take me to the meetings – a twelve-year-old

girl in little Mary-Jane shoes at the board table of some company my father was taking over. Oh, Forrest, you should have seen him. I mean people don't remember, but he was so funny then. And nobody could stand in his way. No girl ever had a better school.

'I mean these,' and she looked around the acre of priceless Ferraris, 'these are just toys. He built a nine billion dollar empire. And they have taken it from him. When I was a baby, he used to hold me by my foot and swing me around the room. I mean, can you imagine, what it felt like? I mean what if he slipped, or let go? I'd scream and he'd just swing me around faster. God, I still feel funny when I think about it. But I have to tell you, I have never been afraid since. Everything else, Forrest, has been easier to deal with than the thought that he was going to let me go and I would go smash headfirst into the wall.

'My father loved me and I love him, and I swear to God,' she said digging her nails into my palm, 'I am not going to let them get away with it. They killed Daddy and nobody cares. Nobody gives a shit. Nobody even knows. Except me.'

We has stopped in front of one of the early cars, a 1954 Type 375 Mille Miglia. Two seats, no top, no radio, no windows. Just a glorious V–12 under a taut, red, hand-formed aluminum skin, designed to be driven to the limit of the car or the driver, whichever comes first.

She put her hand on the door. 'This isn't mine, now. All of these cars, the house, all of the houses. All of the television companies, the satellites, the newspapers and magazines and the radio station, and all of the stock, everything belongs to Global. They are the trustees now. Isn't that a joke, "trustees"? They killed him and the only reason he isn't buried is because when he is, his will says that everything – ' her voice lowered to a whisper '– everything goes to me. I mean you'd be scared too. I don't know anybody I can trust. They don't know where I am now. But they'll find me.'

'Who's they?'

'You met them. Hillburn and Meyer. Except Meyer's name isn't Meyer, it's Mehar.'

'Mehar?'

'It's Iranian. Hillburn brought him in.'

'And you think they'll kill you.'

'Forrest,' she said, with those big brown eyes open wide, 'for God's sake, they've taken control and the only thing to stop them from owning it is me drawing breath.' She took a deep breath as if to reassure herself. 'For God's sake help me.' The she turned and went up the steps, turned out the lights, and I followed her up the steps to the open door.

Outside it was still warm from the heat of the day and there was a last rim of light on the western horizon. The pool was glowing from underwater lights and she stood by the edge, the greenish light making her look almost transparent. 'Why me?' I said.

Caroline moved close to me and I was aware of the fine straight line of her nose and the contrast with the soft curve of her mouth. She put her hand on my chest, smiled, pushed hard, and I went flying backwards into the water. When I came up, she dived straight at me and I ducked out of the way.

The water was deep enough for me to stand and she swam over to me and put her arms around my neck, her hair in a fan around her. 'You big dummy,' she said. 'You are brave and tough and I have brains enough for both of us.'

'Then why are we in the pool?'

'Because I want your attention.'

'You said you wanted revenge. You want your twelve million back?'

'Forrest, I'm offering you tigers and you want to play with pussycats. Forget the twelve million. We're talking about the most powerful communications complex on earth. Or in the sky come to think of it.' She pulled herself close to me. 'If you really want to know, I traced the twelve million. It'll all come back to us anyway. But if we don't . . .'

'How did you know it was me?'

'Oh, God, don't be stupid. How could I miss you? Daddy loves racing and racing cars. We own a team, we watch the races. I saw you on TV the day before at Indianapolis. And before that on TV at the Monaco Grand Prix, and before that in magazines. Just to make sure, I rang Sunwest. Alistair Hampton is fifty-six years old.'

'And you want my help.'

She pulled tight to me and kissed me. Her mouth was soft and warm and she moved against me. 'I want your protection. I want you to stay very, very close to me.'

She started to kiss me again and I put my hand on top of her head and shoved her under.

She came up sputtering.

I started striding out of the pool the way you do when you're two-thirds underwater, using my arms.

'What kind of crap is that?' she yelled, thrashing towards me.

I stopped, the water up to my waist, my faded green T-shirt dripping. 'You are a very bright, sexy, wealthy woman who has had a very big shock. If you want help, I'll help you if I can. But you are a lot more upset than you realize and in about five minutes you'd wonder who the hell I was.'

'I know who you are. You're a prick,' she said. Then her mood changed again and she started to cry. I put my arms around her and she let go, great big sobs that made her cough.

We stood like that for a while, up to our waists in the green pool, the underwater lighting making our faces look like ghouls, the big grown-up boy and the weeping little girl in a woman's body. When enough time had gone by, I led Caroline, snuffling and crying, out of the pool and she pushed me away and stood by herself for a minute, struggling for control. 'Oh, Jesus, I'm sorry Forrest,' she said, taking deep breaths. 'Look, there's a shower and some towels in the guest bedrooms. Let Carla throw your stuff in the dryer and, you know, let's have supper and some wine.'

'How many staff are here besides Carla?'

'Just her and her husband, Bobby. Ramirez. The man who drove you here. They're Apache.'

'Do you trust them?'

'Since I was born. This was originally their land. Or rather their tribe's land. My father said he didn't know they were here until after he bought the place. He said there was no way he was going to say "get off my land". There's 12,000 acres and they have the best part as long as we own it; so sure I trust them. They live here in the house, but they have families back out there in the hills.'

'And Hillburn and Meyer don't know where you are?'

'I don't see how they could. I mean there are thousands of places I could be and I didn't know until yesterday I was coming here.'

'They might have had you watched.'

'How do you watch a jet plane that changes course?'

'So it's not like you are in immediate danger.'

'Not right now. But you know, in a couple of days. I mean, Forrest, in the cities they're killing people for fifty dollars. What do you think they'd do for twelve billion?'

'What makes you so sure they killed him?'

'I don't know what they've done to him. But I know they've done it to him. He's not in a hospital, I can't reach him. There's just those awful tapes on TV and the pictures in the newspapers. I mean maybe they propped him up or maybe they have an actor, but he's as good as dead, Forrest. I can feel it.'

'How do you feel now?'

'OK. Better, I mean. I mean thank you.'

'You run off to the shower,' I said. 'I'm going back.'

'Forrest, please help me.'

'How?'

'I don't know yet.'

'Well let me know when you do.'

'Forrest, do I have to draw you a picture? It's not just my problem.'

'You think they know about me?'

'You fooled Daddy but you didn't fool anybody else. I tried to tell Daddy, but they wouldn't let me talk to him. Anyway, now you know they killed Daddy, they'll have to come after you too, won't they?'

I didn't know they killed Daddy. I thought she was just very upset and her mind was looking for reasons when there weren't any reasons beyond the roll of the dice and the spreading blot on the brain when a tiny vessel clogs, swells up with the pressure until it goes pop, like a balloon.

But if Hillburn and Mehar knew who I was they weren't going to ignore me. I gave Caroline a little pat on the shoulder goodbye and when she closed the door behind me I heard a key turn in the lock. Bobby Ramirez, the Apache, was standing by the Taurus. When he saw my dripping clothes he didn't say a word.

20

'It was a hypo.' The sound of jet fighters three inches off the ground, Indy cars practising, drowned out George's voice.

I shouted, 'What?'

George motioned me to follow him back behind the stands. The backup car was going through tech inspection and we had a few minutes before I could take it back out on the track for the practice I badly needed.

'A hypodermic needle,' he said when we got back into the Fenstermacher garage, 'injected sulphuric acid into the carcass of the tyre. Goodyear said they've never seen anything like it. Turned the inside of that tyre to soup.'

'You check the other tyres?' I asked.

George gave me a don't-ask-such-a-dumb-question look. What he said was, 'We checked every tyre at Indy. Nothing. Good thing it didn't let go when you were on a flyer.'

A big hand grabbed a bruise on my shoulder. 'How're we doin'?' Orrin said in his big beefy drawl. 'You feelin' any better after your rest?' There was an irritation in his voice I hadn't heard before.

It was a hot, oppressive day. The wind was gusting and driving a car I'd never driven before on the limit was going to be difficult. I had finally got back to my motel room at two in the morning. After four hours' sleep I felt needles in my legs, fur on my tongue and an all-over aching soreness that seemed to grow with the day. 'I feel fine,' I said.

'One hell of a mystery, innit,' Orrin said, 'why somebody wanta do that to one of my cars. Never seen anything like it. Not in all my years at Indy. Never heard of sabotage in an Indy car before.' He emphasized 'heard'.

'You trailing any snakes in your wake, Evers? This sort of shit happen to you in Formula One?'

Outside the sun was blazing and the heat was rising off the tarmac in syrupy ripples. A small crowd, backlit so we couldn't see their faces, peered into the garage like the small crowd peering into every garage with a car in it in Gasoline Alley. To them we could have been discussing toe-in and wing settings. I shrugged off Orrin's question, but I did have an idea who might like the idea of sulphuric acid in my tyres.

'Besides us and the tech inspectors,' I asked Orrin and George, 'who gets close enough to the car to stick a needle in?'

George said, 'Don't even have to get close to the car. For every tyre on the car, there's probably another twenty lying around. And they're all marked, "left", "right", "practice", "qualifying", "Evers". So we know which is which, and so's a man with a needle. Look around, you'll see them stacked in the garage, in the pits. Goodyear stacks 'em all over the place.

'But to answer your question. Oh, Christ, there's USAC observers in the pits. There's every Tom Dick and Harriette who's a friend of a friend of somebody in a company that sponsors a piece of one of the cars. They all got pit passes. There's all the people from the sponsors. There's all the other teams, owners, drivers, mechanics. There's actors and actresses, there's sports people, there's probably a thousand people from the car and tyre and accessory companies that all got pit passes. You got advertising agencies, you got PR people. Then you got over a thousand reporters and photographers. Christ, you got to swat them away like flies.'

'Any way of checking the reporters and photographers?'

'Sure, if you got the time. I mean every little dipshit local rag has some guy who gets a free ride to Indy, plus all the real radio, TV, magazine and newspaper people. You go over to the press office when you got a few free hours, they got lists of all of them. Although I bet half of 'em can't read let alone write for some newspaper.'

It was a funny idea, some mild-mannered reporter moonlighting as a contract killer. But the next thought wasn't so funny. A word from Hillburn would give any thug the credentials to go any place he wanted at Indianapolis. The press was indeed free to stick needles in my tyres any time they liked.

Eugene stuck his head in the garage and said the car was being towed to the pits.

'You got anybody watching the tyres?' I asked Orrin.

'We passed the hat. And Goodyear's paying half. We got thirty undercover guys watching every goddamn tyre for every team in this place like a mother duck watching her little duckies in a pond full of snapping turtles.'

Walking to the car, I caught myself looking to see if anybody was acting suspiciously around the stacks of tyres. Everybody was acting suspiciously around the stacks of tyres.

'How did you set up the car, George?' I asked him to take my mind off the picture I had of a shiny needle sliding into my back tyre.

George looked at me like he was trying to make up his mind whether to talk to me or not. 'Well the whole secret to this place is the trade off between speed and downforce. You get too much downforce, you're slow down the straights. You don't get enough, you can't go around corners.'

'This much, George, we know.'

'Well what do you expect, the meaning of life? Christ, how do you set up a car for a speedway? You set the inside front wheel with toe out so it looks like it turns too far, you run a lot less wing than a road course, more tilt, positive camber on the left side of the car, fuck around with the shocks, tyre pressures and sizes.'

'You should write a book, George.'

'I am.'

We walked for a few more steps and George said, 'It's all a fucking guess. I got it set up just like the other car. But it's not like the other car. I know it's got the same engine, the same tyres, the same chassis, and now it's got the same set-up. But I guarantee you, you get it out there it's gonna feel a different car. So you take it out there, find out what it's doing. We'll fuck around with it. You take it out again, bring it in, we'll fuck around with it some more. And if we're lucky we'll get the sonofabitch hooked up right this afternoon.'

I slid into the car, trying to avoid the bruises and be kind to the strained ligaments.

Midwives say that the only reason a mother gets pregnant again is that she forgets how much it hurts to give birth. You could say the same about Indy. It never gets any easier. You build up your concentration, you put your foot down, you drive as if you don't give a damn if you live or die and it's not fast enough. You watch Foyt, or Mario or Michael Andretti, Sullivan, Mears or Al Unser Sr. or Jr. and it looks easy. It looks like they are stroking it, laying back, going three-quarter speed. Then you get out on the track, your perspective changes, the car starts bouncing around and the projector runs five times too fast and you realize there is nothing easy about it. They were just making it look like a Sunday drive.

On the last day of qualifying, nothing comes without pain

at the Indianapolis Motor Speedway. Not for anybody. The big names and the big money are somewhere else, playing golf and lounging around their swimming pools. This is the day of the back-markers, the has-beens and the never-will-bes. This is the last chance for the teams who stretch their budget by using somebody else's worn drive shafts, a three-year-old chassis, and an engine they hope will last the four laps to qualify. If they make the race, even if the car falls apart on the first lap, they can take home $60,000 and face their sponsors, family and friends. If they don't make the race, they get a fist full of unpaid bills and a story nobody wants to hear. So they drive harder than they should. Take chances they shouldn't take. And try to overcome a faltering engine and a sloppy chassis with courage. The wall welcomes them with her white, wide open arms and gathers them in.

I had just got up to speed, playing myself in, when Phil Powell, driver and mechanic from Wilkes-Barre, Pennsylvania, lost it in front of me going into Turn One. I saw his car wobble slightly turning in, not really having enough grip, then let loose, almost straight into the concrete. I got onto the brakes hard as his car bounced back on the track and straight in front of me, as I was turning in on the groove. His car was flinging wheels and fuel as it spun, and out of the corner of my eye I saw one of the wheels skimming like a frisbee across the surface of the track. I eased off the brakes and back onto the throttle, going high on the grey area trying to keep the car from going all the way up when his car began to flip end over end, back across the groove and into the wall again at the end of the chute. I aimed down low again, sure I was going to hit some of the debris. I saw him hit the wall and the engine broke off on the impact, leaving Phil Powell from Wilkes-Barre, Pennyslvania a passenger in a 150 miles an hour plastic and aluminium box sliding along the grey tarmac. He hit the wall head on again a hundred yards later where the wall turns left, glanced off and rolled over and over and smacked into the wall again, with the tub on its side, Phil's head into the wall, his feet towards me. I stayed low down on the track and by a miracle hadn't hit anything although in my mirrors the track was littered with wheels, fibreglass, broken pipes, radiators oozing oil, and all the other bits of scrap that moments ago had been the finest racing car Phil Powell could put together with the mortgage money. Some of it was still moving.

Marshalls and firemen were leaping over the wall, running towards the shattered black tub lying on its side, oozing fluid.

As I pulled into the pits, the anxious faces of George and Orrin pulled into focus. The same thought – Poor bastard. Thank God it wasn't us – written large in their eyes. Peace be with you, Phil Powell.

It would take at least fifteen minutes to clean up the track and I unbuckled and I got out of the car, brushing past George and Orrin. They wanted to know what happened and how the car was handling. There was a surge of reporters who knew I'd seen the crash and they were headed towards me with their pocket tape recorders and their video cameramen. I got on the little pit scooter and left them. I didn't want to discuss the death of a man I'd been inches away from minutes ago. And I didn't want to think about why I would go out there again and put my foot down harder. And I didn't want to conjure up again, I was thinking to myself, picturing it anyway, the sight of the man in the little black carbon fibre capsule, sliding headfirst into the wall for the last time. I was thinking that, getting off the scooter at the garage door, my helmet in my hand when a hand on my shoulder and a familiar voice said, 'Alistair?'

Hillburn had on the same polyester suit, the same dimestore smile on his face. 'I'm so glad you weren't hurt in that crash, Mr Hampton,' he said, his hand still on my shoulder. Looking beyond him there were several men with short haircuts and sports jackets. There is a story that Agnelli, the Chairman of Fiat, always has thirty bodyguards in the immediate vicinity. Some of them may be washing windows, or reaching into a handbag, or riding by on a bicycle, or eating pasta in a nearby sidewalk café, but they are always there. I guessed Hillburn only had half as many, but there were more than enough for me.

'Will you walk with me for a moment?' he said. 'I think we have one or two things to discuss.'

We walked. 'You don't mind if I call you Alistair, do you? I kinda got used to the name. Suits you.'

There is not much you can do when you are caught. All jokes

are weak. There is no place to run, and stories of Robin Hood's noble character do not amuse the King. 'How's Billy?' I said.

'With care and time he may be able to lead a reasonably normal life,' Hillburn said walking slowly. 'It may surprise you to learn that I came to apologize,' he said.

I could think of several things he could apologize for; his breath, his haircut, his arrogance, but none of those seemed likely.

'One of the people who are devoted to me learned of your theft and, I'm afraid, over-reacted. I want you to know it won't happen again.'

'Someone you know stuck a needle in one of my tyres?'

'I haven't the slightest idea what you are talking about,' he said with a little smile he kept for his inferiors. 'There is a saying in business that you may know. "Don't get mad, get even." And what I want you to know, Mr Evers, is that until I am able to recover that $12 million, I am going to cause you $12 million worth of shit.' He smiled his little smile and turned away. Followed by a group of insurance salesmen from Salt Lake.

21

'I've had a hell of a time getting through to you. I told the operator I'm your mother.'

'What time is it?' I said. 'I told the operator I wasn't to be disturbed.'

'Mothers take priority. Are you alone?'

'I'll look.'

'Forrest, you're not still in bed are you? It's eleven o'clock here, ten a.m. your time.'

I took a deep breath and stretched my arms. There was pain in my ribs and my neck and shoulders and forearms. And come to think of it in my legs. But it was better than the day before and the sun was streaming under and around the edges of the curtain. Maybe, for a change, this was going to be a good day.

'I was so worried about you. The news showed you hitting the wall on Saturday. Are you OK? It must be awful going out there again after you've crashed.'

'I keep my eyes shut. How are you?'

'Lousy. Every one of our offices and franchises around the world is on the telex and the phone, trying to reach me. None of the Global-Village newspapers will run our advertising. And that, Forrest, is disaster. We have got to advertise people and jobs or we are out of business.'

'Ellie, slow down a minute,' I said, distracted by a knot of black and blue on my shin that was sending out throbs of distress. 'They aren't the only newspaper or TV station in town. They don't have a monopoly yet. Besides, Global-Village can't refuse your ads. Aren't there laws about that?'

'There's a lot of one-paper towns out there, Forrest, and Global-Village own a bunch of them. Sixty-three major US markets have just one newspaper owner. If we can't advertise in Global-Village newspapers, we'll have to close Seattle, Cleveland, Des Moines, God knows how many . . . As for the law, we're not exactly in a position to throw stones. And even if we were, a big messy lawsuit with the media would be the worst possible publicity for us.'

'What about television?'

'Forget TV. The newspapers are our bread and butter. Even radio doesn't help. People don't listen to the radio to find jobs.

What really worries me is Fraser or whoever is running Global-Village now, what's his name, Hillburn, obviously they know and they are taking revenge.'

'They know. I saw Fraser's daughter, Caroline.'

'God, you do get around, Forrest. Where do you take Caroline Fraser in Indianapolis?'

'She's not in Indianapolis, she's hiding from Hillburn. She thinks they've made her father into a zombie. And she also thinks they are going to come after her.'

'Sounds to me like she's hysterical. Did she sound hysterical?'

'Maybe she was. She changes moods the way most people change expressions, so it's hard to pin her down. There's something unfinished about her, like she hasn't grown up yet or missed her childhood. I mean you never really know who you're talking to with her and I'm not sure she does either. Anyway, she didn't strike me as the most stable person I've ever met. And she is certainly frightened. She says her father has given her the whole of Global-Village in his will. But as long as her father is alive, Hillburn has a legitimate right to run the company. On the other hand, with Caroline alive, he can't own it. So maybe she has a right to be scared. One other thing. I saw Hillburn yesterday.'

'What? Where's he? You didn't tell me. What did he say?'

'He said that until he got his money back, he was going to give me twelve million worth of shit.'

'Obviously he's got me on his gift list. Have you seen this morning's paper? I wouldn't want you to feel left out.'

I sat up. There was a newspaper stuck under the door.

'Hang on, I'll get it.'

There was a small item on the front page.

PINKO AT THE BACK OF THE PACK

Swishy European Forrest Evers, usually seen on the Grand Prix Circus driving the pink Women Unlimited car, was out on the track again yesterday after smashing the Fenstermacher car at the end of Saturday's qualifying session. One way or the other, the Pink Pussycat, as the delicate driver is known in Gasoline Alley, will be on the grid next Sunday, proving that the Brickyard is open to all sexes and opinions, even if no one is quite sure what category Evers fits.

I started to read it to Ellie and she said, 'I've read it. I love the part about your being delicate. I've seen gorillas with more delicacy. Look on the sports pages and see if there's a column by Jack Boyce.'

There was.

WHOSE STANDARDS ARE THESE ANYWAY?

They do things differently in Europe. There it doesn't seem to matter much if the sexual and moral standards deviate from the norm. But there are those who are deeply troubled by one Forrest Evers, recently arrived on our shores to take part in that most American of all our annual pageants, the Indianapolis Five Hundred,

Evers, openly flaunting his outfits up and down Gasoline Alley during qualifying, must give car owner Orrin Fenstermacher pause. Did he know he wasn't just signing a driver but a fashion parade as well? And how do parents feel, whose children watch our Memorial Day Classic, about the Pink Pussycat mixing it up with the men out on the track?

We're all for equal opportunity for women as well as men. But there are laws about the Mr Inbetweens.

Ellie had read that one too. 'Those two items are probably in every Global-Village newspaper in America. Who knows what they've cooked up for the TV news.'

'Oh thyucks,' I said. 'Thooner or later they were thertain to find out.'

'Forrest, that is not funny. This is not some little game. This could finish your career in racing.'

'Come on, Ellie. As long as I win races, who gives a damn if I prefer parakeets? I thought that kind of prejudice went out with black and white television.'

'Well, think again, Forrest. It's hard enough for a woman to get sponsorship in racing. Women's products think they're too butch. Male products say women "don't project a masculine image". What do you think you'd get for a sponsor if the fans thought you were gay? Condoms? Drivers without sponsors walk.'

'I can't believe that anybody cares about my sex life.'

'I care.'

'You're exceptional. But really, Ellie, you have to laugh. I mean what else do you think I should do? You think I should hump the Memorial Day Parade Queen on the start line on race day?'

'Forrest, you have the mind of a twelve-year-old. I don't know how you can fight it. Maybe that's why.'

'Why what?'

'Why they are painting you pink. I was thinking. If they were going to attack you in the press, the obvious thing to do would be to expose your little Cayman Island scam.'

'Our little scam. Well, maybe they can't. Maybe Castleman's lawyers really did sew them up so there's no legal way they can get their money back. I mean if they can't get their money back legally, they're going to look pretty stupid admitting they lost $12 million to a racing driver. It wouldn't exactly get Hillburn off to a running start in his new job.'

'Maybe, but whatever the reason, you can bet it's going to get worse. You could sue them for libel, but if you read those pieces there's not a lot you can pin a lawsuit on. Anyway, I don't think we can fight them. I can't fight them.'

'What do you mean, you can't fight them?'

'I mean that if I can't advertise in their newspapers, I am going to have to close shop all over the country. The effects of one day aren't too bad. But shut out for two days is twice as bad. A week could be a catastrophe. I mean I'm going to ask Castleman to give the money back to Hillburn and Global-Village.'

'Suppose Caroline is right?'

'About what?'

'Suppose Hillburn has made Fraser brain dead? Suppose he's really that kind of a son of a bitch? You don't think he's going to just lean back and forgive you the interest on the junk bonds. He's going to eat you alive.'

'Forrest, we're over our heads here. We've been out of control since you started this whole thing.'

'You know what Stirling Moss says.'

'Who's Stirling Moss?'

'Stirling says if you're in control, you're not going fast enough.'

'Brilliant. I find that really reassuring, Forrest. Any other little kernels of wisdom like that, write them on a plain postcard and send them to my address. I'm sorry I called. I've got to call Castleman.'

'Wait a damn minute, Ellie, if . . .'

'I'm not waiting, I'm frightened. Maybe it doesn't matter to you if people call you a screaming fag. But it matters to me and it matters to my fourteen thousand employees whether or not I close this business.'

'How many people do you find jobs for in a year?'

'Over 875,000, worldwide.'

'And you've got their records on computer?'

'Sure.'

'Do you think any of them might work for Global-Village?'

'Probably. A newspaper here, a TV station there?'

'And do you think any of them might work in air-traffic control? Or a travel agency?'

'Forrest, what are you talking about?'

'Well, there are two things we don't know that could be important. The first is when I saw Fraser take off from the Cayman Islands he was fine. When he landed in Miami, he was brain dead. We ought to be able to find out who was on that plane, and what happened. There must have been radio calls for assistance. There must have been calls for an ambulance on landing.'

'What else?'

'You sound sceptical.'

'Just tell me.'

'Well, the other thing we don't know is why Hillburn is in Indianapolis.'

'To tell you he wants his money back. Watch the race. I don't know.'

'If you had just taken over the largest media complex in the world, would you fly to Indianapolis? I mean he could pick up the phone and threaten me. He didn't have to come all the way out here to do that.'

'So?'

'So maybe we could find out. Maybe some of those people you found jobs for are pissed off at their present employer. Maybe they'd like a phone call from the chairwoman and chief executive officer of the largest employment agency in the world.'

'It sounds dumb.'

'Try saying: "I'm giving $12 million to a murderer." See how smart that sounds.'

'What's that banging sound?'

'Somebody's trying to knock the door down.'

'Sounds like there are a lot of them.'

'I think there are. It's not easy being a star. I'd better find my pink housecoat.'

'What are you doing today?'

'For the first time in a year, nothing. There's a dinner that Fenstermacher's giving for some builders, but I don't know, I haven't a thing to wear.'

'Stop that. Listen, Forrest, why don't you come to New York? See if we can dig up something nasty on Hillburn.'

It sounded like there were thirty people in the hall who wanted to talk to me. They were pounding on my door and calling my name. 'I'll call you back,' I told Ellie.

22

Nowhere is it written that the press has to be fair. But then fairness never lives up to its reputation. Even fairness isn't fair.

Everybody in the room always knows that there is only one perfectly fair point of view. And that's his. Or hers. Including the homicidal maniac. Except, of course, for the goof-ball who broadcasts the Seven O'clock News cocooned in the official corporate belief that the truth lies half-way between the homicidal maniac and the police.

Here then is the authorized Evers version. The true version. The one that is fundamentally different from the story in the newspapers and on television that evening.

I threw on the terry cloth robe hanging in the bathroom and opened the door. And seeing that the hall was almost empty, I had the fatuous thought that of course, most of the national reporters would have flown back to base after Sunday's qualifying and wouldn't return until next weekend for the race. Otherwise there'd have been fifty reporters in the hallway ready to report to the world that the great racing driver was a fairy. Even in a smear, the ego balloon rises.

There were three of them. There was a cameraman with a small Sony on his shoulder, a short stocky man who was trying to cover his acne with a beard, and another man, small and slender, and next to me.

The one with the beard had a notebook and he said, 'Mr Evers, I'd like to ask you . . .' As he said that, the red recording light lit up on the face of the camera, the man next to me took hold of my arm and leaned against me. I turned to look at him to see who he was and he kissed me on the nose. I lunged toward the camera, but the boy, who wasn't more than seventeen, held me back and the bearded one kicked me squarely in the balls. I doubled over a great blue bloom of pain that spread up from my crotch and twisted my stomach, heard the soft thud of their shoes running on the carpet and they were gone.

As I straightened up, the door to the opposite room opened and the mild face of a greying woman in her late forties looked at me. I was nearly fainting with pain and my jaw hung open stupidly, an expression she was later to describe as 'sated with pleasure'. She stared at me for a couple of beats, withdrew her face and shut her door and turned the key. Then I realized my robe had fallen open. I walked bowlegged back into my room, closed the door, sat down on the bed and dialled the hotel operator.

'Omigosh Mr Evers, hi, it's Darla. I sure am glad you called. I don't know if it's true what they've been saying about you in the papers this morning. But I saw you walking across the hotel lobby yesterday and if it is true, I sure envy the boys.'

I thanked Darla who sounded as if she baked apple pies on Saturday afternoons and asked if I could speak to hotel security.

'Sure can. They're off on their break right now but they should be back in around twenty minutes. You want your messages?'

I wanted my messages.

'You sure get a lotta phone calls. Most of them sounded like they were in a big hurry and they didn't leave any numbers. But I do have around twenty-five messages for you. You want me to have them sent up to your room?'

'Did a Caroline Fraser call or Orrin Fenstermacher?'

'They sure did. Two or three times each. They want you to call back urgent. There's also a call from London, just a sec, a Mr Ken Arundel. I just love an English accent, don't you? And I don't know if you want to talk to the *Gay Times* in San Francisco.'

I rang Fenstermacher.

'What the fuck you up to, Evers?' he said.

'Kiss me,' I said.

'Don't fuck me around, Evers. I don't give a damn if you jerk off monkeys at the zoo. Don't see why anybody else would either. I mean we got more gay rights than wrongs. You musta really pissed that Fraser off good. You got any idea what to do about it?'

'You have a good lawyer?'

'I got a lot of people smarter than me workin' for me.'

'If you would, I'd like one of your best lawyers to sue Global-Village for libel for $12 million and see if they can get a cease and desist order.'

'You do that, you better be squeaky clean. There any dirt, they sure to find it. They got a lot of reporters.'

'They set me up this morning. I opened the door to my room wearing a bathrobe and a kid grabbed onto me for the photographer. You can expect to see that on the Global-Village news tonight.'

'I know the chief of police pretty good. I think I better sic him on that one. And there's a pretty good PR girl works for me. I think she better set up something for you to talk to the other newspapers. Maybe coach you to stop opening your door in your bathrobe.'

We talked about that for a while, then he said, 'So you ain't gay.'

'Orrin, you said you didn't give a shit.'

'I don't. But I also like to bet on a sure thing. Are you?'

'It's a bullshit question and you know it.'

Caroline's phone rang fifteen times.

'Yes?' she said.

'You OK?' I said.

'Oh, Jesus. It's you. Thank God. Forrest, I'm so frightened. They're watching me. I can feel it. I know they're up in the hills with telescopes and binoculars and they're watching me.'

'You don't sound good.'

'I'm not good. I'm falling apart. Why did you go away? On the news this morning they were saying you are, you know, gay. Is that why you wouldn't stay here? I mean it's OK. It doesn't really matter to me. I just need somebody I can trust.'

'No, Caroline, it's not why I wouldn't stay with you.'

'Can you come out here now? I really need you. I'll send the plane.'

'I can't come out now, I've got to go to New York.'

'I'll come too. I feel safe with you, Forrest. We can stay in New York together.' I felt uneasy and touched by her childish dependence on me.

'If Hillburn is after you, Caroline, then staying with me is the worst thing you can do. He knows where I am and his reporters are going to follow me wherever the hell I go. Where else can you stay? You have any friends?'

'I got a million friends and I don't trust any of them. Forrest, he knows where all our houses are. He has keys to all of them. Have you found out anything yet?'

'I'm working on it.'

'Working on it? Working on it?' she said. 'Let me put it in simple terms for you, Forrest. If there is such a thing as a Princess these days, then I am it. I didn't choose it and I know

I'm not pretty enough, but you better believe I am rich enough. And I need a knight to save my kingdom before they throw me off the tower. It sounds stupid, but I know what they did to Daddy. And the man who comes charging into Daddy's den to save some silly woman in New York can do the same for me. Or am I overestimating you?'

'You're overestimating me. You should go to the police.'

'What police? Miami? He was brain dead when they got there. Or maybe the FBI. You think I should call up the FBI, tell them Hillburn killed my father? Have them write up some fucking report and file it under loony. I don't have time. I didn't choose you, Forrest, I just need you. Please.'

'What hospital did he go to in Miami?'

'Miami General.'

'How long did he stay there?'

'They kept him overnight for observation. Then they released him in Hillburn's care.'

'Did you see him there?'

'He was gone by the time I heard about it.'

'Do you know where he is now?'

'Hillburn says he's in a private clinic in Beacon, New York. He says he sits in his room and looks out the window.'

'You talked to Hillburn.'

'He called me this morning.'

'Why don't you go see your father?'

'Hillburn said he'd kill me if I went near Daddy.'

'He threatened you like that?'

'Not exactly like that. He said he had a room reserved for me next door.'

'That's not necessarily a threat.'

'Who talked to him, you or me?'

'You were talking about a knight. It reminded me of a place you might stay in New York. It's not exactly a fortress, but it's safe. You ever meet Tom Castleman?'

'I met him once in London when I was seventeen. He tried to feel me up. Why can't I just stay with you? Because you're going to stay with that businesswoman? Jesus, Evers, she's a little shopkeeper compared to me.'

'If you want, I'll ring Castleman for you.'

'I can make my own phone calls. Look, I'm sorry I mentioned it. Don't worry about me. I'll be fine, OK?

'I worry about you.'

'Thanks a lot.'

I dialled Ken at his London flat in Holland Park. There was a terrible wheezing sound when he came on the line which sounded like a dying rhinoceros, but it was only his laugh. When he got his breath, he said, 'Sorry, Evers, but you must admit it is hilarious,' wheeze wheeze. 'You a poofter.'

'It's not funny. This morning they set me up in the motel hallway in my bathrobe with a boy on my arm. You'll probably see it in Fraser's papers tomorrow morning.'

'That does sound unpleasant. You have a good solicitor there? But you have to admit. I mean there must be women all over the world rolling out of their beds with laughter at the thought of you being homosexual.' He started wheezing again, then stopped himself. 'Sorry, no doubt it's not funny at all at your end.'

Then he started wheezing at his joke and I interrupted.

'You bringing two cars to Mexico?'

'Well, just the one for Abbey and the backup. I thought you were driving at Indianapolis.'

'I am. But I think I'll have our sponsor back for Phoenix.'

23

Coming in at cocktail hour, striking the island amidships, the last rays of the sun illuminating the smog and keeping the atmosphere inside the taxi on boil, I felt like an alien coming in to land on a strange planet. But then everybody feels like an alien in New York. First thing the first alien Dutchmen did in 1625 was kick the natives off. Manhattan has been the alien landing pad ever since.

I was in the back of a rolling yellow sauna with the windows down, the traffic on the Long Island Expressway on permanent slo-mo, the tall dark buildings of Manhattan winking their lights on and rising up to greet us as the Long Island Expressway sank down to tunnel under the East River. The driver flung coins into the robot, the light went green, we edged forward and I rolled the windows up, despite the heat. Anybody who doesn't roll up the windows in the Midtown tunnel is nursing a death wish.

Fifty-five storeys over Grand Central Station, most of the Women Unlimited executives had gone home, leaving the glowing green computer scattered among the empty offices the only sign of life. When I turned the corner towards the Chairwoman's office there was a warm light coming from Ellie's office and then Ellie standing in her doorway, smiling and saying, 'Give me a hug, you sexual misfit.'

I gave her a big hug and felt her squish against me. 'Yick,' she said, pulling back, 'you're sopping wet. How'd you get here, walk?'

'It would have been quicker.'

'Well sit down and cool off and I'll tell you what I've been up to.'

I lowered my frame carefully down onto Ellie's wicker settee, the muscles in my thighs and shoulders reminding me that I had crashed two days before, my balls sending up yet another reminder of the kick they had cushioned in the morning. Ellie, lovely long-legged Ellie, was wearing linen trousers and a loose yellow cotton pullover that made her look like the most sophisticated girl on the campus, young and sexy but untouchable. Random wobbles under her pullover (first this one, wobble-wobble, now that one, wibble-wobble) and strands of light brown hair making their escape from down the back of her neck. There are women who are a nest of secrets, hiding thoughts they want no one to know and fearful of smells they want no one to smell. But not dear Ellie. Thirty-eight-year-old Ellie. She was as clear as air. There was a delicious looseness beneath the surface of the buttoned up Chairwoman, a wild streak that wasn't hidden or flaunted, it was just there, easy to see. As usual, no make-up and no jewellery, just those clear grey-blue eyes for ornament.

It had been a week since I'd been in Ellie's office, and for the first time I felt the tension begin to ease. In the distance, through the large windows, the red and white winking lights of the jets descending and rising from La Guardia looked like there was another world out there that worked. It looked like across the speckled darkness of Queens warehouses and tenements, another race of higher intelligence led intricate and orderly lives with scheduled arrivals and departures. It was better from a distance. Up close the pilots call La Guardia 'La Garbage' for the sinkholes in runways built fifty years ago on New York City refuse. Every forty-eight seconds a pilot was landing and another taking off, their knuckles white on the hand grips, half expecting to find a plane stalled on the runway four seconds away.

Ellie's office was cool after the steam bath of the taxi, and the blonde wood floors, big white canvases with their streaks of primary colours on the terra-cotta walls, the green faces of the video screens banked against the wall, all felt reasonable, spacious, relaxing and familiar. Even the mark on the door where Ellie had smashed her ashtray seemed like an old family story, so much had happened in the seven days since then.

Ellie was explaining in her clear confident voice.

'Normally,' she said, 'we do some personality profiling on the people we place. On the lower end of the pay scale it's pretty simple; intelligence, analytical skills, ability to perform under pressure. It helps employers choose the people they want and it helps us place people in the right jobs. As we go up the pay scale,' she said, punching buttons on a console, 'we paint a more complete picture with things like curiosity quotient, ability to invent, imagination, leadership. We even put a numerical value on a sense of humour. Which is pretty funny itself. Most of it is really the guess of the interviewer, matched against the candidate's own assessment, so it's a long ways from being scientifically accurate. But it does give us a picture.'

Ellie stretched for a yawn, exposing an instant of tanned navel. Then she sat down to face one of the computer screens.

'This terminal here is patched into our main frame in Omaha. It holds the files of every single person we placed for the past five years. And it is also connected via satellite and land lines to terminals in every one of our branch offices and franchises around the world.

'Now what I've done is have Bonnie research and draw up a list of all of the Global-Village Companies, run those through against our master files to search out the names of the people we've placed there in the past five years. That's this list here,' she said, patting a foot-high pile of computer printouts on her desk.

'Then I built up a kind of personality profile of the sort of person who might be willing to help us. Adventurous, intelligent, highly curious and imaginative, that sort of thing, and matched those characteristics against the names on the first list.' She tapped a much smaller pile next to the first.

'Finally, I matched the names on the second list against the names of the companies that might know something that we wanted to know; Fraser's travel agency, the Global-Village corporate headquarters (we have three women in there), the company that maintains the company planes, their central accounting unit and so on. And I got this list.' She held up a piece of paper with a hundred and twenty-five names on it.

'But I need clearer direction from you on what we need to know so I can run searches on non-Fraser companies. The Miami airport, for example, to see if we can find somebody who knows when Fraser's plane arrived. The other question is, now that we have these people, what do we ask them and how?'

'You did all that yourself?'

'Forrest, if you ever have the misfortune to become a chief executive officer, the first thing you'll find is that you never do anything yourself. The only thing you ever do yourself is tell people to do what they should have done in the first place. I had our computer department tied up all day working on it. But now that I've got the programs I can run them.'

'What about Castleman, did you call him?

'He rang me. To ask me to lunch next week. And I asked him what it would cost, just in case I ever wanted to, to give the money back. He said he'd be happy to send it back, after he took out a month's interest for expenses.'

'So it would cost you, what was it, another $250,000.'

'I don't think I could hide that much from my board. Not after all the other expenses.'

'So you don't really have much of a choice, do you. You have to fight back.'

'I thought of quitting. Taking a year off in the Caribbean, doing some serious scuba diving, writing the little tract on subversive management techniques that I've got up my sleeve.'

'But you're not.'

She gave her head an impatient shake. 'I'd be bored rigid in a week. What is it you Brits say: "in for a penny, in for a pound"?'

Why is it Americans think I'm a Brit? I'm not a Brit, I'm just British. My mother was American. I grew up here. And there. In Britain, where they can detect an overdraft or a summer in Cornwall in a single vowel, I was absolutely American. In America, I was terribly British. My soul lay moored somewhere over the middle of the Atlantic. 'Brilliant,' I said, thinking that she was much better off before I started all this.

'One thing does worry me, though, Forrest,' she said, walking over to the window. 'You really know zip about finance. You have to admit, this thing hasn't exactly run according to plan.'

'Nothing ever goes according to plan. That's why guerillas win wars. They know that once the battle begins, the plans are obsolete.'

'Let's get 'em, gorilla.'

It was the night we became the Pan Am Gorillas. The long-armed hairy beasts that slept hanging over the side of the Pan Am building, and ate international financiers for breakfast. The night we went ape.

We wanted to know three things. What happened on Fraser's flight from the Caymans to Miami; what was Hillburn up to; and background on Hillburn and the wolf-faced man who called himself Meyer and Caroline said was Mehar. The best way to find out, we decided, was by phone. Telexes could be misunderstood or intercepted. And a direct phone call from the Chairwoman of Woman Unlimited was more likely to get your attention. But that meant cutting the list down to fifty at the most.

For Fraser's flight, we found a woman who worked in the administration office of the Miami airport, a nurse at Miami General Hospital, and a booking agent at Fraser's in-house travel agency. But it was slow going. The programs had been done in a rush and they were full of glitches. Ellie was scrolling through people who might be persuaded to give us an insight into Global-Village recent investments when I switched on the TV to watch the Global-Village Ten O'clock News. 'Want to see me in a bathrobe?' I said.

It has become as common as turning on a tap and seeing water run into a glass. But it still amazes me that a beam of electrons moving across a phosphorescent screen can fool you into thinking you are seeing a face, or a plane flying across a blue sky. But then, as a technological illiterate I've always been dazzled by the flash of science. Shame about the message.

The screen bloomed to life in the middle of a commercial. Two actors fronting for General American Food Corp were sitting on a porch pretending to be good ole country boys, and urged housewives to brighten up their day by getting bombed on soda pop wine.

It had been a while since I'd seen Global-Village News. I'm used to the deadpan British delivery. American TV has a finer screen for news, filtering out the complexities, and allowing only the visually exciting stories to pass through. It bears the burden of having to work as entertainment as well as information. Global-Village in its never-ending struggle to boost its audience figures leans towards more entertainment than hard news, so I don't watch it much. But millions do. Beamed around the world by satellite, the pictures I watched would be seen by thirty million people around the world. Not as many as watch ABC, CBS or NBC, but a considerable number of souls. Tonight, apparently, we were in for a treat.

Over a video of fast cuts of disasters, Presidents, Queens, and movie stars, there was a new signature tune, a single trumpet heralding . . . we cut to a bronzed man who had just had his hair combed and his teeth buffed. He leaned across a vast desk and said in close-up:

'Tonight will go down in the annals of television history. For tonight we, at Global-Village, are introducing a new concept in the reporting of the News. Good evening, my name is John Manning,' he said, his deep voice shining with sincerity. 'And tonight it is my privilege to introduce THE REAL NEWS.'

The signature tune came back again, this time joined by what sounded like a 150-piece orchestra. And the video took us from the star studded blackness of outer space through the atmosphere, down to earth to a series of close-ups of people ordinary people beautifully lit and shot. Over this there were the credits as the announcer reeled off teasers of the evening's main news stories. Then we cut back to him at his desk.

'Tonight THE REAL NEWS presents a simple, powerful new concept in TV journalism. The facts. On THE REAL NEWS we will only report facts. 100 per cent facts. Opinion, right or wrong, has no place on THE REAL NEWS. If some dissidents do not like the facts, they are welcome to their opinion. But their opinion, just like any other opinion, has no place on THE REAL NEWS.

'Now, here are the facts this evening.'

The item 'covering' my escapade in the hallway of the motel was typical. The footage showed me in my bathrobe turning towards the boy leaning against me, and froze as he kissed me on the nose. The voice-over said, 'Meanwhile, in Indianapolis, foreign driver, Forrest Evers, here for the Indy 500, is making new friends.'

In the dim watt light of the motel hallway, I looked sleazy. My expression, which I had remembered as something like, 'what-the-hell-is-going-on', looked guilty as sin.

The rest of the programme covered the major stories of the day with footage picked up from the networks. A bomb in Beirut, a dry spring threatening corn in Nebraska, the last flight of a billion-dollar bomber, crack bust in Chicago, rain expected over Florida and the southeast. Of course it was slanted. News is. Language is. How would you describe a steak, my old philosophy professor used to ask. Cordon bleu Filet Mignon or First Class Piece of Dead Cow? Or, for the next question, try to think of an totally fair way of describing taking a pee. But, it was no more biased than usual, apart from two items. One was the bomb in Beirut. I forget the context, my attention had wandered. But somewhere in the story the announcer said 'Satan'. A weird word for a newscaster, I thought. And later, covering the maiden flight of the bomber, he said 'forces of evil'. Even in a world where it is impossible to describe any event without giving away some point of view, those two phrases stuck out like flashers at a wedding.

24

There is a time before dawn in New York City when the overhead swirl of air traffic descends down to the ground and stops. When jetliners, helicopters, Piper Comanches, Beechcraft Twin Bonanzas and blimps turn out their lights and bed down for the night. It's the one time you can look at the night sky and be sure a distant light is a star and not some ancient incoming overloaded stress-cracked jumbo straining to make up for lost time.

Ellie's face and mine were bathed in green light from a computer screen. Ellie was saying '. . . whacko format like that doesn't just happen. If this, wha'd they call it, The Real News, is a new direction for Global-Village, you know what that could mean. That could mean that Hillburn had it all planned months ago, and you just walked in right before it happened.'

I was bending close to her. We were comparing six women at Global-Village's corporate headquarters in Danbury. One older woman looked promising. She'd been out of work for six months with a child to support before Women Unlimited found her the job. But that was two years ago and the job was in office services, not exactly at the nerve centre. Another woman was in the computer department, but she was a secretary, not an operator. Ellie's hair smelt of warm woman. She had a small mole at the side of her neck. As she bent over her blouse gaped, soft shapes rising out of a valley of shadow. I leant forward, my arm around her shoulder. Her bottom, her small warm soft bottom, moved a sixteenth of an inch into my thigh.

This is the oldest language, the one of absolutes, before words were invented. A soft bottom presses gently against a man's thigh. Yes. A fractional retreat, no. I squeezed Ellie's shoulder and she turned and we kissed. Then we got, slowly and carefully, completely out of control.

Her hand sliding up inside my shirt. Her wet tongue on my neck. My hand, just brushing my fingertips down her long straight back, and sliding down inside the back of her trousers, pushing a little harder to reach the beginning of the valley where the spine dives down to hide the tip of its shy, inward curling sensitive tail. A shocking touch.

Her hips thrust against me, and her mouth on my mouth.

She pulled away. 'Wait,' she said. 'I've always wanted to run around naked –' she kicked off a small mahogany shoe in an arc into the corner – 'in the Chairwoman's office.' Second loafer flew in an arc into another corner.

'So have I,' I said, pulling my polo shirt over my head and throwing it behind me.

'From the time you walked in here?' Ellie was unbuttoning her shirt. I helped, starting from the bottom.

'Not that quick. Not for at least two or three minutes.' I was having trouble with the second button.

'You men are such babies. All you have to do is ask. Nine times out of ten the answer is yes.' Her long fingers brushed mine aside and undid the button in a flick. She was unbuttoning her cuffs and I leant forward to nuzzle her nipples. Just the tip of my tongue . . . she pulled back. Then stepped back, and threw her blouse in my face, making a grunting sound.

Then she was on her knees, in front of me, unbuckling my belt, unbuttoning my trousers, sliding the zip down, and pulling it all down around my ankles. I pulled out the hair clips that kept her hair piled on top of her head, and her hair fell half over her face and around her bare shoulders. She stood up, in front of me and slid her trousers down and stepped out of them, her silk panties a little white island on the floor. 'You smell,' she said, 'like a gorilla.' Ellie leant into me, her face burrowing in my chest. She made a snuffing noise sniffing my chest and her hand, her hot hand with the long fingers, slid down my stomach to my cock, wrapped around and squeezed. 'A very sexy, wild gorilla.'

We had been working side by side, non-stop, for eight hours in the same room. Maybe it's what animals feel in the cage; half sex, half aggression. Ellie let out a strange gorilla-like noise, a grunt that came from some dark, prehistoric time, and leapt back. Leaning back against her desk, her legs wide apart.

The same old primitive sound came out of my throat and I started forward and tripped. My trousers were around my ankles, the last ankle chains of civilization. There is no graceful way to take off your trousers and shoes when they are bunched around your feet. A gorilla drops down to the floor, and first one foot. . . Ellie, making snorting noises, pushed off the desk, was standing in front of me in two steps, put her hands behind my head and pulled my face into her silky, musky dark honey muff.

Still struggling with a pants leg tangled around a shoe, I roared and she leapt back. I stood up, naked and Ellie climbed onto her desk, on her hands and knees, knocking the telephone off onto the floor and kicking over a red leather cup that held pencils and pens. She bared her teeth, and took a clumsy swing at me. I grabbed her hand and she wrenched free, standing up on her desk. She looked down at me, breathing hard, then let out a howl and leapt at me knocking me over backward, sending the settee skidding back to the door.

She was quick and much stronger than I'd thought. Tangled on the floor, something was squeezing my neck hard, a knee was in my stomach. I rolled and she slipped loose. I caught Ellie's ankle as she was about to stand up, she fell forward and I was on her back. She rolled underneath me, put her arms around my neck and we kissed, both of us out of breath. She moved underneath me and pushed away. Slowly she got up, moving with a languid, dream-like grace as if sleeping, and pulled the cushions off the cane settee, arranged them on the floor, and crawled onto the cushions on her hands and knees.

It was a game and it wasn't a game. As if we were the first players, and the first lovers, inventing the rules. I crawled onto the cushions and we began the long and slow exploration that new lovers do. The sniffs and the touches, the hmms and groans of pleasure and giving pleasure, finding all the sweet places. She had a small knot of muscles above her left shoulder-blade, a light blonde fuzz down her spine, a small mole in the hollow behind her knee, long delicate feet and nipples like red raspberries. She was wet to the touch of my fingers and my tongue and she came before I went inside her. She came again and again. And so did I.

Later, lying like two spoons, watching the first light pink the black sky, we invented the last of the urban gorillas, the secret night creatures who swing from skyscraper to skyscraper in a never-ending search for their diet of international financiers, junk bond dealers and takeover sharks. Then Ellie said, 'What's she like?'

'What's who like?'

'Caroline. Fraser.'

'You're not jealous?'

'Not yet.'

'I don't know what she's like. She's had a hell of a shock and I don't know if it's knocked her sideways or if she's always falling apart. She's like little bits of girl and woman shaken up in a bottle, and the pieces come out one by one. One minute she's a spoiled little brat, the next she's sexy like she can't wait to get you into bed, and then she's a frightened little girl who just wants her Daddy.'

'You didn't, did you?'

'Didn't what?'

'Go to bed with her.'

'You're not worried?'

'Well, you didn't wear a condom. That's plenty to worry about right there.'

'For all I know she's a virgin.'

'Caroline Fraser is nineteen and she was married for six months before her father had it annulled. So I don't think I'd buy her little girl act. Do you think she's right, about her father?'

'I don't know. Probably.'

'You think she's in danger?'

'If she's not in danger from Hillburn, she's in danger from herself. There's a girl who could do herself a serious injury.'

25

It was after eleven, Tuesday night, when I got back to the Speedway Motel. Caroline Fraser was in my bed.

She had been reading a paperback and the shade of the reading light was tipped so the soft yellow light spilled across her face and down along the roller-coaster ride of her body. Caroline's hair was soft and silky and fell half across her face down to her shoulders. She had brushed her long black hair partly across her face half hiding her half smile. A cream satin nightgown was full to overflowing with creamy white breasts, and she had pulled back the cover so I could see the soft curve over her tummy, a little dent for her navel, the rise of the mons, the silky slope down between her thighs. 'Hi, Forrest,' she said, a little breathy catch in her voice.

I leaned against the wall, and looked at her for a moment, her big brown eyes looking up at me, moving her thighs with a little squirm, making a moaning sound. It was a performance, but it had power. Dear mother nature, the pushy old broad. I felt a surge of desire, inhaled the delicious scent, visually traced the wide expanse of a satin-covered nipple. I said, 'What the hell are you doing here?'

'I came out to prove the stories they're telling about you aren't true.'

I leaned against the wall, something to do. 'I don't know how you got here, but it's the worst place you could be. Hillburn knows I'm here. So now he probably knows you're here too. Damn it Caroline, he's in Indianapolis.'

'Don't be grumpy, Forrest, it was easy. I made a phonecall, that's all. To a friend who happens to be the sister of the man who owns the company that owns the majority shares in the Speedway. You get up high enough, Forrest, everybody knows everybody else. You're not angry, are you? Aren't you even a little glad to see me? I'm not afraid of Hillburn or anybody when I'm with you. Oh Forrest, I could give you so much.'

'I know you can, Caroline. But I'm afraid they're true.'

'What do you mean, true?'

'I mean the stories they've been spreading. I'm gay.' I gave her a big, wistful, sad-but-brave, Evers smile. 'Some of my best friends are girls, but I love boys.'

'Forrest, you can't be. I know I could turn you on.'
'I'm sorry Caroline, but tits turn me off.'
Caroline dropped the pose, sat up and pulled up the sheet.
'You crude bastard,' she said.
'I told you not to come.'
'Well I did. And I'm here. And I'm not going back to Carefree.'
'Poor little girl. She's only got eighteen other houses to go to.'
'Why don't you take me seriously?'
'Believe me, Caroline, I take you seriously. I was up all night, taking you seriously. By tomorrow morning it's just possible that we'll know what happened to your father.'
She was out of bed in a flash. Standing in front of me. Her breasts pointing straight out. One, one way, the other, the other. Long breasts, pointing, saying hold, fondle, lick, kiss . . .
One day when I grow up I will admire women's minds or shoulders, or necks or knees, before I get around to lusting after their breasts. Breasts are silly, helpless, everyday things. Half the human race has two. And it is a baby passion, a confusion of love, warmth and food. About as sophisticated a passion as a tantrum. It is childish to let them pull so hard. But pull they do. And like a compass rising to point true north I could feel an erection rising. I went into the bathroom and shut the door and ran the cold water.
'Forrest, are you OK? What happened? What'd you find out about my father?'
I was too exhausted to sleep on the couch. And it seemed ungentlemanly to make Caroline sleep on the lumpy, cigarette-burned, knobbly upholstery. Besides it was a big bed. So we slept side by side, chaste as nuns.
Except in the middle of the night I woke to feel her hand reach across, trailing her fingertips down my stomach and down my thigh and back up slowly to cup my balls. Her hand was warm, and slid up slowly and wrapped around my, by then, throbbing hard-on. 'Oh, Forrest,' she said.
'Oh Frank,' I said, heavily feigning sleep. Her hand withdrew like a shot. I rolled over and a mere hour and a half later was relaxed enough to go to sleep.
The bottom half of a full moon shone through the window. The cars going by outside, from time to time, on Sixteenth

Street, made a swishing sound, as if they were going by in the rain. And alongside me Caroline said, in her sleep, sounding like a little girl, 'No, Daddy. No no no no no no no no no no.'

26

I raised my head to see Caroline was dressed in a t-shirt with toucans on the back and a pink mini-skirt. She was looking out of the window at the parking lot, smoking a cigarette. The dingaling sound came into focus. The phone was ringing.

I picked up the godawful instrument with the goddamn tinkle bells, rolled over on my stomach and mumbled hello. I am not at my best first thing in the morning.

'Hi,' Ellie said, 'wanna go ape?'

I made a grunting noise. Caroline turned round and looked at me.

'Want to hear what I've found out? Of course you do. The first thing is that both Hillburn and Meyer or Mehar as Caroline calls him, graduated from Cornell in 1961. So they must have known each other. And they both worked on the College newspaper. I got this from a woman in outplacement at Fraser. She says that Meyer is Iranian and went back to Tehran and worked for the Iranian National Bank. But he returned to America with the bank three years ago. And Hillburn hired him last year.'

'What about Hillburn?'

'I couldn't get a lot on him. His CV at Global lists, and I'm quoting here, "experience in Iran", whatever that means. It says he was employed by the State department from '62 to '79. And that he joined Fraser as "Director of Internal Management" in 1980. So it's very possible he met up with Mehar when the Shah was in power, because they were both in Tehran at the same time and must have known each other from Cornell. And thinking about it, they're both fundamentalists, Moslem and Mormon. You know, different religions but the same attitudes. Anyway, I think Caroline may be right.'

'What do you mean?'

'Well, the good news is that Fraser's plane landed at Miami at 10:57 p.m. That's over three hours after you said he took off. And it's only an hour's flight.'

'So there's two missing hours,' I said to Caroline as well as Ellie, 'between the Caymans and Miami.'

'Yup. The flight log just registers Cayman to Miami, but unless they flew around in circles . . .'

Caroline said, 'Tell her to try Haiti. Daddy owned a lot of property in Haiti.'

'What about . . .'

'Haiti,' Ellie said, 'I heard. Who the hell is that?'

'Caroline,' I said. 'Caroline Fraser.'

'Where the hell did she come from? I thought you said she was hiding.'

'She is. When I came back she was in my room.'

'You sonofabitch.'

'I told her I was gay,' I said.

'And you didn't touch her all night. Had to sleep on the floor, didn't you? It's really been a treat to know you, Forrest.'

'Why don't you come out here? See for yourself.'

'Goodbye, Forrest.'

'Ellie, stop this. You have to believe me.'

'Why?'

'You don't have any choice.'

'I have plenty of choices. You're just not one of them.'

Then she hung up.

'You have to go,' I said.

'Who the hell do you think you are to tell me what to do?' Caroline said. 'You're an impostor, Evers, a fake. You don't even make a good faggot.'

I put my hands on her shoulders to calm her. This was a mistake. 'Just because that old bag who runs some fucking business thinks she owns you, you want to get rid of me.' Her face was two inches from mine and she was screaming. I kissed her forehead.

'I don't want to get rid of you and I don't want Hillburn to get rid of you either.'

'I want to stay with you.'

'I think we can expose Hillburn. But I can't do it if you're here and I have to spend all my time protecting you.'

'Bullshit,' she said, but she was already pulling open a drawer, pulling out a handful of brassières, starting to pack.

No, she didn't want to stay in Ellie's apartment in New York. No, she loathed the thought of staying with Castleman. She had a couple of friends in Ojai, California she said. No, she didn't need to call them. They didn't have a phone. She rang her pilot at the airport. 'How close can we get to Ojai,' she said.

She didn't have a suitcase. She carried her few things in a Bergdorf Goodman shopping bag. Poor little rich refugee. We went out of a side door into the parking lot and she got into the Malibu rentacar and slid over beside me, like a teenager on a date. I started to pull out and she kissed my cheek and squeezed my thigh, and another car rammed us from the side.

There was a flash of yellow on my left. A bright yellow toy baseball bat smashed into my window, exploding the transparent glass into a mushrooming cloud of shards, followed by a pair of arms in a leather jacket reaching inside on the follow through and sticking the toy bat under my chin and pulling hard to lift me half out of the jagged mouth of the window frame.

People who come back from nearly drowning say there is a moment, when you are deep and sinking, of immense peace, a black and liquid tranquillity when you accept that you will never ever have to do a single thing ever again; you are descending into the perfect endless, carefree holiday.

Until the shards of light began to pierce my eyelids, I felt like I might have slept for ever. I opened my eyes and the car was surrounded by people with cameras. Most of them looked as if they were just tourists, but some of them must have been reporters. The dark sky was telling their sensors to flash while a big red balloon was blowing up to bursting size in my throat. I tried to speak, to ask what happened to Caroline, but the balloon turned into a Brillo pad. Her shopping bag was on the seat beside me, spilling pink panties, brassières, and a red, patent-leather, spike-heeled, sling-back shoe.

'Goddamnit Evers, you're more trouble than a basket of snakes at a picnic.' Fenstermacher loomed over me. In the background the mechanics were bolting on the front suspension to the tub that had arrived by air-freight from England that afternoon.

Kidnapping is a Federal crime and the FBI were on their way to talk to me. They would have to do all the talking since my neck still looked like puffed up turkey wattle and a thin stream of air in and out was the best I could hope for. Speech, it seemed, was still a way off.

Thank God for Orrin Fenstermacher. He had heard the crash

as he was brushing his teeth, thrown on a shirt, charged out of the Motel and peeled away the curious and the police. 'Out the way,' I heard him say, 'out of the way, he's a friend of mine.'

The Speedway, Indiana police, naturally, were curious. Who was in the car with me? Could I describe the perpetrator? What was my estimated speed at the time of the incident? Could I furnish any details of the other vehicle? Registration number, make, model and year? Did I hold a current US driving licence? And on and on it went, in the drizzle, while, at the edge of the cleared off space, the crowd swarmed with reporters and the blank eyes of cameras – TV lenses waited for their chance at some good close ups of me and the spilled underwear. It took the police just a little while to realize I couldn't talk.

And when they learned that the best I could do was to guess that it was probably grey and maybe a Chevvy, they gave up trying to read my scrawled answers. Fenstermacher bulled his way to his car and drove me straight down West 16th to the Methodist Hospital where, in the glass and white panel maze of the emergency room a doctor sewed up two slits in my cheek in two minutes and a slim, tall, blonde nurse with freckles on her turned-up nose and a name tag that said Paula swabbed out my cuts and said she was betting on Al Unser Jr. but you couldn't count out Bobby Rahal although you'd be a fool not to bet on a Penske. But wouldn't it be great if A. J. took it again?

In Indianapolis, everybody is a fan and A. J. Foyt is a saint. And the Methodist Hospital can fix up a mangled body faster than anywhere else in the world. A few cuts on the cheek and a squashed throat they can do with standing on their head, whistling 'Moonlight on the Wabash'.

When we had got back to the garage in Gasoline Alley, it was nearly two-thirty in the afternoon, and the mechanics had just taken the tub out of its crate and put it on stands. The tub is the torso of an Indy car, the one part you cannot replace and still claim to have the same car. Sitting on its stands without wheels, suspension, engine, brakes, hydraulics or electrics it looked as naked as a bathtub. After two hours of intense activity from George and five of the best mechanics in the world, it was starting to drool hoses, and electric wires. But it was a long way from a race car.

George had said it would be ready to go for the practice tomorrow, Thursday, Carburetion Day. Normally Carburetion Day is a last chance to check all the final settings and run a few laps on three-quarter tanks. Then the cars are parked until Sunday. 'But it's the same goddamn story all over again,' George said. 'I'll set it up just the way it was before you touched the wall. But it won't be the same. We gonna be starting from scratch all over again.' So they would work non-stop all night, with zero margin for error. Every nut torqued to the exact torque, every wire perfect.

'Yeah, I ain't so worried about the car. It's the goofball driver, worries me,' Orrin said, looking suspiciously at a coiled brake pipe. 'You gonna be able to drive tomorrow, Evers? We skip tomorrow, we haven't got a rat's ass.'

'Tomorrow's fine,' I wrote on a yellow pad. Hunky dory. You betcha. Indianapolis wasn't as physically demanding as most Formula One races. There weren't the constantly changing heavy g-forces between accelerating and braking, there wasn't the constant sawing at the wheel. The track was smooth and the adjustments you made to the throttle and the wheel were almost infinitesimal. The only part of your body that really came in for a pounding was your neck. There was a strap that kept your helmet cocked to the left. But the bruised and swollen muscles that connected my head to my shoulders were not looking forward to the experience.

'Hiya,' said a high, feminine voice. A shadow at the door which moved into the light of the garage. 'Hi, George, Orrin, Eugene, Jack, Fred, Tony.' Nobody looked up, they'd all seen her before. 'Hi,' she stuck out her hand at me, 'I'm Charlotte Rapp, PRO for Fenstermacher Lumber.' She was wearing a gauzy lilac pants-suit that swirled when she moved. And white Reeboks. Her hair was a dark mop of curls and she had a chipmunk face and intense little black eyes. She was pretty in a soft and chubby way and she had a voice like a screech owl. I nodded hello and worked up a smile.

'I gotta say, you do have a talent for publicity, Mr Evers,' she said, rummaging in a black leather handbag the size of a suitcase. She came up with a pocket tape recorder. Short, stubby little hands with dimples to mark where the knuckles were. 'OK to call you Forrest? Boy, there were some really cute things we were going to do with your name. You know, Forrest and the Fenstermacher lumber company, I mean it's a natural, but that's all blown out of the water now.'

I nodded, unable to say Thank God for small favours.

'Course you know what the media's gonna do with this morning's little escapade.' Orrin raised a hand to deflect her, but there was no deflecting her. 'They're going to say "Indy driver can't drive his way out of the parking lot". They're going to say "kinky fashion show". They're going to say "pretty in pink".'

'For God's sake shut up, Charlotte,' Orrin said.

'Well I think it's important to be prepared for this. This is blockbuster stuff and once they get their teeth into it . . . and my God if they ever get a whiff of who was with you and is probably kidnapped! I gotta say, you really got a talent for PR, Forrest.'

'Charlotte, we're a little busy here, and Mr Evers has had a difficult morning. Why don't you just outline what you told me on the phone?'

'Sure, Orrin. No problem.' She looked at me as if I was a lump of abstract bronze in a museum, squinting, making a this-is-a-tough-one-to-figure-out face. 'Well there's two ways we could go. I mean we got a problem, right? Well maybe it's an opportunity. On the one hand, we got Carburetion Day tomorrow, and you got to go to that. Then, for the rest of Thursday, Friday and Saturday, there's a lot of picnics and dinners, there's the fashion show with the racing drivers' wives, there's the parade, and the breakfasts, luncheons, press conferences, barbecues and picnics. Did I say picnics before? Never mind. What we could do is have Forrest go to all of them with some well-known starlet, you know, like Dyanna, what's her name, Bell. I think she's on a $500 per diem, but I can check that out. That way at least we're up front, in the public eye. But given your track record so far, Forrest, the downside of going public like that is that it lays us open to situations we may not be able to control. I mean they set you up once, they could set you up again.

'So the other idea I had,' she said, 'was after Carburetion Day practice, you just disappear. I mean if I was going to be objective, from a PR stand-point I have to say that on balance right now your PR value is pretty negative. I don't know what kind of budget we're talking here, or if Dyanna's under contract, or maybe you know some lady who could go with you to someplace like Mr Fenstermacher's cabin, that's a super place,' she paused to toss a grateful smile to Orrin who caught it without flinching, 'and take a film crew with you. You know, film walks in the forest, no pun intended Mr Evers, take some shots of the two of you having breakfast in bathrobes . . . things like that that we could scale out to the networks. Burn in the idea that you're really a very sexy, masculine hunk.'

Good idea. Call Ellie, I scrawled on my notepad. *No film crew.*

'Forrest, you do understand you have a major problem,' she said, her voice rising up towards a screech. 'And I am trying to help you. I mean you've got the whole Global media complex portraying you as a raging faggot. And the public are starting to believe that you *are* a screaming faggot. I mean uh, no offence. Really, it doesn't make any difference to me one way or t'other. But you've got to agree it is an issue we have to address, pronto. I mean you have no *idea* how a smear like that can affect your image.'

Frankly, Charlotte, I wrote out in my best Rhett Butler scrawl, *I don't give a damn.*

27

Forget about Caroline. I said. I said. I said. Never mind. Nothing I could do for her. Or about her. No way I could change what happened. I pictured her terrified, locked in a room in a farmhouse in Michigan. I pictured her laughing by a pool in California, pouring the man with the big forearms and the yellow baseball bat a tall frosty one. Forget about her, I said again for the forty-third time. Let the FBI worry about her. Racing is another story and the race goes on.

It wasn't easy pushing her out of my mind, but then nothing is easy at the Indianapolis Motor Speedway. There are men who have the talent and the grace to make it look easy, but nothing is easy. Not even good ol' Carburetion Day, when every car on the track has already earned its place in the race, and the race is still three days away, and the sun is shining in a clear blue sky and all you need to do is check your settings on race tyres with fuel in the tank. Even then it is hard.

Two things catch your eye. The first is speed. Pure, unadulterated, massive speed. Low-flying flamingo-pink and candy-flake grape machines turn into the corners at 230 miles an hour with the foot on the accelerator not the brake . . . accompanied by the full orchestra of jet whine, tyre screech and eight hundred turbo-charged horses at 12,500 rpm, their thousands of whirling bits screaming, their exhaust pipes on full *vroom*. These men love to race and they are out there under the blue sky to show who is the fastest of them all. No pressure, just foot to the floor, balls to the wall. No pressure at all, except from the car coming up behind you and the other one pulling away. So long, sucker.

Then there is the wall. The wall is the next item of interest and yes, indeed, it does engage your attention. The wall rises three feet high at the edge of the track and it goes all the way around. There are no escape roads, no gravel runoff areas, no piles of tyres or even a little forgiving ribbon of grass. There is the groove, the black line of rubber the cars leave in their passage, there is the grey area of track beyond, and then there is the unloving, unforgiving wall. At Indianapolis, like most Superspeedways, the wall is reinforced, thick concrete. At Pocono it is inch-thick boiler plate. Concrete or boiler plate, it doesn't make much difference. Either will tear your wheels off at the first kiss. Or ram your thighs behind your ears should you have the misfortune to hit it head on.

The art of keeping a car off the wall while turning left at, say, 225 miles an hour is a fine one, not practised by the unbrave or survived by the heavy-handed. I was standing in the pit lane, waiting for George to make another one of his infinitesimal adjustments. He had set up the car, as he usually did, for slight understeer. 'Just a little push,' he said. 'So you know where you are.' But I was used to my oversteering Formula One car and I'd asked him to set it 'just a little more neutral'. Out on the track, there was a yowl of engines as the green lights went on. The cars were frozen in the distance for an instant and then, in the next, were streaking by like low-flying aircraft in ragged formation, banking into the first turn, three abreast. In the next instant they were gone, leaving in their wake the acrid smell of burned alcohol, and the distant scream of several million pounds of intricate racing machinery. Forty seconds later, they were back and Texas Stimson had a lead of a hundred yards, just under a second.

If any of the drivers had read the papers or seen the slurs against me on TV, they weren't showing it. Except for a little jibe here and there. We were now all on the same hazardous journey, trying to stay in the groove, out of the grey area and off the wall. Charley Dobson Jr., third generation of Dobsons to race at Indianapolis, had been giving me a 200 mile an hour driving lesson. He had to shout over the passing cars. I nodded from time to time because I couldn't shout. Although my whispering was getting stronger all the time. Goddamn her.

'Lookit ol' Texas out there. I bet you $500 he's got his baggy trousers on,' Charley said.

'That makes him go fast,' I whispered my hoarse whisper in his ear, 'baggy trousers?'

'Damn straight. Ol' Texas won so many times here they don't check his pop-off valve, they don't check him at all. You watch when he gets out of his car. He's gonna be wearing baggy pants and you look close you gonna see a big lump on his shin.'

'What's the lump?'

'Nitrous oxide. He's got a bottle of nitrous oxide, laughing gas. He feeds that into the fuel line and that car takes off like a big-ass bird. Christ he does all kinds of things. That mechanic of yours, George?'

I nodded to show I knew George.

'When George was working with Texas he got sorta confused, screwed on a stockblock pop-off valve, you know, give that thing around two hundred extra horsepower. Well, they go to qualify and Texas come off of Turn Four like he was shot out of a cannon. They reckon he was doing 250 mile an hour down the straight.'

'So what happened to Tex?'

'Jesus, don't ever let him hear you call him that. He hear you call him Tex and he'll about tear your head off. His name is Texas, like the state. Which he thinks is something to be proud of. Anyway just as he was turning into One the engine with all that extra boost blows up like a grenade and George and Texas say they real sorry, musta just got confused over the pop-off valves.'

'I thought you played by the rules.'

'There's only one rule you gotta remember,' he said. ' "You ain't cheatin' if you don't get caught." Everybody out there is going 99.999%, looking for that last thousandth of a per cent. If you go outside the rules to find it, just don't get caught, that's all.'

I nodded as if I was looking for a thousandth of a per cent instead of the last two per cent.

Charley looked off into the distance, down to Turn Four, his childish face turning serious. His spread his big hands out in front of him as if he could feel the atmosphere with his fingertips. 'This here's my favourite, you know, my favourite course. It's the smoothest course in the world and probably the simplest. And it can kill you that quick. But I gotta tell you, if I could just drive here and noplace else, I would. That's the only reason I drive these Indy cars, to drive at Indianapolis.'

In the distance I could see Eugene towing my car back into the pits. Twelve oh five, fifty-five minutes of practice left. Every second was precious. Robby Kokorian joined us. 'Hi sweetie,' he said. 'I was watching you out there,' he said with his famous gap-tooth grin. 'You weren't doin' too bad.'

Robby has won the Indianapolis Five Hundred, won the CART Indy car championship twice, and won the Daytona twenty-four hours. He has raced at Le Mans and in Formula One and he knows whereof he speaks.

'Thanks, Hot-Lips,' I croaked, 'but that car is still faster than I am.'

'Don't feel bad,' Robby said. 'The first time I drove on a Superspeedway, I couldn't believe it,' he said. 'Nothing, and I mean nothing, I had done in road racing prepared me for the intensity and the speed. I mean when I realized what these guys were up to I thought, Sheeeit, maybe I'll go into advertising.'

The yellow light came on and the cars started diving into the pits. Robby had been out, was satisfied with the car and had parked for the day. 'No point wearing it out,' he said.

He took a pull on a plastic cup of Coca-Cola and spat it out. 'It takes time, Forrest, to get up to that kind of speed and concentration. On a road course if you make a mistake you can get into serious trouble. But you know, you've usually got some options and some room. And usually you can drive your way out of it. On an oval, nine times out of ten you're fucked.'

Over in the Fenstermacher pits George held up two fingers. Two minutes and I could get back into the car.

'I don't know,' he said, crumpling the cup and flinging it in a long high arc into an oil drum, 'I don't think there's much point comparing Formula One with Indy cars, they're just two different animals. In an Indy car you are working with very fine increments. Of course it depends on the track, but usually you'll keep your foot down right up to the apex and use the lateral forces in the corner to scrub off speed. But it needs a very fine touch. Delicate, you might say.'

The most delicate thing I did on Carburetion Day was lower myself into the cockpit. My neck was better but it still claimed serious attention, particularly with the helmet feeling as heavy as a bowling ball.

At first out on the track it wasn't too bad. There was too much to think about. But when I got into traffic, and my head started to bounce around from 220 mile an hour gusts that came boiling off the spoilers from the cars in front and the rear end started to go light because the downforce had suddenly disappeared, and my neck felt like it had a couple of spears stuck through it, then it wasn't what you would call fun. After ten laps, I would come in and ask for another touch of downforce on the front or a little less or this or that just for the rest it would give me. For the chance to take my helmet off, catch my breath and massage the bruised and swollen cords of my neck.

Somewhere out there, across the track in the miles of stands cluttered with spectators, journalists and photographers, somewhere out there, along the wall or on a tower high above the track there was the wink of the sun bouncing off one of the thirty-seven remote-control television camera lenses turning, pulling focus, zooming in.

28

The sun was rising behind us, turning the sky pink and pale blue. Somewhere below us, the dark waves were rolling in from Asia to crash into the rocks on the shore. Two and three hundred feet above us, the wind was ruffling the tops of Coastal Redwoods that had been standing in the wind since Mohammed was a shepherd boy in Mecca.

It had taken some planning, but not much time. Ellie had caught a TWA flight, JFK to San Francisco. I had taken Orrin's jet, we had met at the desk of a little feeder line called Pacific Air and flown an hour north up to Eureka, rented a car, picked up some groceries, and we were in time for the sunset over the dark blue sea, among the oldest and tallest living things on earth, watching the sun go down.

Orrin Fenstermacher's log cabin sits on the western edge of Fenstermacher State Park, on 1,500 acres 'reserved' by and for the Fenstermacher family. You drive in the main entrance of the park off Highway–101, past the administration buildings and campgrounds and after a mile's drive through the redwood forest, turn off on an unmarked trail, enter a code to unlock a gate, drive through, and behind you the gate shuts on the twentieth century. Three miles further down the dirt track, on a promontory over the Pacific, 'the cabin' bears the same resemblance to a cabin as the Baths of Caracalla bore to a bathroom.

Orrin said his family built it in the 1880s to celebrate the hook-up of the railroads across the continent. The cabin's scale was taken, not from the men and women who might spend their weekends there, but from the three-hundred-foot-high, two-thousand-year-old trees that make up its beams, walls and floors. With ceilings forty feet high, and a porch with redwood pillars eight feet in diameter, facing the sunset over the sea, it is the world's largest front-row seat at the geographical end of America's frontier, built when we thought America and the old redwoods went on for ever. When we thought we were big enough to inhabit rooms three storeys tall.

We arrived in time to throw open the windows to blow away the mouldy air, to see the labels peeling off the cans of soup and corned beef hash on the kitchen shelves, sweep away the rust from a cast-iron stove big enough to feed a battalion, and wipe the cobwebs from the windows. Then we sat, as small as two children, on the wide front steps and watched the sun turn from gold to an immense red fireball, burning the sky behind as it sank out of sight.

We cooked a simple supper in a pan, and ate by kerosene lantern light. The soft light from the lantern flames made pools in the darkness, our faces shining at the edge, our bodies lost in shadow.

Ellie put on flannel pajamas and we crawled into dank sheets. Tired and sleepy, we snuggled around each other, and Ellie said 'no' five times before I went to sleep.

Our bedroom had forty-foot-high floor to ceiling windows at the back and at the front, so when the sun rose we could see the snow-capped coastal mountains behind us and the Pacific in the distance at our feet.

I woke up with Ellie stroking my throat with her fingertips.

'She did this to you,' she said, 'didn't she?'

'Ellie, she's just a kid. What are you jealous of a kid for?' I said, dragging myself up.

'She's twenty-one and that's just one of the reasons I'm jealous of her. It's obvious, Forrest,' she said, following her fingers down to kiss my chest. 'You told me she was looking out of the window to the parking lot. She was signalling someone. And she grabbed you just before the other car hit you. Think about it, Forrest. She set you up.'

'I've thought about it. And I can't think of a reason why she'd do a thing like that.'

'You wouldn't. But look at it this way. Suppose she doesn't want you to race? Suppose she wants you all to herself to get revenge on Hillburn? Or protect her? Or both? I mean she is a very spoiled woman who is used to getting what she wants. At the very least, Forrest, doesn't it occur to you that she wants your attention?'

I rolled over on top of Ellie, feeling her soft thighs loosening. 'I wonder how I get your attention. How are things at the office?' I said.

'She's probably just using you,' Ellie said, wrapping her legs around mine.

'Think you can hold out for three more weeks until you get

your money from Castleman?' I said, pushing my cock slowly
into her.

'Forrest,' she said, 'for God's sake, stop it.' She put her arms
around me and pulled my face down to her. 'Didn't anybody
ever tell you you can't make love to a woman before you take
her pajamas off?'

I bent down and pulled on her pajama string with my teeth.
Oysters and champagne for breakfast.

When the sun shines on a redwood forest, it is filtered from a
single light source ninety-three million miles away into the
finest of golden shafts. High overhead, there is a scattering of
blue sky in the dense green needles and branches. Underfoot,
the ground is spongy from millions of years of sequoia effluvia
and not much else. For *Sequoia sempervivens* is a fascist and
nothing else can grow in its shadow. Its high branches block out
the light and the acid from its needles poisons the competition.

95 per cent of these ancient 'live for ever' trees are gone now;
two-thousand-year-old trees cut down to make houses, shingles,
and salt- and pepper-shakers that look like outhouses and say
'souvenir of the Redwood Forest'.

The stupendous soaring columns of trunks and the high
overarching branches made us feel hushed, as if we were walking through a cathedral. We were intruders, temporary. A speck
of time.

The stand we were walking in had never felt an axe. The
tallest tree, twenty feet in diameter at the base and nearly
four hundred feet high, was probably the tallest in the world,
Fenstermacher said. 'But we like to keep it a secret. I'd like to
think it might hang on for a few more centuries before some
turkey nails a plaque on it and folks start stomping around on
their roots. They have real delicate roots, don't ya' know.'

Ellie leaned against the tree, just a plain little lumberjane in
a check flannel shirt, blue jeans and tan leather work-boots,
her hair held with a ring of stretchy stuff in a pony tail that
swished behind her. I leaned against her and we kissed. 'Does
it have a name?' she said. 'You know, like some of the big trees
are called Captain Miles Standish, the Dyerville Giant . . ?'

'Fenstermacher said he thought it probably did have a name,
but so far it hadn't told anybody. He said sometimes the family

called it Frank. After some uncle who was supposed to have an enormous schlong.'

'His wife probably called it "wishful thinking".'

'I thought women didn't care about the size of cocks.'

'It's a limited subject.' She held her head to the side for a moment, then pushed off and we walked, our boots making no sound on the forest floor. 'Forrest, what are we doing here? Orrin made it sound like you were dying on the phone. I know you said you were OK, but your voice sounded so awful I cancelled six meetings, lunch and dinner, grabbed my things and ran. But really, darling, couldn't we have just seen each other in New York? Or even Indianapolis?'

'Maybe. I don't know. Fenstermacher has a PR lady who thought it would be a good idea to lay low for a few days before the race. Apparently I'm not exactly a PR asset. She wanted to send along a camera crew to prove I'm not gay.'

'So that's what you were doing this morning, showing off for the camera.'

'Ellie, really. Certainly not. That was just the rehearsal.'

Walking in a primeval forest is not easy. Trees the size of office buildings create chaos when they fall; broken limbs, trunks ten feet wide lying flat, roots erupting out of the ground, and yet the forest was as still as a locked church. As if whenever it had happened, a moment or a thousand years ago, the chaos remained suspended in time. We picked our way around a tree that may have fallen when Columbus stumbled on America. Ellie stopped. 'I just had the eeriest feeling,' she said. 'When you just said "a rehearsal", my first thought was what about an open-air performance? And I had this silly picture of us ripping our clothes off and then, I got this awful feeling we're being watched.'

'Must be the Abominable Lumberjack.'

'Don't you feel it?'

'Not really. Maybe we make the trees nervous. They're not exactly used to visitors. It's a good thing we're not carrying chainsaws. One of them probably would have dropped a limb the size of a bank on us.' I put my arms around Ellie and gave her a hug. 'I'm glad you're here,' I said, my voice still rasping from the yellow baseball bat. 'And it's not a bad idea to keep out of Hillburn's sight until we can nail him. Did you find out anything else about him?'

Ellie gave me a soft kiss, then turned away. She found a foothold on the side of a gigantic fallen trunk and pulled herself up and stood on top of it. Then she stretched out on her stomach, looking down at me from four feet above my head. 'Our computer lady in Danbury has been terrific. Global bypassed her for some man who used to report to her. Apparently she thought she was going to be promoted to the head of her department and let me tell you she really wants revenge. She's accessed all kinds of interesting things.'

'Isn't that illegal?'

'When did that ever hold you back? It's illegal if you can prove damages, but I don't think they are going to want to press charges.' Ellie stood up and walked along the back of the trunk, holding out her arms as if she were balancing on a high wire.

'Because . . .'

'Because right after Mehar was hired by Hillburn, there was a huge injection of cash into the company.'

'Could you find out where it came from?' I found a series of broken-off branches sticking out like the rungs of a ladder, climbed up and started walking behind her, holding my hands out. High-class high-wire act with a three-hundred-ton log for a wire.

Ellie said, 'The Iranian Office of Information bought the franchise rights for a Fraser TV station and newspaper chain.'

'Which means?'

'I don't know what it means. Except there was no TV station and no newspaper chain. It was money for nothing. Or something. I don't know.'

'Was this around the time of Irangate?'

Ellie stopped and turned round to face me. 'Oh shit, don't say that. This is complicated enough as it is. I just want my little $12 million bundle back so I can keep my company.' I gave her a kiss, a nice big long one, turned her around and lifted her up on my shoulders. Ellie made a little shriek of surprise, then stuck her arms out, balancing.

'What do you mean, complicated enough?' I said, walking again, making it seem as if the high wire was shaky.

'Well, right after they got the money, Global went on a buying spree. They bought a Hong Kong film company, a

Korean radio and TV manufacturer, an English bank, all kinds of companies all over the world.'

'Did you ever find out why he's in Indianapolis?'

'Not really. We've been monitoring his movements through his travel agency. He left Indianapolis on Wednesday for London. He should be back in New York tomorrow.'

'He moves around.' There was a big vertical branch in our way. I stopped and put Ellie down.

'Moguls move around. Just like racing drivers. It's what they do. Do you really think we have any chance of stopping him, Forrest? I mean you don't seem to be that upset, but how many successful racing drivers are called fairies?'

'I don't know, maybe plenty. I mean you'd have to be from another planet to think only he-men play football or drive racing cars.'

'He probably has terrible sexual problems but I sure wouldn't want to know about them.'

'He could be worse.'

'How?'

'There's something we haven't thought of. Maybe our darling Philip is from Mars. Can you imagine him kissing anybody.'

I jumped down to the ground and held my arms out to catch her. 'Ooof,' she said. 'I'll tell you, Forrest, I can hold out for a month without the Fraser newspapers, but after that, that's it. I'll be looking for work. I mean, I think we've found out a few interesting things, but what do we know that could stop him?'

I unbuttoned her shirt, put my hands on her breasts and looked into her clear eyes. 'Nothing yet,' I said.

The sequoias were a time filter. Events had been ripping past us so fast they blurred. Now they slowed down to the speed of a dust mote, floating through a shaft of sunlight. We made love slowly and quietly, whispering in that vast outdoor cathedral as if someone might be listening, two tiny naked figures at the base of a towering tree, me leaning back against the rough bark of a redwood, Ellie leaning into me.

I pulled the elastic ring out of Ellie's hair, and her hair fell, loose and fragrant around her bare shoulders. We spent a long time or a moment, time didn't matter, kissing the soft way that slow kisses do (here, where she was blushing and there, where she was apricot and peach), aware of all of the different sensations, the warmth and softness of her smooth thighs, the redness of her nipples in the sunshaft, the sound of a distant bird, the light on the fine gold hairs at the back of her neck. When we had kissed and touched each other and my cock was rising between her legs, I knelt down in front of Ellie and she leant on her arms against the tree, while I parted her lips with my tongue and found her endlessly soft and wet and delicious. And when I stood up and leant back against the tree as she knelt in front of me, I held her head in my hands as she made sucking sounds that were the only sounds in the high arches of the trees. When Ellie stood we kissed again and I held her bottom in the spread of my hands and lifted her up and lowered her down slowly on me, lifting her up and letting her slowly down again, teasing a little until it was easy. And as we made love, standing with our feet still and the rest of our bodies moving, tiny at the bottom of the forest, we closed our eyes and it seemed as if we grew large in the sun until we were for a moment as large as, even larger than the trees, bursting out into the clear open sky and the sun. Somewhere in the far distance, a flock of birds answered our cries.

Later we walked in the stillness of the forest, not saying a word, listening to the small brushing and whispering sounds of the witnesses, the trees.

The sky clouded over and there was no sunset. We lit the kerosene lanterns early, and wandered through the rooms, finding framed photographs of Fenstermachers at Horace Greeley High School. Finding fishing rods with tangled lines and rusting reels, and cartons half-full of ancient *National Geographic* magazines with fading pictures of astonished tribal faces, faces that had never seen a white man before. We found a huge bed made from a single log, unframed watercolours fading and blooming with mould and empty chairs in empty rooms. At night, the great halls echoed with emptiness and the scurrying of mice nibbling away at the vast structure. There was fog on Saturday morning, and we left early, making excuses about needing to be back. The truth was we wanted to go back. Our lives were wired to phones, faxes, TVs, PCs, modems, videos, telexes, microwaves, mainframes and CDs and we missed the jolt. We were from another time and there was no way we could daytrip back to another century. Ellie 'had' to get back to her company. I 'had' to get back to my race. We needed to be on our Superspeedways, flat out, going round and round.

29

Memorial Day Sunday started with a bang. I was half awake when I heard the WHOOMF of the bomb they set off to announce the opening of the Indianapolis Motor Speedway gates. They say it's a military bomb and for all I know, they dropped it from a B–52. My watch said 5.00 a.m.

Outside the Speedway Motel on West 16th, Pontiac Trans Ams, Ram Chargers, Bronco IIs, Cadillac Eldorados, Winnebago Campers, Vettes, Bimmers, Tauruses, Buick Rivieras, stretch limos, Harley Hawgs, Gold Wings, Ninjas and Kustom Kruiser Private Buses started their engines and nudged forward among the pedestrians wearing baseball caps and lugging coolers fulla Millers and Buds. In the weak grey light before dawn, the Indianapolis Motor Speedway looked like a giant model of the Coliseum and a half a million fans wanted in. My motel room filled with the mumble of cars and trucks shifting from PARK to LO and back to PARK again, the throb of idling motorcycles and the up and down whine of police motorcycle sirens escorting another gaggle of biggies with big connections (and $100 per motorcycle cop plus $25 per car) down the centreline and straight into the infield. And above all the *Fans* heading for the *Snakepit* were warming up: HEY FUCK NOSE. SHOW US YOUR TITS. YOUBETCHERASS, MOTHER-FUCKER. *Go Foyt*. Bye, bye, sleep.

The Early-Morning-IND–TV-Weatherwatch-Central–Indiana Forecast said it was gonna be a Hoosier Hot One up there in the high eighties. I showered and dressed, taking my time. A year yawned in front of me, a bottomless hole in time to fill before the start of the race at eleven. Unlike Formula One, there is no half-hour warm-up on the morning of the race. So there is no chance to check the settings or make any last-minute adjustments or repairs. And there is no chance for the driver to get the feel of the car again before the race starts. The last time the cars had run was last Thursday afternoon. Sunday morning, just before eleven, you started from the grid, did a couple of pace laps behind the pace car and, if it all went according to plan, the green light went on and thirty-three cars raced flat out into Turn One. I like to wind down before a race, to empty my mind and to be as empty as a cup, with no emotions, no other thoughts except the start and the car. But without the release of the morning practice session, today would be one long winding-up of the springs inside the nervous Evers nervous system.

I met Orrin for breakfast at 6:30 in the dining room. It was a big plain open room with a buffet full of corned beef hash, flapjacks, grits, sausages, bacon, eggs, prunes, pineapples, bananas, Danish pastry, grapefruit and tomato and orange juices and I wouldn't, couldn't touch any of it. If you crash, you don't want to do it on a full stomach. So your vomit doesn't clog your windpipe or your stomach doesn't split open and dump breakfast bacteria inside the peritoneal cavity. Don't tell me racing drivers don't have a vivid imagination.

Orrin half stood up to greet me. A plate of eggs and sausages in front of him had suffered a serious attack. 'Glad to see you lookin' so much better, Forrest,' he said. 'Siddown, siddown. A little time at the cabin appears to have done you a world of good.' He poured me a cup of coffee which I thanked him for but wouldn't drink. No food, no caffeine. It helped to go into a race hungry. And I was wired tight as it was. 'What'd you think of our little ol' Villa De Log?' Orrin said, swabbing his plate with a piece of toast. 'Place still standing?'

'It's tremendous,' I said.

'Yeah, tremendous. It's too damn tremendous. We hardly ever use it nowadays. I keep thinkin' we ought to turn it into a museum, give it to the park. But there are so few stands of coastal sequoias that don't have tourists carvin' their initials in 'em, or some dumb lumberman like me lickin' his chops and thinkin' a million and a half clear board feet. So I hang on to it mostly for the land around it. Just let those ol' trees do what they do. Little luck, maybe five hundred years from now, those same trees will still be there. You hear about your friend? Little Miss Fraser?'

'What about her?' I said, suddenly interested.

'She rang me to tell you that she's OK. Said she took off when you were hit in the parking lot because she thought they were kidnappers. I told her to call the FBI.'

'She say where she was?'

'No. She did say she missed you and hoped you were OK.' Orrin chased the last lump of scrambled egg around his plate with another piece of toast. 'You do lead a colourful life. You must tell me about it sometime.'

He pushed his chair back and stood up. The dining room was wall to wall American Businessmen. Corporate officers large and small who have an interest in Indy cars. You could say they were fans, and you'd be right. But some of them had fifty to a hundred million tied up in advertising and marketing products they had put on the backs of Indy cars. Buick, for example was giving their Indianapolis engines to any team willing to take them. But most teams preferred spending the $100,000 to $150,000 for a Cosworth, a Judd or a Chevvy. 'Bullshit walks, money talks.' 'Win on Sunday sell on Monday.' Homegrown Indy phrases invented right here at the Indianapolis Motor Speedway where 'business is in the winner's circle'.

Orrin was nodding to them. 'Howdy Bill, howyadoin' Harry, goodtoseeya, Lou.' He whispered in my ear, explaining, reverently, 'That's Big Bill Faulkenberg, Chairman of Chrysler, Harry Memling, Chairman of General Motors, Red Taaffe, Chairman of Ford.' On the way out Orrin nodded to the chairman, president or CFO of Champion Mobil, Domino's Pizza, Quaker Mills, Goodyear, Quaker State, Raynor Garage Doors and Trench Shoring. All of them just having a raceday breakfast. Where the drivers have breakfast. Where the big, broadshouldered men with the short haircuts and the bulges in their sports jackets stood six deep at the doors.

The businessmen, wives and bodyguards stopped looking at us and turned towards the side door. T. D. Jackson was making his way through the tables. 'Howyadoin, Forrest?'

'Good to see you, T. D.'

'Pedal to the metal.' His famous grin was fixed to his face.

'See you there, T. D.' He hadn't come in for breakfast. He'd come in to shake hands with his sponsors and their very important customers. Make them feel good. Make them glad they spent their money. I took some comfort in realizing that he was just as nervous as I was.

You mind if I drive?' Orrin said in the parking lot.

'You pass your rookie test?'

'Third try,' he said. He was as edgy as I was and the weak jokes helped. We got on Orrin's golf cart and headed out of the back of the motel parking lot to tunnel three, under the track at Turn Two and out into the infield. Orrin liked driving his cart because he'd had it modified with special batteries. Given a long enough straightaway it would trundle right on up to 22 miles an hour. But with the crowd shoulder to shoulder on the road and off it we rolled along at walking speed. Half of the coolers in the western world seemed to be inside the Indianapolis Motor Speedway. No alcoholic beverages are sold inside the grounds, so the serious beer drinker had to do some serious logistical forward planning. Fill the bathtub with some serious icecubes from the motel ice machine the night before. Buy beer by the goddamn case. You betcherass, boy. Don't fuck around with no dipshit little six-packs. Gotta have backup. Gotta have a lotta backup. One man with arms like thighs carried three coolers stacked one on top of the other, held in place by his chin and a no-lip hippo grin.

When we got to the garage, the Fenstermacher Specials looked like they were giving off light. Gorgeous. Candy-apple red and chrome. STP, CHAMPION SPARK PLUG, DIE HARD, MONROE, VALVOLINE, PPG: decals. Every surface, every nut and screw was polished, checked, polished, rechecked and polished again. Jack was bent over the cockpit and looked up when I walked in. He had his usual sore-tooth expression. 'What's this crap I hear about you being a fuckin' fairy, Evers?'

'What you said.'

'What?'

'Crap, Jack. It's crap.'

'Well, I don't like it.'

'Don't kiss me then.'

Jack scrunched up his bread-roll face and dived back into the car.

In the distance we could hear marching bands parading on the main straight. Eight o'clock. Three hours to go. But who was counting. 'Jack, if you're ready. Oh Jesus, look who's here.'

George Gavoni had been working on T. D.'s car, running electrical checks. 'You touch that car, Evers, you wear gloves. I don't want to get no fuckin' AIDS.'

'George, for God's sake. Evers is no more a homosexual than I am.' Orrin boomed behind me.

'You too, huh.' Then George started laughing. A joke. Very funny. Ho. Ho.

'George, take your finger out of your ass and you won't get AIDS.'

'Oh hi, T. D.' said George.

'Hey, Forrest, my man,' Eugene said, in his low baritone. 'It's about time we towed the cars out to the pits. Anything you want me to check or anything?'

'If you could make the clock rev a little faster, I'd appreciate it, Eugene,' I said.

They towed the cars out, Orrin and T. D. went over to the motorhome and there was nothing to do but wait. I waited. Then I waited some more. I could have waited in Orrin's motorhome. Or I could have gone out with the car to the pits. But I didn't want to walk through the crowds and have to deal with the reporters. Just before a race, most of them would leave you alone if you were in an empty garage. But out walking in the crowds, you were fair game for every fan and marketing man who had a pass to the pits. So I waited. At 9:45, the Purdue University Band Played 'On the Banks of the Wabash', and the cars were pushed into place on the grid. I stayed put, inside. Waiting. I idly wondered how many thousands of loudspeakers there were at Indianapolis. And how many gigawatts of power it took to drive the Purdue University Band marching through them at full honk.

I looked down at my watch. 10:01. The announcer was fawning over celebrities. Harry Brill was here. His new movie, 'Free Fall', was breaking box-office records. And Sally Thighs. And Greg Hummer. 'And Ladies and Gentlemen here he is, taking a well-deserved break from his incredibly busy schedule, to see the Greatest Spectacle in Racing, ladies and gentlemen, I am honoured to present to you the Vice President of the United States, *Dan Quayle*.'

'Great to be here, Wally.'

10:06.

10:06 and a half.

Slow timecrawl. Outside, the heat of the day was rising in wavy lines. A couple of ticks past 10:30 I walked out to the car. Past the peering eyes, past the hundreds of photographers, through the solid mass of people, wall to wall, autograph albums held out like alms dishes. I walked under the Gasoline Alley sign, through the break in the stands, past the pits and out onto the track.

30

A sea of humanity rising on both sides of the track had parted for a narrow strip of asphalt and thirty-three parked racing cars. Last Thursday the track had seemed bigger than life when the stands were half-empty. Now to emphasize its size, it held the power of five hundred thousand people. Their murmur was deafening. I felt like a gladiator walking into the Coliseum, half power and half dread. On your toes, Evers. The lions could come from any direction.

I could just see the top of T.D.'s head on the outside of the front row. The rest of him and his car was hidden behind photographers, mechanics in the Fenstermacher red and white, businessmen with soft bellies and t-shirts, businesswomen with chunky gold jewellery and suntans, and a TV soap star with a Barbie Doll face and breasts like cartoon bananas was using her elbows to get into the photographs with T.D. I edged in without much effort, the crowd parting for the driver's suit.

T.D. was the calm at the centre of the storm. For as much notice as he took of the fans and journalists staring at his every expression and every gesture he might have been standing in the middle of a pasture in Oklahoma. 'How you doin', Forrest?' he said when he saw me. 'You looked jumpy as a one-legged rooster this morning.'

'Not my best time of day. Looks like a few people came to see you.'

He looked beyond the crush of people around us, up into the ten-storey-high main stands. 'Yeah, well it does get to you,' he said, with a kind of distant, far-off look, as if he was thinking of his ranch and his horses. Then he looked back at me. 'It's a hot track. Last surface reading I heard was 134°. So it's going to be a little slicker than what we've been used to. Up here in front row, going into Turn One shouldn't be too bad. But you be cautious, hear? Especially on the first lap or two. Five hundred miles is a long drive. You can't win this sucker on the first lap but you sure can lose it. Tell you the truth, I'd be real cautious the first 50 laps. Get the feel of it, stay out of trouble. This track gets awful crowded when somebody gets out of shape in front of you.' He took a deep breath. 'Time to go to work,' he said and began the slow and painful process of getting into his car, his old injuries reminding him of too many sledgehammer impacts.

Orrin was standing by my car in the middle of the seventh row, surrounded by a few curious gawkers. As I made my way through the crowd towards him, the announcer was saying:

THE GREATEST SPECTACLE IN RACING EVERY YEAR SINCE THE
INDIANAPOLIS MOTOR SPEEDWAY HELD ITS FIRST FIVE
HUNDRED IN 1911 APART FROM THE YEARS WHEN THE TRACK
CLOSED FOR THE WAR. NOW HERE'S A MAN WHO HAS SEEN
EVERY SINGLE INDY 500

In the background another band was playing 'Sweet Georgia Brown'.

Row seven out of eleven. Dead centre. The car on my right was Sam Babonaugh in a Popeye green Corl Welders Lola—Judd, number 26. He was already in the car, helmet on, visor up, staring straight ahead. On my left, Jon Ward, in the chrome yellow and metallic blue Kissin' Kousin Fried Chicken March—Cosworth. Between them they had raced for fifteen years at Indy. Jon's best finish was seventh in 1982. Sam had finished ninth in 1986. Good solid drivers, hoping for a break. I felt reassured that the men next to me weren't rookies. I wondered how they felt.

'Might as well get in the car,' Orrin said. 'It's what we're here for.' He was wearing bright red trousers and a crisp white short-sleeve shirt with red epaulettes. He looked like the service manager at the world's most efficient service station. Which, in a way, he was. I settled in, my old seat fitting like a second skin, Eugene did up my straps and handed me my helmet.

Up ahead, out of sight the Chief Steward started out in the Pontiac Titan Trans Am Pace Car to make a final inspection of the track.

10.52. I closed my eyes, and held the wheel. The car would be my instrument, the four wheels, sensory antennae. I imagined the whole chassis, the electrical system, the hydraulics, the suspension all linked with me.

AND NOW, LADIES AND GENTLEMEN, THE PURDUE UNIVERSITY
BAND AND OUR NATIONAL ANTHEM.

Five hundred thousand people began to sing.

I signalled to Eugene and he handed me my helmet and I slipped it over my head, a hard-shell cranial cocoon, soft on the inside, plugged into the radio and a supply of freon gas to keep my face cool during the race. And the world went quiet again. Faintly I could hear, 'and the rockets' red glare, the bombs bursting in air' but I tuned it out, settling back into my seat, feeling at home in the driving position.

There was a rapping on my helmet.

And another.

Eugene's face was in front of me, mouthing the words 'Off. Take it off.' I took off my helmet.

HOME OF THE BRAVE.

A million hands clapping. 500,000 fans, cheering and whistling.

'Don't it work?' Eugene said.

'What doesn't work?'

'The radio. Didn't you hear me on the radio?'

I shook my head, *no*.

AND NOW, REVEREND RANDALL CRADDOCK, LEADER OF THE INDIANA

'Shit.'

CHRISTIAN COUNCIL OF THE UNITED CHURCHES OF CHRIST WILL DELIVER

'Orrin, have you seen the radio guy?' Eugene was screaming to be heard. 'Where the fuck is the sonofabitch?'

THE INVOCATION.

THANK YOU. LET US PRAY.

Eugene went off to find the radio guy. A radio, I thought, is not essential. An Indy car only carries forty gallons of fuel. At 1.8 miles per gallon, that could mean six or seven stops for fuel for a five-hundred-mile race. But with as many as a dozen yellow flags there would more likely be nine or ten pit stops in the race as teams took advantage of the slow down to top up, get fresh tyres and make a few adjustments without losing much time.

Either way, there would be several pit stops and each one needs communication between the driver and the crew. And the radio is a way of giving the driver the news. Who is leading. How far behind or ahead he is. With the telemetry giving the pits detailed information on the engine, cornering forces and tyres on each lap, the crew may notice that the car's temperature is rising and the fuel is leaning out and tell a driver to look at his temp. and come in before his engine blows up. And the driver can let the crew know if he is going to need more wing, or a new tyre or has a problem.

So a radio is useful, but it is not a necessity. The crew can hang out pit boards to tell you your position and to come in, say in two laps. True, going down the straight between two other cars at 225 miles per hour with a 90° turn coming up in a couple of seconds doesn't give you a lot of spare time for reading.

But the damn radios never work right either. They're full of static, and they only really work well when you are in front of the pits. Although, there can be times, when you are coming into a corner, right on the edge, just on the verge of losing control, trying to pass another car, and you hear with perfect clarity that they'd like you to pit in two more laps and the distraction makes you lurch towards the wall. Like you are an acrobat spinning through the air with no net, in the middle of a triple, and you suddenly hear this loud voice in your ear saying you split your tights. Still, a radio is an advantage and it is better to have one than not.

Orrin stuck his head in front of me. 'We've found him, he'll be here in a second.'

Behind him I could see Orrin's red gaberdine, knife-edge knees and hear his booming voice, 'Listen, if the radio's not right, don't mess with it, stick in another one.'

AND LET US ESPECIALLY HONOUR AND REMEMBER OUR SONS AND

'What the hell are you waiting for?' Orrin shouted, reaching in, unbuckling my harness, 'get it out of here.'

OUR DAUGHTERS, OUR MARINES WHO DIED IN THE BOMBING OF OUR

Orrin disconnected my helmet and I hauled myself out of the car. The 'radio man' was about twenty-three but he had hung on to his teenage pimples. Shaving, apparently, was a problem. He had that blank, watered-down look of a life indoors, at home with 3D circuit diagrams, resistors and ohms. Six radio units, looking like mobile phones, dangled from his waist, a battered red toolbox hung from his hand and there was a 'KoGai Radio' badge on every radio, on his toolbox and on his yellow coveralls. Just above the KoGai badge on his coveralls it said 'Ballard' in a red script. 'What's the problem?' he said, looking at Orrin's feet sticking out of the cockpit of my car. Orrin had dived head-first into the cockpit and grabbed the radio out from

EMBASSY IN BEIRUT AND WHO HAVE DIED GUARDING THE PEACE ON OUR BASES

its hiding place alongside the pedals and handed it to Ballard who was ready with a plug-in tester.

IN SPAIN AND IN FRANKFURT AND IN GREECE. WE KNOW THE PRICE

'Nothing wrong with this one,' said Ballard on his knees, 'what about the transmitter?' Orrin handed him his transmitter-receiver.

OF FREEDOM IS HIGH, LORD. WE PRAY TODAY THAT THOSE WE ASK

While Ballard was plugging his test equipment into Orrin's radio, I took off my helmet, thinking how good it would be to feel a fresh breeze. Wearing two layers of Nomex, a driving suit, and a Nomex sock over my head makes standing on a hot track on a hot day, hot work. Something caught my eye. Hanging from my helmet.

TO PAY THAT HIGHEST OF ALL PRICES NOT BE FORGOTTEN

In the clear plastic radio earplug, there was a dab of what looked like grey-blue clay. Imbedded in the clear plastic tube leading into the earpiece were two silver wires. It looked as if the plastic was blocking the tube.

BUT BE HONOURED AND BE REMEMBERED NOT JUST ON THIS MEMORIAL DAY

'I think I've found the problem,' I said. I handed the helmet with the dangling tube and earpiece to Ballard. 'What's that grey stuff blocking the tube?' I said. The small blob was the size of a pencil eraser inside the earpiece.

BUT HONOURED AND REMEMBERED ON ALL DAYS FOR THEIR

'Oh, yeah,' he said, holding the helmet, inspecting the ear-piece. 'That could be it. That's a kind of sonic shock absorber,' he said, 'Supposed to absorb some of the high frequency static. Musta come loose.'

THEIR PRICELESS GIFT

He reached into his toolbox for a probe. 'That's not some kind of sonic shock absorber, Ballard,' I said just loudly enough for him to hear, 'that's Semtex.'

TO ALL OUR DAYS OF PEACE AND FREEDOM. AMEN.

'What's Semtex?' he said.

31

'You're crazy,' Ballard said, standing up, looking at me as if I were contagious. 'You're the fruitcake, right? The foreign fairy.' He turned to Orrin. 'He's nuts. It's just some plastic stuff. You don't even need it, I can take it out easy.'

THE COMBINED US ARMED FORCES COLOUR GUARD PAYS HOMAGE ON

Orrin stepped between me and Ballard and put his arm around my shoulder. Big Daddy Fenstermacher. 'Now look here, son.

THIS MEMORIAL DAY WEEKEND TO OUR WAR VETERANS WITH TAPS.

You just relax, we got a race to run. What do you know about Semtex?'

'That's Czech, grey-blue with metallic flecks. American is snow-white. Soviet is ochre, Dutch is orange. It is 33 per cent more powerful than TNT, invented in Britain in the Second World War, and debris thrown from a Semtex explosion travels at eight times

TA TA TAA. TA TA TAA. TA TA TAA. TA TA TAAAAA.

the speed of a bullet from an M–16 rifle, about five miles a second. If that little gob there went off inside your ear it would blow the side of your head off. If you were wearing a helmet it doesn't bear thinking about. Sir. Now for Christ's sake find out what T. D. has in his ear and get Security. Get the head guy. Somebody who knows something about bombs.'

Taps finished on a long flat note.

Ballard looked at me as if he had a mouthful of map-pins. 'You're really nuts.'

'That's right, I'm a homicidal maniac, so don't you move, Ballard,' I said. 'How many cars have your radios in them?'

AND NOW LADIES AND GENTLEMEN, FRANKLYN PORCH IS BACK HOME, HERE WITH US TODAY, FROM HOLLYWOOD, TO SING AS ONLY HE CAN, FRANKLYN PORCH IS, 'BACK HOME IN INDIANA'.

'I don't think I . . .'

'Don't think, just tell me.'

'Twenty-four.'

'And who owns KoGai Radio?'

'How the hell should I know? They just hired me. I've only been working for them for a week. I don't even know that much about radios. I just stick 'em in and remove 'em if they don't work. Look, all the radios have the plastic in them. They're supposed to. It's not a bomb or nothing', you're just fuckin' nuts.'

'What the hell's going on out here? Why aren't you in the goddamn car?' This was a big man in a blue blazer and a face as wide as most men's shoulders. He looked like an all-pro defensive tackle for the Chicago Bears.

'I am not in the goddamn car because my goddamn radio is stuffed with Semtex.' I showed him the earplug dangling from the helmet.

'Get the hell off the track. Push that car off the track.' He waved to some USAC observers and they began to push my car off the track. It rolled easily.

'You don't understand.' I grabbed his arm and he jerked it away, steering the car past the front of Jon Ward's Kissin' Kousin Lola–Cosworth. 'There could be twenty-four of these. You have got to stop this race.'

'The only thing I gotta stop is you from fuckin' up this race. You stand in my way, you goddamn faggot, you'll spend this race on your ass in a jail cell.'

'For God's sake,' I said, 'just test it.'

196

Orrin grabbed him by the necktie and stood him up. 'You push that car back or you're finished at this race track.'

Bigface squeezed Orrin's arm just above the elbow and Orrin let go with a surprised cry of pain.

FRAGRANCE FROM THE FIELDS I USED TO ROAM

'I'm sorry, Mr Fenstermacher, but nothing is going to stop the start of this race.' By now there were several men in blue sports jackets crowding around us, helping the big one push the car. I didn't think, I just hit him on the jaw.

WHEN I DREAM ABOUT THE MOONLIGHT ON THE WABASH

He looked at me for a second, dazed, then sat down on the track heavily, holding his jaw. 'Orrin,' I shouted, 'get T. D.'s radio.' I wasn't sure he heard me in the uproar as they grabbed my arms and frog-marched me off the track to the Fenstermacher pit in the pit lane.

THEN I LONG FOR MY INDIANA HOME.

I tried to break free, and somebody hit me hard, on the forehead. For a moment I thought I was seeing stars, but it was the cloud of balloons dotting the mild blue sky. As the balloons rose behind the electronic VALVOLINE sign, there was a roar from the crowd that grew as the balloons rose.

NOW THE MOMENT WE HAVE ALL BEEN WAITING FOR,

'What's the problem?' My eyes focused on a USAC badge. USAC Chief Steward, Lloyd Wilkinson, his badge said. In his late seventies, wearing earphones with a mike, Wilkinson had the walnut tan of a man who has stood by the side of racetracks since he was old enough to squint. He looked at me, not saying anything, slim as a guard rail, balding, deep grooves in his forehead and his cheeks, a long turkey neck and sunglasses reflecting the sun.

MRS MARY FENDRICH HULMAN ...

'He went nuts out there, Lloyd. Hit Kirk Kekorian. We had to pull him off.' This from a voice behind me. Probably the one who had my arm in a hammerlock.

The USAC official turned his shades towards the startline

platform, his sunglasses reflecting the sky and the balloons and the endless circle of grandstands jam-packed with humanity.

As reasonably as I could, I said, 'There was, there is a gob of Semtex in my radio earpiece. I think every other driver out there with a KoGai radio could have a bomb in his ear. Think about it. In about five minutes thirty-two cars are going to be thundering down the straight with 300,000 people in the stands and another 200,000 in the infield. Suppose it is Semtex. They'll be going over 230 miles an hour across the startline, with twelve hundred gallons of fuel and the drivers' heads blown off. Suppose I am right.'

GENTLEMEN, START YOUR ENNNNGINNNNES.

'I suppose you are a fuck-up. But it should be easy enough to find out. Where's the KoGai rep?'

Ballard edged in front of the USAC official. Lloyd said, 'You got Semtex in your earplugs?'

'The guy's nuts. It's just a little dab of plastic.'

'All your earpieces have 'em, these little dabs of plastic?'

Ballard nodded. It was getting difficult to hear. The engines had started and the drivers were blipping their throttles. Twenty-five thousand six hundred turbocharged racing horsepower warming up makes a deep, wide, rising and falling scream, an awesome noise. But you can only hear a whisper of it when half a million people stand on their feet and holler.

THE FENSTERMACHER CAR DRIVEN BY FORMULA ONE DRIVER FORREST EVERS APPEARS TO HAVE A PROBLEM AND HAS BEEN PUSHED OFF THE

'How can we test one?'

'Four double–A batteries and a switch is all you need,' I said.

STARTING GRID. TOO BAD, WE WERE LOOKING FORWARD TO A FORMULA ONE DRIVER ATTEMPTING TO RUN HERE, BUT THAT'S RACING.

'We're not having a bomb going off in these pits. Got any other ideas on how we can test this "theory" of yours?'

NOW THE CARS FORM BEHIND THIS YEAR'S PONTIAC TRANS AM TITAN PACE CAR WITH THREE-TIME INDY 500 WINNER BOBBY UNSER AT THE WHEEL FOR THE PARADE LAP.

Orrin said, 'Get a bomb expert who knows Semtex when he sees it.'

'I don't want an opinion.'

THE SEVENTY-FOURTH INDIANAPOLIS FIVE HUNDRED IS ABOUT TO BEGIN.

Then Orrin said, 'Then get the best radio guy from one of the crews to open up one of these damn radios and see if they've got a detonation system.'

ON THE POLE, FROM BEAMUS, NEW MEXICO, ERNIE EMMERLING LOOKING FOR HIS SECOND WIN. ALONGSIDE HIM,

The best radio man was bound to be in the Packer pit. Ronald Packer has the most money, the best cars and the best people and backups for all of them. Orrin ran three pits down and I could see him talking to Ronald. It can't have been easy. Packer is a dedicated, single-minded billionaire. I saw him glance at Orrin and then look back at the track. The race was about to begin and Ronald Packer fully expected to win it. His attention was not to be deflected. But Orrin can be a difficult man to ignore. Orrin took Ronald's earphones and microphone off Packer's head, which is, at Indianapolis, like lifting the Queen's crown while she is addressing Parliament. Ronald listened to Orrin explain why the most powerful man in American racing should give up his communications engineer while he is talking to his drivers. Yes indeed, Orrin can be a persuasive man. It only took him the time it took for the cars to crawl down the main straight, parade into Turn One, through the south chute, into Turn Two and down the back straight, warming up.

NUMBER TWO, FROM VENTURA, CALIFORNIA, VETERAN FRANK CHASSON. AND ON THE OUTSIDE STARTING FROM THIRD POSITION, FROM SAPULPA, OKLAHOMA, THREE-TIME WINNER, T. D. JACKSON.

And when Orrin brought the man back to our growing crowd in the Fenstermacher pit, the first thing we noticed was that the Packer electronic communication wizard spoke almost no English.

Which is not surprising. Telemetry is a three-dimensional analysis of a car's behaviour, broadcast from the car while it is on the track. Every time a car passed the pits, the teams who could afford the hardware and the technicians to run it, received a coded transmission of data. The data is numerical, and since the Japanese have been at the leading edge of the technology, it wasn't that unusual that a telemetry hotshot didn't speak our language. After all, most of his conversations were with racing cars not people.

None of which stopped fifteen people giving Aguri Takahashi advice on what we were looking for and how to find it. Fortunately I don't think he understood any of them because when he picked up the radio he had the back off in seconds. He stared into the intestines of the radio, a 3D plan for the city of the future; transistors, transducers, printed circuit boards. The new universal language that only technicians speak.

ROW TEN. HARRY BENFIELD FROM OAKHILL, MICHIGAN. ANTONY DRYER FROM BELSIZE, MISSOURI AND TOM MARTENS THE FLYING DUTCHMAN NOW LIVING IN GREENHILLS, OHIO.

Aguri looked up, frowning. 'Two,' he said.

Then he peered down again.

When he looked up again, he said, 'Two weceiva.' He paused.

'Hey listen, they told me one of them was the back-up, in case one of them goes down,' Ballard said. But no one was paying attention, we were watching the small Japanese man in the purple Packer jacket struggling to find the right word.

THEY'RE COMING OUT OF TURN FOUR NOW AND WHAT A SIGHT IT IS. THIRTY-TWO OF THE FINEST RACING CARS IN THE WORLD FOLLOWING THE PONTIAC TRANS AM TITAN PACE CAR, NO, WAIT, NUMBER THIRTY-SEVEN, JORGEN BERSTROM FROM MATTEWAN, MINNESOTA IS DROPPING BACK AS THEY COME OVER THE START/FINISH LINE AND START TO ACCELERATE FOR THE PACE LAP.

He pointed to his ear. 'Weceiva,' he said and then pointed to the batteries. Then he pointed to his ear.

'Sweet Jesus Christ, Howard. Howard.' Lloyd was yelling into his microphone.

AND THEY'RRRRRRE ON IT, ON THE PACE LAP. FORMATION HOLDING BEAUTIFULLY AS THEY ACCELERATE AROUND ONE THROUGH THE CHUTE AND INTO TURN TWO.

'Howard, goddamn it get me the control tower. Goddamn it

Howard get me through to the control tower now or I will rip your balls off.'

LOOKING GOOD DOWN THE BACK STRAIGHT. STARTER BENSON ELLIOT HAS THE GREEN FLAG READY, THEY ARE UP TO 135 MILES AN HOUR

'Lloyd. Wilkerson.' He was screaming.
'Lloyd Wilkerson, Bob. for God's sake stop the race.'

COMING INTO TURN THREE THE PACE CAR PULLS DOWN LOW ONTO THE APRON AND THE CARS ARE ACCELERATING HARD INTO TURN FOUR.

'What? Say again. I can't hear you. Neverfucking mind. Stop it.'

BOBBY UNSER IN THE PONTIAC TRANS AM TITAN PACE CAR PULLS DOWN LOW ONTO THE APRON ON THE WAY INTO THE PIT LANE AS THE CARS ARE IN FORMATION, HEADING DOWN THE STRAIGHT AT 200 MILES AN HOUR AND ACCELERATING AS STARTER BENSON HOLDS THE GREEN FLAG UP AND NO. NO HE MUST HAVE SEEN SOMETHING, COULD BE ONE OF THE CARS OUT OF FORMATION AND THEY WILL GO AROUND AGAIN FOR ANOTHER PACE LAP.

32

'Woco.'

'Walk. Wilco. Crazy.'

'No. Woco.'

The Japanese telemetry expert was trying to tell us something, and we couldn't make it out. Out on the track, the red light had gone on, the cars had come into the pits and the race was delayed while we found that of the twenty-four drivers who had KoGai radios, seventeen had Semtex in their plastic ear-plug, wired to their radio batteries.

The Motorola Rep had been 'real happy' to supply radios to the teams that needed them. Orrin had even persuaded USAC to allow me back into the race, 'as long as he apologizes to Kirk'. So I wasn't 'the crazy, flaming, foreign faggot' any more. I was just 'the flaming foreign faggot'. I said, 'Sorry, Kirk,' and it had seemed a relatively easy thing to do, to restart the race. Not according to Preston Fulbaker it wasn't.

'Used to be we had every goddam government security agency in the country,' Lloyd said, 'tripping over each other. CIC, CIA, FBI, SAI, VBAS, NSA. This country has more security agencies than I've had hot dinners. And they all want to come watch the race. Every time we had a bomb threat we had to talk to fifteen different guys and they stood around and argued about whose job it was to go see if there was one. Then we got smart. Now we just got the one guy from the National Security Agency. We talk to him, he gets what he needs. Isn't that right, Preston?'

Preston was leaning back in his chair, making a show of being relaxed. 'I'm not sure what we got here. You see, sometimes you get something like this and think you got a little ol' rat and you pull it out by the tail. And when you pull it, you find out what you got ahold of, it's not a little ol' rat it's a goddamn thirty-five-foot-long anaconda. If you know what I mean. Anyway this is bigger than we thought it is, and until we know what it is and how big it is, we're going to have to be real careful.'

'Preston Fulbaker,' he said, to the Japanese technician as he came in the room. 'Indiana State office of the National Security Agency. Call me Press, please,' he said. He didn't like the name

Preston. And he didn't like the fact that at 8:15 a.m. a camper had exploded on the infield near Turn Four. 'My friend, Captain Commaccio and his men have found two more of these,' he held up a tiny KoGai radio, 'stuck to the gas tanks of campers. The trouble is, there are over 80,000 vehicles out there in the infield, and these little radios are a bitch to find. They are especially a bitch to find when you're trying not to alarm anybody by not letting *anybody* know that what you are looking for is a bomb.'

So there were five of us: Press, the boyish looking blue-eyed man from the National Security Agency, Lloyd, the USAC Chief Steward; Herbert Commaccio, the chief of Police of Indianapolis; myself; and Aguri Takahashi, sitting in a bare conference room painted fish-restaurant green in the Speedway administration building. Outside, the Purdue University Marching Band were stomping through 'My Old Kentucky Home'.

Commaccio had said, 'We don't get this sonofabitch cooled down right now we are going to have so many State, local, and Federal police agencies walking around it you won't be able to see the ground for special investigators.'

Press had said, 'That's why I'm here. Until I ask for them, they won't come.'

Press had said, 'Until we know if there are more of those little bombs out there, and where they are, you'll have to cancel the race.'

And Chief Commaccio had said, 'Oh shit, don't even say that word. We got half a million people here, plenty of 'em drunk enough to be belligerent, and if we tell 'em we think their campers might blow up, we got a riot on our hands. And if we don't give 'em a reason why we're delaying the race, never mind cancel, we got a riot on our hands. Besides, if some of them cars and campers are carrying bombs, no way I can let 'em back on the public highway. But cancel? Shit, don't even think about it. Never mind the riots in the snake pit. You're talking a couple of billion dollars tied up in this race.'

And I said, 'If we find out what those radios were tuned to ... and if we can shut down the broadcast, we can stop worrying about bombs.'

And Herbert Commaccio said, 'That's just what I'm thinking.'

So we brought Aguri in. And he had plugged one of the driver's radios into a little black box and said, 'Woco.'

Finally Press said, 'Local?'

'Hai. Woco wadio station.'

'Jesus, it's probably that goddam rock and roll FM station my kids play all night. Some shit like that.' Commaccio was standing up, pulling on his belt. He had a little roll of flab that hung over his belt and tended to keep checking it to make sure it was still there. But he didn't look too bad for a man of fifty who spent most of his day at a desk.

Aguri wrote down 98.6 A.M.

'Christ, that's the big one that's the uh, uh . . .'

'Global network station,' I said.

'What do you say we hop over there,' Press said.

'Mine or yours,' the police chief said.

'Mine,' said Press.

A helicopter in flight makes an awful phonebooth. You can barely hear yourself think, let alone somebody else talk. But I rang Ellie anyway. Down below, the race track looked green and pink in the middle. Grass and people. Dotted by 83,000 cars, trucks and campers that might go boom anytime. All at once or one by one.

'Who?'

I screamed again.

'Oh, it's you. Forrest. What happened to you? They took you out of the race. I've got it on now. Are you OK?'

'Peachy. I said, "PEACHY". I'm fine. Listen. What? I said listen. Can you remember the name of that Korean radio company that Hillburn bought?'

'Mojo, Fugako,' she said. 'No, I don't remember. Hojo? Something like Hojo. But that's not it.'

'Well, do you have a link to your mainframe at the office?'

'Sure. Me and my modem. Follows me everywhere.'

'See if the company is called KoGai. Capital K, o, capital G, a, i. And see if there's anything more on Hillburn. Because I'm in a helicopter. Me too. Listen, ring me at— ' I leaned over to Commaccio and he told me the letters. 'Ring me at KIND in Indianapolis. Soon as you can.'

We were flying south of the Speedway, over Eagle Creek and Rockville Road. We crossed Interstate–70 and banked east and dropped down just south of West Morris Street, near the stock-yards. KIND roared up from the ground to meet us, a low flat dark brick building with a lawn in front and the sign that said,

KIND
INDY'S KIND OF TV

We ducked low under the chopper blades, like medics from M*A*S*H. 'I thought we were looking for a radio station,' I said to the chief.

We got to the front door and Chief Commaccio paused to realign the strands he kept over his bald spot. 'It's both. TV, and radio.'

The three of us went in, Commaccio leading. There was a dark green soft carpet, dark wood panelled walls, a wide receptionist's desk, and nobody home. Signed framed publicity photographs of TV stars smiled on the walls, and a glass coffee table was piled high with old TV and radio magazines and surrounded by grey leather sofas. The room was silent, as if it was a place where people met and things happened, but not on Sunday afternoons. Over the receptionist's desk a TV monitor showed the on-air broadcast, an aerial shot of the Indianapolis Motor Speedway. There was no sound, but nothing was hap-pening either. The door on the right said KIND TV. The one on the left, KIND AM & FM. We went left.

Down the corridor the doors were all in the same dark wood as the reception room and marked Studio 1, Studio 2, and so on. We opened the doors and they were all empty until the last one, Studio 5. 'Hey my man, how you doin', what you doin', and is it fun?' he said. 'Well don't just stand there lookin' blue, gimme some news?'

He was a handsome man, around twenty-six or seven with a long thin nose and a long thin neck, and big wide eyes that looked sorry to see us. A skimpy green t-shirt that said 'Hutch-ins Productions' and spotless white jeans.

'Who the fuck are you?' said Chief Commaccio, flipping his badge.

'L. H. Hutchins, DJ and Audio Extraordinaire, with the KIND Sunday afternoon blues. But you can call me L. H. What can I do for you gentlemen?'

'I thought you were broadcasting the race,' Press said in that flat, bureaucratic voice of his. As if he could tone down the DJ by sheer contrast.

'Indeed we are, that's a fact. But that's AM. I am the funky FM. Although, as you know, not too much happening out there at the track so the AM folks been patching into my show. Change of pace, you might say.'

He swivelled in his chair, turning his back to us, pushing his headphones up on his ears and leant into the microphone. ' "Juicy Fruit", from that juicy group, Mtume. Hope that wasn't too racy for you fans joining us from KIND AM while they straighten out the oval. 'Cause I'm gonna continue down the Juicy Fruit tracks with two more on the album by the same name, "Hips", and "Would You Like to Fool Around". For the Sweet Lady who I hope will still be there when I get back from my long dark journey, high in the sky, flying with the satellites over Indianapolis, a town that's got bad drains and railroad pains and Yuppie bars to hide the scars of yesterday. I'll be back.'

He swivelled around again, to face us, his earphones a necklace. 'Now gentlemen, as I said before. What ever can I do for you?'

'Who's handling the AM broadcast from the track?' Press asked leaning toward the black man.

'Fred Shively at trackside. The radio voice of the Indianpolis Five Hundred for twenty-three years.'

'Anybody else out there?'

'Yeah, he's got Dave Arno his producer and Phil Corrigan the engineer in the van.'

'They both been with the station for awhile?'

'Since the dawn of time.'

'Who handles it here?'

'I do.'

'Now we're getting somewhere,' said Press.

'You tell me where you want to get to, maybe I know a shortcut.'

'How do you handle the race broadcast, L. H,' I said.

'Easy, no trouble at all. We got the commercials on tape here, it's all programmed on the computer, Fred keys it in from trackside. If the computer doesn't fuck it up, or a thunderbolt strike the transmitter there's nothin' for me to do except make sure it's turned on and running.'

Press said, 'Can you get the computer to print out the program?'

'Done.' L. H. turned to his console, pressed a few buttons and behind us a screeching announced the birth of a printout. I tore it off, looked at it and handed it to L. H. 'Weird.' he said. 'Definitely weird. They got some strange interrupts programmed here. You know, like one of those Civil Defense, "this is a test, this is only a test" warning tones? Only this is ultra high frequency. And they got it sourced from outside.'

'From where?'

'From our TV station next door.'

'Let's have a look next door, then, for Christ sake,' said the Chief.

Press was talking quietly as we rushed through the reception room. 'When you think of the organization and money that it would take to set this thing up. I mean usually a terrorist act, usually it is perpetrated by some poor deranged slob looking for a day on the front page. Or it's some small political group with a specific grudge. But I don't see one person setting this up. This is too big.' He furrowed his brows for emphasis.

'The old conspiracy theory,' I said.

'You wear that driver's suit everywhere you go?' said Press. 'Maybe if I had the outfit, I could be a racing driver too.'

There is not a lot going on at KIND–TV on a Sunday afternoon. There is one small sound stage with a curved desk and a weather-map for a local newshow. And a kitchen, bedroom and living-room for a locally produced soap opera. All the furniture was on wheels so it could be rearranged in a couple of seconds. I wondered if people noticed that Susan, the philandering doctor's wife, had the same sofa as the long-suffering Camilla. Maybe they altered the colour by chroma key. I was losing concentration. Back at the track, a bomb could be blowing ten teenagers, sitting on top of a camper, high in the sky.

The stage with its cameras and lights on stands with wheels, and its coiling tails of electrical cables took up most of the space behind the radio studios and reception. But there were other rooms. There was also a video edit room with a bank of computer keyboards and the wall lined with monitors. And, in a grey metal cabinet in a small room of its own, a reel-to-reel one-inch tape dubbing machine. And a control room with a computer console and display. They were all empty. Nobody home.

L. H. led us into the control room. 'How do you run the TV station at the same time?' I asked L. H., squeezing into a small, windowless room with one door, one chair in front of a desk with a computer terminal and three video monitors. It was cramped, but we all fitted in.

'Easy,' he said. 'It's all on tape and a computer runs it. When we have a live broadcast out on location like this afternoon, like I said, the guys on site punch in the commercials. Shall we,' he said, 'have a look?' He sat down at the computer console and began to access the day's TV programmes. The printer ground out a series of instructions to the computer. L. H. translated.

He let out a low whistle. 'This,' he said, 'is some shit. Look at this batch command.' We looked over his shoulder at a series of letters and numbers. 'It accesses a hidden dish stack on a pre-programmed interrupt.'

'You want to try that in English? I got more trouble under-standing your technical bullshit than I do when you do that jive crap.' Chief Commaccio, the voice of authority.

L.H. looked up, with the poker face of a man who knew the cards but didn't know the game. 'Why is it,' he said turning back to face the computer screen, 'that cops thinks they got the right to be rude. Probably go to too many cop movies. Go to a cop movie and know what you see? You see a whole audience full of dumb cops learning how to act nasty.'

'Goddamit, what does it say?' said Fulbaker. 'If you would, please.'

'See, my Daddy said: "son, you gotta get a college education. You don't get a college education you gonna be illiterate and have to do some dumbass menial job. Like Chief of Police." '

'You wanna bet,' said Commaccio in a tired voice, 'that there is an automobile in the parking lot owned by one L. H. Hutchings that contravenes the Indiana Highway Code in sev-eral expensive respects.' Moreover, I got some good friends at the State Tax department be happy to enquire after the little payments the record reps give you for playing that shit. And I'd be careful driving home after a late night show. The streets of Indianapolis are not as safe as they used to be.'

Hutchins stood up, putting his sharp nose an inch from the

wide, soft, red and blue veined nose of the chief. 'Don't nobody never teach you, Lunchmeat, don't never mess with the power of the press.'

'Maybe,' I said, 'we should tell Mr Hutchins that we are talking about several thousand lives. Time counts.'

'We think a number of bombs have been planted at the track,' Preston Fulbaker said, 'and that a radio signal coming from this station could set them off.'

'Why didn't you say so in the first place, 'stead of all this monkeyshit?' said L. H., pulling his shoulders back, still giving the Chief the bad eye. 'What I'm sayin', there is an outside signal, or at least the thing is programmed for some outside signal, that will come into the station and do two things. It will get magnified and rebroadcast from the radio station. The other thing it does is play a tape for TV broadcast. What I'm sayin', the same signal that gets sent over to the radio station, boosted and broadcast by radio, on its way through, it kickstarts some videotape I don't know about.'

'And where,' I said, 'does that outside signal come from.'

'Where it all comes from,' said L. H., looking at the Chief and pointing a brown finger straight up. 'Comes from the sky.'

33

It took five long minutes to find the tape. It was unmarked, but L.H. traced it through the encoded computer commands. 'This one,' he said, pointing to the third down out of five three quarter inch Sony cassette decks mounted in the edit studio.

'Like I was saying,' he said, taking the cassette out of the deck and putting it into another, 'the command that sends the signal out to the track, also starts the tape. But the tape doesn't start broadcasting until five minutes after the signal.

'Let's assume that somewhere, the bomber or whoever the hell they are, is watching the race on TV. He could be anywhere, could be Idaho, could be Afghanistan. Wherever, when he sees the start of the race he presses his button to send out a signal, relayed by satellite to here and by radio out to the Speedway while the cars are crossing the startline, all bunched up together, loaded with fuel, going over 200 miles an hour.'

'So what you would see before this tape plays,' I said, 'would be the live broadcast from the track at the start of the race. Cars smashing into each other, exploding, spraying fuel into the stands and Lord knows how many gas tanks blowing up in the infield. I mean they have 37 cameras and they would cover it, wouldn't they? Five minutes of people on fire. And then you'd see this tape. Is this a national broadcast?'

'National and 53 countries,' said L. H. 'This is a big day for us.'

'Speaking of that outside radio signal that is going to be broadcast out to the track,' Press said.

'First thing I did,' L. H. said with a little smile to the Chief, 'shut that sucker down, erased the program. But I got another one pointed at the Chief's house in Spring Hills just in case. Joke, Chief. Sit down.'

L. H. fast-forwarded the unmarked cassette to the start of the picture and I switched off the lights. On the big monitor over the control board the screen bloomed into life. A jumbo jet was taking off into the blue sky. We watched as, from a distance, a smoke trail made its shaky way to the plane and the jumbo shuddered then burst into a dirty ball of fire. The video cut to close-ups of the bloated corpses floating in the water, the severed arm of a child bobbing in the bright blue choppy waves.

The film had the shaky feel of a home video. And the bruised and jagged edge of street violence. Varnished mahogany speedboats with raked windscreens, looking as if they should have been picking up fallen water skiers, were picking up bodies and pieces of bodies. Some of the bodies were charred and naked, and some still floated with grey and black robes spreading in the water like angels of death. The speedboats were awash with bloody, ripped, grey bodies, legs at broken angles, mouths yawning. The film went on for some time with the boys on the speedboats, they couldn't have been more than fourteen or fifteen, hauling more charred and staring bodies of men and women and children out of the bright blue water. This was followed by footage of Arab houses after a bombing (probably Libya, I thought, but it was impossible to tell), the broken buildings with the women screaming inside and the battered head of a man protruding from a pile of plaster and stone. The tape ended with little schoolboys carrying rifles, walking away from the camera, carefully on tip-toe and suddenly springing into the air under a mushroom of mined earth and finally an Arab boy was hit repeatedly in the face by rifle butts.

The voice-over was cultured and British. The kind of deep, male, aristocratic 'care for a brandy?' voice we're used to hearing sell expensive German automobiles. What he said was, 'The crimes of Satan America against Islam can never be forgotten. But they will be avenged. Today's corrupt, materialist American Memorial Day Ceremony of useless and obscene racing cars in the middle of America has been transformed into a fitting Memorial to the Martyrs of Islam. The force of truth now controls the sky and can now make the force of Allah's revenge felt anywhere, any time. This small demonstration of the fire of Allah is by way of encouraging you to accept Allah and the Truth of Allah and to mercifully help you to prepare to atone for the horror of your crimes against Islam.'

'May the power and the truth and the fire of Allah cleanse the world of the works of Satan.' Then the screen went black.

'In other words,' Press said as I switched on the light, 'they can set off their bombs any time and any place they feel like it, by satellite. Large or small bombs, doesn't matter.'

'Is there any way of tracing the transmission?' I asked.

'It will take a little while,' L. H. said. 'You see we go up to the bird and downlink again, from the track to here. Sounds crazy, but it's cheaper to make the 50,000 mile round trip to a satellite parked over the equator and back than to go a couple of miles by land line. Then we uplink again to another satellite and down to New York. From New York it goes up to one satellite for North American broadcasts and another for European broadcasts. Each of those up and down links has an encoded name tag, so it just takes some back-tracking once we get the signal. But you know, the signal could come from anywhere. These satellites, got a big footprint.'

'And you'll get the signal,' I said.

'Once you folks start the race,' L. H. said. 'Unless they get tired of watching the dumbass stadium just sit there and decide, "Fuck it let's blow that sucker *now*." '

In the distance a phone was ringing. As I went out to reception to answer it, Press said, 'Make it short. We need help.'

'Don't let that call hold you back,' said L. H. 'We got lotsa lines out of here.' He handed Press a phone with one hand, leaned forward, flipped a switch with the other hand and said into the microphone, 'Mtume. Still a whole bunch of nothing happening at the track. So here's Maypole. From Motown.' He pressed another series of buttons. 'It's easy when you know how,' he said.

When I got to the phone, Ellie was in high gear. 'What is going on, Evers? I have the race on television and they keep saying the track signals are screwed up. Typical, isn't it? I mean it is their only race of the year, you'd think they could screw in the light bulbs or fix the switch or whatever it is.'

'What'd you find out?'

'And what the hell are you doing at a stupid TV station? Why aren't you in your little racing car, defying death?'

'Ellie—' I said, sounding impatient.

'Right. Mr Big Secret. The mushroom theory of management. Keep 'em in the dark, feed 'em shit and watch 'em grow.'

'I can't tell you about it on the phone.'

'You know Forrest, there are times when you are so uptight. And other times . . . Anyway, you were right, the Korean Radio company bought by our friends at Global is KoGai. And the transfer of funds from Iran to Global took place on the day that Mehar joined Global. The money came from an account in Mehar's name in Switzerland. But the real news is that fifty million of it didn't stop for breath. On the same day, Hillburn transferred fifty million out of Global's Swiss account into Hillburn's Swiss bank account.'

'How the hell did you find all that out? I thought Swiss banks were confidential.'

'Not if you know the right bankers. Women Unlimited is very big in Switzerland.'

'You mean you got Swiss bankers their jobs?'

'Not all of them,' she said with a little laugh. 'But we have placed a lot of their secretaries and book-keepers.'

'Ellie, if you have the bank account numbers and all the other stuff, the details of buying into KoGai, and Hillburn's flight from the Cayman's to Haiti and Miami, let me write it down. Some newspaper will print it.'

'OK, but don't let them know your return address. You could wake up in the morning and find that Hillburn bought the paper.'

'Thanks for the tip, smartass. You OK?'

'I'm OK, Forrest. You?'

'Anybody ever tell you, you make love like a gorilla?'

'That's what they all say.'

When I came back into the control room, Chief Commaccio was saying, 'One nuke, that's all it'd take. Nuke the fuckers in Tehran or wherever the fuck they hide out. Let 'em know we mean business.'

L. H. let a smile widen across his face and said, 'Who you gonna bomb, Commaccio? They got 50 million people in Iran. Only 8 million of 'em are what you call Fundamentalists. And they ain't the ones set this up.' He swivelled around in his chair, his arms folded, facing the chief. 'That last statement, on the tape? About the power and truth and fire of Allah cleansing the earth of the work of Satan? That's the Alzhia Shiites. You ever hear of them? Dumb question. You probably never heard of Tuesday.'

'If we could get beyond this schoolboy shit . . .' the chief said, his eyes closed.

L. H. went on, arms folded, in control. 'Alzhias are a small sect, a few thousand maybe, but they supposed to control the private banks in Iran. So they got connections in Iraq, Syria and Lebanon, and they make the Mullahs seem like pacifists.

They believe in the Firestorm of Nostradamus. You know about that one Chief, the Firestorm of Nostradamus, where a storm of fire is going to engulf the earth? Burn all us sinners down to the ground?

'The Alzhias, though, in their version, say the earth shall be burned clean and only the one true sect of Islam shall flower. Suckers are pyromaniacs in robes. You see Chief, you go to University, study Moslem studies, you know shit like that.'

'Well they are just another buncha dumbass sand niggers if they think that blowing up half a million people at the Indy 500 is going to change anybody's mind,' said the Chief.

'Didn't you hear the suckers?' said L. H. 'They ain't stupid. They control the satellite. And they don't want to change nobody's mind. They want to cleanse the earth.' He pushed his earphones back over his ears and swivelled back to his console, talking into the microphone, pressing buttons, running his DJ show.

'Press,' I said, 'there are a couple of things you should know. This station and KoGai are both owned by Global-Village. The man who runs Global-Village was in Indianapolis last week. At this station. His name is Phillip Hillburn.'

'Are you saying he set this up?'

'It's worth looking into. You could, for example, see if that tape has his fingerprints on it.'

'Where did you get this information?'

'He spoke to me at the track on Thursday.'

'And he told you all that?'

'Told me what?'

The Chief stood up and walked out of the room and stood in the hall, framed by the door. 'You sure you blocked their signals?'

'Well I can't stop them sending,' L. H. said over his shoulder. 'But the signals can't be relayed from here, cause I erased the program.'

'So they can't set off the bombs.'

'Nooo,' L. H. said. 'No way. You see, the strength of a radiated signal falls off at the rate proportional to the distance travelled. So by the time our dish picks it up, the poor little sucker is down to a few hundredths of a watt at the outside.'

'Well let's get this goddam race started,' the Chief said.

34

Outside the KIND building, on the lawn, it was Memorial Day Weekend again. The first weekend of summer. The weekend we honour the dead of our wars.

The grass had just been cut and was wet from sprinklers. Cicadas buzzed in the hot, still air, and Harding Street was innocent of traffic, the cars parked here and there along the kerb; Buicks, Toyotas, Escorts, pickup trucks and Aerovans, baking in the sun. It was a day for parades and boring patriotic speeches, picnics, Hoosier Hollers, swimming and softball games. A day for floating down the river in an inner tube with the sun hot on your head and the riverwater still clear and chill from spring rain.

Four miles away, magnets held Semtex tight to the gasoline tanks of campers and family sedans. And 22,000 miles above the equator, a satellite held still, balanced between gravity and centrifugal force, a mirror in space, winking down on a still peaceful Indiana summer noon. Where an olive-green Army Sikorsky S–76 helicopter rested on the lawn, its rotors drooping in the heat.

Once we had risen a couple of hundred feet, Press leaned on the joystick and the helicopter veered sharp left, west, away from the stockyards. When we gained enough altitude to see for thirty miles across the flat green hazy countryside, Press pointed to a convoy of Army trucks heading south on Interstate–456. 'There they are,' he said, tilting the helicopter back towards the northeast and the track. 'If you don't check yourself, they never show up.'

'Who's "they" this time?' I shouted over the roar of the rotors and the turbine.

'National Guard trucks from Camp Dellwood. They are going to meet a bomb unit flying in from Fort Harrison. While you are out there on the track, they'll be running their scanners and X-rays over the parking lot.'

'Who else did you call?'

'You want the Marines?'

'Whatever it takes.'

In Formula One, we start a race with twenty-six cars parked

on a grid in thirteen staggered rows, one car slightly in front of the other. It is an appalling, dangerous way to start a race. When the green light goes on the cars are turning 6,000–12,000 rpm, the drivers pop the clutch and twenty-six times 700 horse-power engulfs the track in noise, dirt, clouds of rubber and smoke as twenty-six berserk ground rockets accelerate from nothing to 150 miles an hour in the time it takes to breathe in and out and in again. Or twenty-five cars or twenty-four. Because dumping 700–horsepower all at once onto a racing clutch tends to make them explode. And men have died while stalled on the grid, impaled on the nose of the wildly accelerat-ing car from behind. There is a berserk charge to the left and the right as cars fight to gain a place, or an inch. If their wheels touch and they launch themselves up into the air to land upside down or sideways, still travelling at over 100 miles an hour, a whole slew of race cars can smash out of control, shorn of wheels, cartwheeling through ᵗhe air.

But, for all of that, the start of a Formula One race is relaxed compared to the start of the Indianapolis Five Hundred.

The Indianapolis Motor Speedway feels too narrow for thir-ty-three cars: and we don't start from rest, but from 200 miles an hour.

We are stacked three wide, inches between us, dodging and weaving. As the white pace car drops down low onto the apron coming out of Turn Three all thirty-three of us have our foot jammed to the floor and all of us have a single desire: more. More power, more speed, more room. I am the jelly in a nine-car doughnut. In the middle of the seventh row as we come off Four into the straight, there are eighteen cars blocking me in front, twelve behind wanting to pass, and, inches away, one on each side. There isn't the variety of wails and roars of Formula One as the cars go up and down the gears, but one roar, as if we are all sucking power from the same mother-engine, none of us getting enough, all of us screaming for more, one scream-ing mass accelerating into the main straight, nosing forward, half-inches from the car in front, at 200 miles an hour, looking for a place to pass. Seeing gaps open in one instant and close in the next. The concrete wall is on both sides of the track down the main straight and it is like being catapulted through a tube at hyperspeed, knowing there is a sharp left coming up and knowing you will be in it before you see it, surrounded by men driving as if they don't care whether they live or die.

My head is twenty-four inches off the ground and I see the green light go on through the syrup of exhaust haze and heat waves. The car is unstable, jumping from side to side as the wind comes hurtling back in choppy swirls of sudden vacuums, updraughts, downdraughts, sideswipes. And the wind punches my helmet like a boxer hits a punching bag.

So I didn't see, behind me, in the last row, Duane Moomaw, slow, fall back behind the pack and drive carefully along the outside wall, sheering off his wheels, the body of the car staying tight along the wall all the way down the main straight and finally coming to rest at the end of Turn One, still tight against the concrete. Eugene told me when the rescue crew arrived, there was no Duane. There was no face and not much of a neck. Just a flood of blood and pulp and char, the visor of his helmet blown away and the helmet gaping like the bloody socket of a molar after the tooth has been pulled.

'Poor Ol' Superstitious Duane,' Eugene said. Duane Moomaw had entered the Indianapolis Five Hundred every year for the past fourteen. For the past five he had qualified and started from the back rows. And for the past five he had worn the same helmet. Last year he had his best Indy ever. Best all-time Indy finish, still running after 500 miles, nineteen laps down, classified eleventh. This year, this was going to be his last run. Just one more. Then he'd hang up his lucky silver helmet in his garage in Schuyler, Ohio. Watch the race next year on television out by the pool with Darlene and the kids.

Because Duane was superstitious and because a smack into the wall at Turn Four in '81 had left him deaf in one ear, he handed in his spare helmet when the helmets were checked. He didn't want anybody, absolutely nobody, touching his lucky helmet. He kept that one hidden in a locker in his garage. And so he started the race with a charge of Semtex plugged into his good ear, the left one. The odds that the signal from the satellite would have set it off without a boost from the local radio station were infinitely small. His receiver must have been pointed in precisely the right direction on the nano-second when the signal was sent from the satellite. Or maybe it was simply a short circuit, like the short circuit on Manuel Romeriez' camper.

I didn't see the column of smoke from the Romeriez camper in the middle of the parking lot. Or the two soldiers who were blinded in the blast, and I didn't see Duane crash. But I did see the yellow light go on and settled in for a long race. When the yellow goes on you slow down to pace car speed and do not pass. You conserve the tyres and the fuel. And dive into the pits if you need fresh rubber or a top up. It's a chance to come down from the plateau of absolute concentration you need to drive at over 200 miles an hour around an oval track. After the chaos of the start and three-quarters of a lap at speed, I welcomed the rest. 199 laps to go.

They took Moomaw's remains away in an ambulance. And they hoisted his gleaming yellow car in the air behind a wrecker that had enough blinking lights to light up a disco . . . hauled the broken machine away to be sold to another man of limited means who dreamed of racing at The Brickyard. The green light went back on. 194 laps to go.

I followed T. D.'s advice, and kept out of trouble for the first 50 laps, learning the track, setting up a rhythm. At one point I was baulked by two slower cars in front of me and Al Unser slipped by all three of us as if it was the easiest thing in the world, into a gap that I could have sworn wasn't there before he got there, and disappeared behind him like water closing behind a stone.

I was working with very fine increments. The engine was flat out at 12,550 rpm in top gear and it was like a sewing machine, there just wasn't any torque left. And I was never on the brakes except coming into the pits or once when Phil Gerstenmeyr lost it in front of me and spun once before going up into the wall on Turn Three. Even then I couldn't come off the throttle too quickly because I'd upset the balance of the car.

There is a moment in Formula One, at the apex of a corner, when you and the car are on the limit of centrifugal force, when you are poised on the edge. An nth degree more speed, or lifting or turning the wheel and the car is gone. That one moment is stretched at Indy, on and on and onandon. Coming into each of the four turns and driving through them, if you aren't balanced right up there on the edge of the knife all the way round the turn, you aren't in the race.

Driving into the corners I didn't really turn, I eased the car in, keeping the accelerator flat to the floor right up to the apex and using the side forces to scrub off speed. Even though my head was pounded in the dirty air from the cars in front and my shoulder, hip, shins and thighs banged into the side of the car on every turn, the car needed a watchmaker touch in the midst of the violence. As I began to get the feel of it I was calm on the outside, relaxed and fluid in my movements. Inwardly I was vicious, voracious, looking for openings, stealing somebody else's air, trying to keep the guy behind me in dirty air, upsetting his aerodynamics. Once I was relaxed at those speeds, I found that the fastest way around a corner would change. On a road course, there is usually just one line. But at Indy, there are several. On one lap I might find that a flat arc, or going down low, or staying high along the wall gave me an extra 100 or 200 rpm coming out of the turn, depending on the fuel load or the traffic or even a cloud passing in front of the sun and lowering the temperature of the track. Up there, poised on the edge, all the way through eight hundred long left-hand turns.

Racing at Indianapolis it is not so much a question of getting a car to go fast as it is getting your mind moving superfast. You have to anticipate everything. Bobby Rahal says coming into Turn One, with the wall of stands rising up in front of you, is like driving into a broom closet. It is too crowded, visually. The mass of faces stacked ten storeys high as you drive into them at 230 miles an hour drags your eye off the track. Turn Three feels much more open with a longer radius. The two turns, One and Three, are virtually identical now that they've flattened the bump coming out of Three. But in setting up for One and Three, judging the speed and where and how you turn in, you are also setting up for turns Two and Four which are nearly half a mile away. The mind has to anticipate both of those second corners because once you are into One or Three, there just isn't time, and there isn't the margin to set up for Two and Four. The car is committed and so are you. Entering into Turn Three at nearly 230 miles an hour you make a bet with the physics of motion, adhesion, and with the indifferent gods of fortune that you will exit Turn Four, over half a mile away, eight inches from the wall. If your mind is there before you, there is plenty of time, and the wall at the edge of the far turn comes rushing towards you at 210 miles an hour, comes within a foot or six inches of your wheels and, whoof, runs alongside you like a 200 mile an hour concrete freight train on the southbound track. If you misjudged the wind which was gusting across the track into Turn Four at 15–25 miles an hour, because you were too busy to check the windsock that flies behind Turn Three, you can find, as you exit Turn Four that the little extra puff of wind pushes the car up towards the wall, past the buffeting barrier of turbulence, over the last twelve inches of free choice and find the letters of your tyres begin to brush the concrete and all the bets are off as your car enters into a brand new, violent and unpredictable path down the main straight, up into the air or wherever the hell the wall wants to throw you.

By lap 165 the car still felt good. My neck was sore and it had a 400lb pendulum swinging from the top of it going from left around corners at 3g's. And I was tired. But I was back up on the same lap as the leaders, lying fifth. George had set the car up with mild push which made it easy to get up right onto the edge and stay there. But, at any time, it could get like balancing on a high wire in high winds over Niagara Falls. Especially up on the grey area, above the groove, getting out of the dirty air to pass on the corners. The grey area was littered with little rubber pellets scuffed off everybody's tyres, lying there to roller the way into oblivion. Up on the grey area the whole car went light, nervous and indecisive in my hands, telling me it could feel the magnetism of the wall.

But I had just come out of the pits with fresh tyres and enough fuel to finish. I had a chance.

Every automotive column wrote about whose fault it was. And the TV cameras covered it from every angle. I should have ... He should have ... they said. But I was there, and what happened was this. First Sayers and then Gravetts went into the pits for fuel which put me up to third behind Duero and Brooks. I ws almost a full lap down on them until, on lap 177, Bill Meryer's Cosworth blew up and sprayed oil on Turn One. So the next eight laps ran on yellow. You can't pass on yellow, and you have to slow down. But you can go fast enough to close the gap between you and the car in front of you and I closed right up behind Brooks.

I've always had a sixth sense about lights. Even in the street I can anticipate the tenth of a second before they change. On the track, I had my foot down and driving low down into Four when the green changed. Brooks and I went side by side down the straight, but I had to edge going into One and when we came out of Two, I was second, ahead of Brooks, behind Duero.

Duero is a former Formula One driver who has been driving Indy cars for ten years now, and he was a bear to pass. Coming into the corners if I moved down or up he would move down or up, in front of me, stealing my air, robbing my car of downforce. But in his last pit stop, he hadn't changed his tyres, and I could feel I had a little more grip in the corners. Coming down the main straight on lap 196, looking into his big chrome exhaust pipe, like the exhaust of one of the old F-85 Jet Fighters, the whole car tapering to a point in the rear blasting sweet, acrid, methanol exhaust in my face, his big rear tyres, blocking my view, flinging grit shrapnel back into my visor, I moved low and stayed there. He had given me enough of a tow for me to move up even on him and I just put my nose in front of him going under him into One. He had to back off. His tyres were too soft and I came up high between One and Two in front of him. I was leading down the back straight and I was going to win this race.

I wouldn't be the first Formula One driver to win the Indianapolis Five Hundred, but I would be in very good company. World Champion Jimmy Clark should have won it in 1963 when the officials refused to black flag Parnelli Jones. Maybe it was Clark's little rear-engined British Lotus that made them hesitate. It looked like a freak among the big front-engine American roadsters. Maybe it was its green colour which was a taboo at the Brickyard. Maybe they just could not stand the thought of a rookie and a foreigner taking home first prize. Whatever the reason, Parnelli was spraying oil all over the track for the last lap and should have been black flagged. Should have been but wasn't. And Clark's tyres (Dunlops from Formula One, too soft for Indianapolis) were in shreds. But Clark didn't make another pit stop and he didn't complain. And he didn't slide off the track, he finished second and came back in 1965 to win in another rear-engined Lotus–Ford. Formula One World Champion Graham Hill was a rookie at Indy the next year, in 1966, and he won too. Of all the Formula One and Indy drivers today only Mario Andretti and Emerson Fittipaldi have both won the World Championship and the Indianapolis

Five Hundred. I hadn't won either, I thought two laps from the checkered flag, but I was about to win one.

At 235 miles an hour down the back straight, I was travelling the length of a football field a second. Plus an end zone. In the intricate mosaic the eye normally sees, I would pick out one detail, like a yellow shirt of a USAC observer behind the wall a hundred yards away, and the one detail which would flow past, the one identifiable object in a high pressure visual stream. The world liquefies at that speed, and all of your movements, in relation to Technicolor hose-stream of the world outside the cockpit, are hopelessly slow. Whatever anybody says, you are hanging on. You think you hold the wheel and the wheel holds you.

Like most incidents at the Indianapolis Speedway, this one began long before it happened . . . forces set in motion to collide at a later, predetermined, fixed point. Duero was in my mirrors, losing ground. But I had to lift for a moment going into Turn Three for two back markers going in on the groove, and in that almost imperceptible slow ease off the throttle, Duero's gold and white car was right behind me again, coming up fast. He went down low, getting his nose just alongside my back wheel as we eased into the turn. Neither of us was going to back off. From that moment our paths were as fixed as two men on a pendulum. I went up high in the grey area to go around the back-markers and Duero went low. I knew he was going to lose it. I knew there was no way he was going to make it going around the corner that low at that speed and on those tyres. As I got around the two cars, I eased down, back into the groove, the fastest way around, thinking that I would try to get past Duero before he came up. But half way around Three, headed towards the chute, he came up towards me. He couldn't help it, there was a slower car in front of him and he was starting to lose control. I saw the gold nose of his car, streaked with oil, looming up out of the corner of my eye. His front tyre was pointing down the track, but it was sliding across the asphalt heading for the numbers on the side of my car, coming coming right up into my lap. He was out of control and I could feel him get on the brakes as he thought he was going to hit me. His front wheel locked. My foot was already trying to push the accelerator pedal through the floor, but I stood on it even harder, hoping to get ahead of him. His car began to slow, his tyres scrubbing off speed and I began to pull away. There was no sound, there was no time to listen to the scream of our engines or the sound of Duero's tyres dragging across the track at 220 miles an hour. We were both of us, as he headed towards me, in an envelope of silence.

Then, a second and a half after I had first seen him in my mirrors on the back straight, when I had been lifting for the two slower cars, his front wheel kissed my back wheel, and the world exploded in a whirl of sound and frenzy. Duero's back end started to come around, but he held it in a long dirt-track slide. Just like you are not supposed to be able to do. My car snapped around twice and hit the wall two hundred yards down the chute. Just before the impact I thought of the Evers pattern on the edge, that the whole wall around this damn track was going to have the imprint of Evers and his car. And I thought, just like the jet pilots do, before they nose into the ground, *Oh fuck.*

But it wasn't so bad. The car glanced off and my shoulder and my shins were bruised, but I wasn't hurt. I was out of my car in time to see Duero take his victory lap.

It wasn't his fault, I could have backed off. It wasn't my fault, he could have backed off. It was just racing. But it almost broke my heart, I had wanted to win so bad.

Back in the Pits, Orrin was jumping up and down. We hadn't won the race but we were third. (The last lap had been run under yellow, and only Brooks was on the same lap.) 'Did you know,' he said, 'the last five laps you were going faster than your qualifying laps? You ran three laps in a row over 222 miles an hour.'

George was miserable. He made a show of being concerned about me, but his heart was in the car, swinging from a two-truck, a crumpled mess of junk he would have to take apart, piece by piece, and rebuild in the two weeks before the next race. But Orrin was happy because we had won $327,756 in prize money. I felt as if someone had pulled the plug out of my heel and let the life drain out. Five hundred miles is a long way to drive just to crash. The TV monitor in our pit showed Duero in the winner's circle, grinning and weary, an ill-fitting Budweiser baseball cap on his head, his arms around two cuddly blonde girls in pink bubblegum satin swim-suits, and talking into the camera about how it really felt to win the big one.

I couldn't watch. I knew how it felt to lose the big one. And the marshals were urging me to the Speedway hospital for a check-up. But before I could leave, Orrin handed me a phone. 'It's your little friend,' he said, 'via satellite.'

'Forrest, are you all right? Please, tell me you're OK.'

'I'm OK. Who is this?'

'Forrest. Really. Is this a bad connection? It's Caroline. Calling from London.'

'Cheers.'

'Oh, Forrest, please don't be like that. Don't you want to know how I am?'

'You sound fine.'

'Forrest, I need you.'

'If you need a bodyguard I can give you the name of a firm in London.'

'Stop being a shit, Forrest, I really am frightened and I really do need you. Hillburn just rang and he says he has to talk to me. I need you with me. I can't face him alone.'

'What did he say?' I was having trouble hearing. In Victory Circle, which was almost behind our pit, someone had handed a trophy the size of a pontoon to Duero and the live cheering was echoed on the TV in front of me. The track and the pits were covered with people the way an Indiana cornfield is covered with corn and every one of them was cheering Duero. 'He says he wants to settle with me. He says he wants to make a deal.'

'He's not in a position to deal. Call the police and your lawyers.'

'Forrest we could settle this if you were here. Please. For me?'

'Where are you supposed to meet him?'

'Here, in London. He says there has been a terrible misunderstanding and he wants to straighten things out. That's what he said, "straighten things out". Look I'll buy you a house or something.'

'You don't have to do that.'

'Then please, just this once, do it for me?'

'Give me your father's address, that place where they are keeping him in New York.'

'Does that mean you will come?'

'I guess I owe your father something.'

'You owe him $12 million.'

'And he owes Ellie the twelve million he stole from her out of their blind asset trust fund they set up off-shore. Suppose we call it even.'

'That's asking a lot. You'd have a tough time proving my father owes that little businesswoman a dime. But OK, Forrest. Whatever it takes to get you out here.'

'Then I need you to do something for me. Do you have a pen? I want you to write a few things down.'

Then, when I told her my idea she said, 'Brilliant. No problem. You got it.'

I rode with one of the marshals on a red golf cart over to the Speedway Hospital. It was slow going, with the reporters and video cameras blocking our way, wanting to know what happened out there on Turn Three. And wanting to know if there were other gay racing drivers. And what did the race look like, out there, from the gay perspective?

'From a gay perspective,' I told one of them, 'the straights are pretty straight, and the turns are all bent.' He drifted away.

An hour later, when I got out of the Speedway Hospital ('You're fine, Evers, nothing broken. But if you start getting headaches or start feeling a little woozy, call a doctor'), I walked out of the hospital with a headache and feeling a little woozy into the Great-grand-daddy of all traffic jams. The stands had emptied but the cars and campers and pickup trucks were locked up solid, bumper to bumper, sidewall to sidewall. Men were leaning out of car windows, their faces red, their kids screaming in the back seat, looking for something to move.

Nothing was.

I found Press by the military helicopter display, where we had taken off and landed. He was yelling at an Army Colonel. The Colonel wasn't yelling back.

Evidently the bomb squad, once they had checked a car and found that it was OK or removed a bomb from its gas tank, had put a red sticker on the car to mark it as checked, so that the police stationed at the exits could let the car back on the road. But they hadn't put the stickerss in the same place: some were on the bumpers, some on the windshield, some stuck on the doors . . . and they hadn't told anybody what the stickers meant.

Some fans, coming back to their campers and cars had seen the stickers and torn them off. A few had lifted off the sticker and put it on their neighbour's car. Which meant that every car had to be checked again when it rolled up at the gate. Some drivers were drunk and belligerent and didn't want anybody touching their camper. Five angry drunks kicked an Army Bomb Squad specialist unconscious when they found his feet sticking out from underneath their camper, trying to remove a bomb.

It had been a long Memorial Day Sunday in the hot sun, and the Polar King Koolers were sloshing empty beer cans and sandwich wrappers around with the last of the devilled eggs and burger buns in the dirty melted ice water. Hangover thunderstorms were rising up from the base of the fans' skulls. The kids were whining and the wives were pissed off and nothing was moving. Preston Fulbaker was not a happy man.

'How many bombs did you find?' I asked when he had finished yelling at the Army Colonel.

'I don't know yet,' he said, looking distractedly off at a camper that was nudging a stalled Oldsmobile Cutlass Supreme. 'I think around eighty-five so far. We don't even know who stuck them on. Or when. You know, they could have just walked through at night. Reached under. You'd hardly even have to bend your knees. The little suckers will stick anywhere. Or it could have been at some of the gas stations on the way in. I don't know.'

The camper driver started leaning on his horn. As if, wedged on all sides, there was someplace the Supreme could go.

'Hillburn,' I said. 'The man who owns KIND and KoGai, Hillburn, Phillip Hillburn is going to be in London Tuesday morning.'

'What do you expect me to do about it?'

'Pick him up. Talk to him. Ask him if he enjoyed the race.'

'Look, you give me some fucking rumour about some media mogul setting this thing up. Sure, I'll check it out. But tomorrow's a holiday, my office is shut. I have to file a report. Talk to the CIA, or the FBI, they're on it now. Along with the Joint Chiefs of Staff, for all I know.' He started to walk away.

'You make a hell of a traffic cop,' I said to his back.

35

When British explorers found the Hudson River in the seventeenth century, they said they'd found paradise. They said the river was as transparent as the blue sky, and as wide as an inland sea. There were oysters and clams, they said, for the scooping up by hand, and fish shoulder to shoulder for hauling out by net. Deer came to the edge of the clear running river to drink. And badgers, raccoons, turkeys, and foxes greeted you with innocent curiosity. And the infinite variety of virgin trees sang with abundant, exotic birds. They said. In the world's first travel brochures. They wanted settlers, and they didn't stick around for winter with the ice on the river two feet thick and the temperature −10° F with forty mile an hour winds. They shot at the first Indians they saw, and sailed home to write up their reports of the promised land.

Driving up the Hudson River Valley, once you get past the perfect front lawns of Westchester County, route 9D climbs up towards Bear Mountain in a gentle reminder of the paradise the Hudson Valley must have been in the spring three hundred years ago. Mountain forests rise up on each side of the river and the road twists along a cliff edge.

Another fifteen miles up the road, seventy-five miles north of New York City, Beacon is a rundown rivertown, stranded between the farthest reaches of a commute to New York City and the largesse of IBM's World Headquarters in Poughkeepsie. So Beacon doesn't have much, but it does have Mt Beacon with a lighthouse on top and an aerial tramway for tourists in the summer and skiers in the winter. At the foot of the tramway, across 9D on 400 acres stretching down to the railroad tracks and the riverbank, the Millbank-Arlington Home hides behind a high stone wall. There is no sign out front. And in downtown Beacon, if you can find anybody on the street, nobody has heard of the Millbank-Arlington Home. But they have heard of it in the White House in Washington, and in the corporate suites and boardrooms of New York City.

You drive down the crushed blue stone drive, through lawns the size of a golf course, past copper beech, oak and blue spruces to a beautiful, white, sprawling, Victorian mansion, built by Clive Vanderbilt as a summer retreat for one of his mistresses. Nowadays it is where the bombed-out refugees of the fast track go to hide and to die. On the porch there is the alcoholic mistress of a former President, still as a statue in the rocking chair that does not rock. Her pale hand rises in greeting as I pass. Inside, in the library lined with books no one reads, the former Chairman of US Steel weeps, and the toughest financial officer Chrysler ever had stares out the window with his finger in his mouth as if there is something he is trying to remember.

The woman behind the polished mahogany reception desk has a narrow face, freckles and an abundant body tightly confined in a business suit. She smiles the relaxed smile of a fifty-year-old woman who has nothing to prove. Yes, Miss Fraser had rung the day before, and they were expecting me. Mr Fraser was in his room and a nurse would show me up.

The nurse was a pretty teenage girl with a pony tail in blue jeans and a checked shirt. She bounded up the grand staircase, her sneakers making no noise on the carpeted steps. 'If he's asleep,' she said, swinging open the tall, panelled door freshly painted glossy white, 'just wake him up. He's got nothing else to do.' It was a large, corner room, and the view was breathtaking. To the north you could see the broad expanse of the Hudson River looking like a glittering promise three miles wide and stretching to the northern horizon. To the south, the river narrowed for Bear Mountain and Sugarloaf, looking like a fairytale version of the Rhine. They had parked him facing out of the window, but I doubt that he saw the view.

'Good morning, Mr Fraser,' I said, turning his wheelchair around.

'Hrrrrrrrr,' he said.

They had dressed him in a fine soft dark blue jacket with a crisp new white button-down Brooks Brothers shirt and a dark red paisley tie. And grey flannel trousers, and dark loafers that had the shine of brand-new shoes. It was the uniform of boys in Prep School and what rich old men wear when they venture forth to the restaurant on Sunday afternoons. His face was a mess.

It was if his expression had been frozen in grotesque pain or anger or both. And at the same time his eyes were blank. As if this man with the translucent bluish skin, and the heavy five o'clock shadow, this man with the wild arched eyebrows and the drooping, drooling lower lip had just slipped away for a moment. But don't go away, he'll be right back, after this.

'Hrrrrrrrr,' he said again.

I looked around the room. A museum of Victorian antiques. A carved four-poster bed, with a white embroidered bedspread, an oval hooked rug on the polished oak floor, a large old armoire, and a chest of drawers with a bevelled mirror that he would never look in. A pleasant mausoleum for the dead who remain among the living.

'Is there anything I can do for you?' I asked, knowing there would be no answer. 'Anything I can do to make you more comfortable?' A stupid question, really. He was one of the world's richest men and wanted nothing. Nothing in his face moved except the blink of his eyes. I have never seen a man look so dead and still take breath.

I sat down in a wing-backed chair opposite him and thought of things I might say. That he would have the money I had taken from him back soon. For all the good it would do him. That he had been a tiger when I had seen him.

Ah, the world is full of tigers and we let them have their way, thinking that is the way of nature. The satellites and the TV news go to the highest bidder because the old tigers never were much trouble. They built their castles in the air to enrich their fortunes on the ground. And if they were monsters when you got up close, you could always keep your distance. They didn't seem so bad now. They weren't even tigers any more. They were pussy-cats compared to the men who planted Semtex and pushed the buttons on the dark side of the globe. I could have said.

What I did say was, 'I will get your business back for you, Billy.' Good old air-head, philosopher Evers. I was getting good at getting things back wasn't I? Evers, stirrer of other people's lives. Boaster. Fumbler. Liar.

I stood up and took his head in my hands. His flesh was cool, unresisting. Tilting his head first on one side, then the other, I saw them. The healing little pin pricks, one on each temple. I straightened his head and wheeled his chair around and left him to his view of the river or whatever it was he saw with blank eyes.

London looked like a blocked drain. I'd got back to New York, just caught the 13.45 Concorde from Kennedy and landed at 20.45 at Heathrow, right on time. It was raining heavily and the traffic on the M4 stopped two miles before the Hogarth Roundabout. The taxi driver said it had been like that all month. 'Summer don't bear thinking about, do it?' He pronounced the word 'finkin'.

My flat in Holland Park was, for lack of a better word, home. It wasn't far from my old house in Edwardes Square. Where Susan, no doubt, had redecorated, thrown out or painted over all the reminders of our life together. Bright new colours for her bright new life. No doubt, no doubt, no doubt.

My flat was large and clean, Zilna the Cypriot fascist cleaner saw to that. And it was empty and it was cold. I threw my luggage in the bedroom and went out to dinner. On the way out of the door, I saw the answering machine winking under the burden of a month of messages. They could wait.

Where does a gentleman on his own go to dinner alone in London? He goes to Green's on Duke Street St James, and sits at the oyster bar where the oysters are fresh and Beth Coventry cooks proper English food far better than it deserves. Nothing like a crisp Chablis to wash down the oysters, said the gentleman in the white apron behind the mahogany bar. Shall we say the Le Clos Chablis Grand Cru '85? No, thank you very much. Let's just say the Malvern Water, Wednesday, last disgusting week. So frustrating being a racing driver. All the temptations are within reach. But grasping them relaxes the grip.

Fish cakes to follow? Very good sir.

Very good indeed.

Fortified by Beth, and in the shine of the rain, walking along Pall Mall, London had regained some of its old gloss. The bulky granite façades of the clubs along Pall Mall and the colonnades of the National Gallery looked like castle walls, bastions to hold back the future while we suck the past for all it's worth. 'Never be another war like the old one, mate.' By the time I got to the foot of Big Ben, I was tired of walking and hailed a cab. Big Ben said 'BONG'. Announcing one.

36

Do not go to Wapping. Wapping used to be on the north bank of the Thames. Wapping isn't there any more. And even if it were, you still wouldn't want to go there.

In Queen Victoria's London the friendly folks of Wapping lived off the pockets of the dead. Sliding out from under the piers at night in their skiffs and sculls, they picked over the floating corpses bobbing up and downstream with the tide. Here, look, in this one's mouth, a golden tooth. And, oh lucky, lucky, in this one's pocket, a slippery coin.

It's a story they still tell the tourists. Adds to the local colour. As if there were any local colour. Now the midnight rowers and the old slums and docks of Wapping are gone, blasted, bombed, flattened, blown away. Colour The Wapping Of Today grey. Wapping is new now, rising high from the rubble. Wapping is exclusive flats built in old warehouses, dwellings designed to extract the maximum poundspersquareinch. Isolation cells with no corner shops, no cafés, no fruiterers, butchers or bakers. No newsagents, no chemists, no stationers, no ironmongers, no electrical shops, no kids on the street. Wapping is noplace. Wapping is big new shining office buildings. Wapping is hi-rise. Wapping is where the electronic money comes down from the sky freshly laundered and squeaky clean. Wapping is the bigtime developer's dream of the future. Wapping is where you will now find the newspaper that still claims to be 'The Standard of the World'.

Winston Churchill read his speeches printed in full in *The Empire*. Gladstone consulted *The Empire*. When Queen Victoria was crowned, she retired to Buckingham Palace to read about her coronation in *The Empire*. When a Gentleman grumbled in public, he did in A Letter to *The Empire*. For generations, *The Empire* stood for Britain's moral right to rule the world. It was intellectual, it was thorough, it was dull, and above all, it was fair. *The Empire* was more than a newspaper. *The Empire* was Britannia in print. And when Billy Fraser bought it for $95 million he swore he wouldn't change a dot of Britain's 'Independent and Distinguished Journal of Record'.

He changed it totally. Now struggling to boost its dwindling circulation, it is undistinguished in any way except that it can be relied on to say whatever the government wants it to say. 'Well,' I thought as the guard at the gate peered at my passport photo and consulted his list, 'there are worse crimes.'

Ten years ago, shortly after he bought the paper, Billy moved *The Empire* from its sagging Gothic building in Fleet Street to the desolate wasteland of Wapping where land was cheap. To what Billy called, 'the most modern newspaper production facility of our time'. Walking towards it, at a quarter to two on a drizzling Tuesday morning, across the floodlit acres of tarmac that surrounded it, the building looked like an exhumed bomb shelter, a dirty, white, twelve-storey, windowless, concrete cube.

When it was built, Fraser surrounded the building and the empty lot around it with a ten-foot-high chain-link fence topped with coils of barbed wire to keep out the union workers his automated printing presses had replaced. The fence is rusting now, but it is still up. In case, I suppose, any of the old workers ever tries to come back. Or any of the new ones inside tries to escape. When I pressed the buzzer on the heavy grey steel door at the side, a bored and sleepy guard let me in and directed me to the executive lift. 'Fifth floor,' he said, 'can't miss it.'

Indeed, you can't. The lift opened to reveal a red carpet leading down a long hall. There was a row of glass office doors on either side but the red carpet led your eye down its length to the warm yellow light coming from the office at the end, the one with the huge carved oak door swung open and Caroline standing in the doorway, her shadow reaching towards me.

She waited for me to walk the length of the hall until I got to her, and her little face was looking up at me. Then she threw her arms around my neck and kissed me hard on the mouth. She must have been out to an expensive restaurant or a club because she was wearing a simple black silk little nothing that looked like a slip and emphasized her heavy breasts. She wore big gold hoop earrings and a gold necklace and her long black hair fell down to her bare shoulders. Her neck smelt of perfume and she felt soft and warm. She squirmed against me then pulled away and half ran into the office, and stopped and did a pirouette like a little girl glad that Daddy's home. 'Oh, God, I'm glad to see you, Forrest. I'm so glad you came. You sure you're OK? That crash was gross on TV. They replayed it about six times and I kept thinking you were dead.'

'Apparently I'm alive.'

'Isn't it wonderful?' she said, sweeping her arm out slowly like an actress on a stage. 'I mean, you know, it's great you're OK and everything. But isn't this an absolutely fabulous office? Out of all his offices all over the world this was Daddy's favourite. Daddy had it brought over from the old *Empire* building. All the panelling and marble floor and the refectory table and well, everything.' She walked around the edge of the room, touching the panelling with an outstretched hand, feeling the wood of the table. 'I mean when I think of the people who have been in this room. Did you know Churchill sat in that leather chair?'

'Maybe he won't mind if I sit in it now.' It was an impressive room. A press baron's baronial hall. High Gothic arches, books lining the oak walls like a library. No wonder Billy loved it. It was his favourite set, the backdrop he liked behind him when he was photographed.

'I saw your father,' I said.

'Did he say anything? Did he ask about me?' Caroline sat down behind the big desk, framed by a Gothic stained glass window that was lit from behind. Behind the window, you could make out the pattern of concrete breeze-blocks.

'You know how he is.'

'I know,' she said, looking down at the desk, 'but I can't help hoping.'

There was a vibration and a buzzing. Then a dull roar and the office shook as if a freight train was passing underneath. 'Tomorrow's paper,' Caroline said happily. 'That's the 500,000 ton Gutterbergen my father installed. I think it's what they mean when they talk about the power of the press.' She laughed at her joke, brushing her hair back over her forehead. 'Want to see it?' She pressed a button on a control panel on her desk, and, at the end of the room, a video screen flickered to life, monitoring the giant rolls of paper and the twenty-foot-high printing drums. By pressing buttons, Caroline could watch the whole length and breadth of the machine that was a block long and five storeys high.

'We print *New Day*, *Sports Day*, *The Globe*, *Stadium*, *The Flag*, *The Evening Record* and *The Empire*. Six million news-papers a day here. Isn't that fantastic?' She was staring at the screen, pushing buttons, watching the tons of steel turn a forest of twelve-foot-high paper rolls into newspapers. Then she looked at me, the way a child looks up from a favourite toy to a parent, eyebrows raised, waiting for approval.

I gave her a smile. 'Did you get it?' I had to shout over the roar of the machines.

'Sure,' she said, giving her smile a wicked twist, 'it's just . . .' her face froze. I was sitting with my back to the door so I didn't see him come in.

Evidently he didn't see me either because he said, in that flat Utah twang, 'We gotta move on this . . .'

'Hillburn,' she cut him off, 'we have a guest.'

I stood up. 'Hello, Philip.'

He looked rapidly between us, his brows coming together over his long, flat face. 'What is this? You let him in here, Caroline? Whataya want, Evers? You got some complaint, write a letter.'

'I thought you'd like to see this morning's *Empire*.'

Caroline handed him a paper from a stack on the top of her desk. The headline wasn't big. *Empire* headlines could be long, but, short of a declaration of a World War, they were never big. The interesting item was the lead story on the front page. It said GLOBAL CHIEF IN MURDER LINK.

As they had said on 'The Real News', it was just the facts. The landing time in Haiti, the electrodes in Fraser's temples, the link to the Alzhia sect, the Semtex bombs at Indianapolis, the number of his Swiss bank account. I was standing alongside Hillburn and I could see the red flush rising up his face. He started to move towards Caroline, ignoring me. 'You fucking bitch,' he said quietly. His voice started to rise, 'You stinking . . .' He started a wild swing at her, reaching for her across the desk.

I was pushing up, out of my chair, but Caroline was ready, and she moved towards him, slashing at his face with a letter-opener. Blood gushed out of his eye and he held his hand up to his face, staring at her with his one good eye, then at me, his face white against the leaking blood. The press was roaring under our feet, and we had to almost shout to be heard. But Hillburn's roar, his mouth open, blood running down his cheek, dripping off his chin, Hillburn's roar drowned out the printing presses for a long moment. It was a scream of rage and frustration. A scream of an animal that is cornered and will fight its way out. He charged past me, out of the door, pressing the heel of his hand into the socket where his eye had been. I ran after him and he disappeared into one of the offices along the corridor.

The non-stop thunder of the presses came flooding out of the open office door and when I got there, there was no office. The door led out onto a catwalk over the whirling printing machinery. Billy must have loved it, to have walked from his office with the chair where Winston Churchill sat, to stand over the presses. To smell the hot metal, machine oil and ink. To feel the power of his editorials rising up like the vibrations through the soles of his feet. Hillburn was thirty feet away, running. I ran out on the catwalk, five storeys over the concrete floor, after him.

The metal catwalks were painted brown, with open waffle panels for a floor and flimsy hand rails, a spider-web network wrapped around the huge machine for maintenance. I couldn't run flat out because my feet slid on the vibrating metal. Goddamn Italian shoes, I thought, and their useless paper-thin soles. Hillburn disappeared down a flight of steps. A few moments later through the haze of dust, machine oil and heat I saw him running down a cross walk and up another flight. The catwalk shook with the power of the immense Gutterbergen press, and the noise had the same heavy vibration, shaking my head so hard my vision blurred. I ran after him.

I didn't have far to run. On the other side of the cross walk, he was waiting for me at the top of the next set of steps. Blood and sweat were running down his face, along with a greasy liquid from his sunken eyelid. I started up towards him and he kicked at my face. 'It's a fake,' I shouted. 'The newspaper article is a fake.' But I might as well have tried to shout over the noise of a freight train. If he had been standing next to me he wouldn't have heard me. I assumed he was headed for a control panel to switch off the presses and stop the story. But the article was a fake. Half of it was guess-work, rumour, and what strangers had told Ellie on the phone. I had wanted to threaten him with it, force him to tell me the missing parts, the link with Mehar, and their contact with the Alzhia.

I started up towards him again and he wiped his face with the palms of his hands before he grabbed onto the rails and kicked at my face again, this time with concentration and power. I saw the kick coming so there was plenty of time to pull back and see the force of the kick carrying him forward off balance, to see his bloody hands slip off the railing and see him slide forward feet first and to the left just far enough for his shoe to catch in the whirling drum and fling him upward. I grabbed at his hands in the microsecond they were thrust towards me like a mad acrobat and for an instant I thought I might save him. But he was jerked away, his head smashing against a steel brace on the way up. His body was flung into the paper path and for a few moments I could see it bounding along on its wild obscene up and down fairground ride before it stopped, juddering at the mouth of two twenty-ton rollers. The paper ripped with a cracking sound like lightning, and in the next instant something caught between the rollers, a hand, the toe of a shoe, and Hillburn disappeared in a horrific pulp of blood. I ran up the stairs to find the control panel he had been running towards, but by the time I got to the top of the stairs, the presses were beginning to slow down. I caught my breath and walked down the metal steps. The presses had stopped and I could hear voices below me shouting. I walked carefully across the cross walk and up the flight of steps on the other side of the rollers, being careful not to slip on the gobbets and sprayed blood.

When I got back to Caroline's office, she was sitting at her desk, relaxed, with the telephone wedged between her shoulder and her ear. 'Just a sec,' she said on the phone. Then she looked up at me, her eyebrows raised in an unspoken question, as if I was interrupting. 'Hillburn,' I started, still shaking with the horror of it.

'I know,' she said. 'I saw it on the monitor. I've phoned the police and they said about five minutes.' She put a hand over the telephone. 'I told them you could tell them all about it. In the meantime, do you mind waiting outside?' Her eyes went around the room as if she was taking inventory. 'I need the space.'

37

Her long, oily fingers slipped up the back of my neck, around my throat and squeezed. 'You've had enough,' she said, 'wake up.'

I opened my eyes a fraction and shut them again. The azure pool was too dazzling. 'Just once more,' I said. 'Down my back. And between the shoulder blades.'

'You're a lazy, spoiled, rotten, Toy Boy.'

'Lower,' I said.

'You're a lazy, spoiled, rotten, Toy Boy,' she said in her fake, he-man voice. I raised one lid a crack. Beyond the pool, half hidden by saguaro cactus, there were rows of gold Cadillac convertibles, BMWs, Mercedes, Corvettes, Porsches and the big dowdy Lincoln Ken had rented. If you have to stay in Phoenix for the Grand Prix, I thought, don't stay in Phoenix. Stay in Carefree. At the Carefree Inn. At the aptly named Carefree Inn.

'Didn't you say she had a house near here?'

'Mmmmmmmmmm,' I said, 'just like that, only harder. She does indeed. Have a house about a mile from here. You want to go see if she's there?'

'I wouldn't touch her with a stick. But I thought you might want to talk over old times. Wasn't there something they could have charged her with?'

'She didn't break any laws. Unless you could prove conspiracy and you'd have to bring Hillburn back to do that. Or find Mehar in Teheran or Isfahan or Beirut or wherever the hell he buggered off to. I thought you admired her managerial skill. She got Hillburn to get rid of her father by promising him control of the company. Then she got me to get rid of Hillburn. So she even got revenge for what she did to her father. She gets everybody else to do her dirty work and the kingdom is hers.'

'Or queendom.' Ellie made an unladylike noise. 'Well maybe I should be a little more generous towards the little shit. She's Chairwoman of Global now so she holds my junk bonds.'

'But you paid her.'

'Oh sure, I paid her. Castleman gave me the twelve million you gave him and I gave the money to Global to pay the interest. Tinker to Evers to Chance. Or Evers to Tinker to Chance to dear little Caroline, if you prefer. Anyway she seems happy to forget the whole thing. It's not exactly in her interest to stir it up again. And I suppose she'll be a better media mogul than that lunatic sect the what's their names.'

'Alzhias.'

'Alzhias. What's she going to do with them? Give them their own news-slot?'

'Ouch,' I said. 'I don't think she has to do anything with them. Without Hillburn, and without a satellite they are just another bunch of loonies with big plans. From now on they'll have to set off their bombs like everybody else.'

'Come on, Forrest, get up. I've had enough of this slave girl routine.'

I rolled over and looked up at Ellie. A tan became her. She gave me one of her nice even executive smiles. 'Don't you wish you'd taken her up on her offer? Of the kingdom, I mean.'

'Would you want to live with a woman who turned her father into a vegetable?'

'I don't want to live with anybody. But c'mon, Forrest, weren't you just a little tempted.'

'Well,' I paused, 'you have better legs.'

'You'll have to do better than that, Evers. And ... And, qualifying fourth in the Phoenix Grand Prix really isn't good enough either. If you can't do better than that I may have to fire you again.'

I stretched and closed my eyes, my head in Ellie's lap. The Phoenix sun overhead was stunning, turning me into a lizard. 'Just below the left shoulder blade,' I said, 'there's an itch.'

A shadow darkened over us and I squinted up at a pair of short unshaven legs. Strong, heavy thighs, and a fury of black hair where a white swimsuit intervened to make a soft purse. Up past a deep belly button and a white shelf of a chest hiding her shoulders and neck and blazing black eyes surrounded by a wild halo of black curly hair. Abbey looked down at us and frowned. 'What do you want to fool around with this dork for?' she said. 'I'm gonna blow his doors off tomorrow.'